Copyright © 2024 Samara Saward

All rights reserved.

This book or parts thereof may not be reproduced in any form or by any electronic or mechanical means, including information storage and retrieval systems, without prior written permission from the author, except for the use of brief quotations in a review.

This is a work of fiction. Names, places, characters, and incidents are either the product of the author's imagination or are used fictitiously. Any resemblance to actual persons, living or dead, businesses, companies, events, or locales is purely coincidental.

Cover designed by: GetCovers

Formatting designed with Atticus

Crimson Haunts the Soul

Samara Saward

To the inner demons:
Fuck you.

Content
Warning

A Guide
to Radelea

AUTUMN COURT

Rennyn — *WREN-in* — High Lord

Kerym — *keh-RHYME* — Bria's father

Fayeth — *FAY-eth* — Rennyn's mother

SPRING COURT

Nyana — *NIGH-ar-na* — High Lady

SUMMER COURT

Ad'Starrag — *ADD-stah-rag* — Summer Court keep

Iker — *EYE-kerr* — Former High Lord; deceased

Tohminic — *TOM-in-ick* — High Lord

Chlora — *CLAW-rah* — Tohminic's lover

Xaler — *ZAY-ler* — Selkie leader; Tohminic's second

WINTER COURT

Ruith — *ROO-ith* — High Lord

Uma — *OO-mah* — High Lady

Tarathiel — *ta-RATH-eel* — Guard at Kol

NIGHT COURT

Maude — *MAWD* — High Lady
Bim — *BIM* — Soldier

DAY COURT

Warakoris — *WAR-rack-oar-iss* — Zentha's home
Zentha — *ZEN-thuh* — High Lady
Elmon — *ell-MON* — Zentha's son
Kyra — *KIE-rah* — Betrothed to Elmon
Nikolai — *NICK-oh-lie* — Bria's lover, deceased

DAWN COURT

Jonik — *JOHN-ick* — High Lord
Leilani — *LAY-lah-knee* — Jonik's mate
Tasar — *t-SAR* — one of the triplets; Prince
Ulakas — *YOU-lah-cuss* — one of the triplets; Prince
Larrad — *Lah-RAHD* — one of the triplets; Prince
Xaria — *ZAR-rea* — Jonik's niece

DUSK COURT

Bria — *BREE-ah* — Our main character
Vander — *VAN-dah* — High Lord
Wynetta — *WIN-et-ah* — Bria's best friend
Torin — *toh-RIN* — Vander's second
Nyree — *nigh-REE* — Leader of the Ill-fated
Penna — *PEN-nah* — Healer

Chapter 1

J ADED.

It is a word I have often used to describe myself, though Father claims my belief is misguided, that I am little more than a rebellious wretch. I will admit there was a small part of me that agreed with him, but that was before Tohminic threw me in that cage. After enduring the iron bars and suffocating heat of the Summer Court, I do not believe I can feel such an emotion as jaded again, let alone feel the pull of rebelliousness.

Tormented.

It is my new and unwanted title. It is the single word many fae have used to describe me since I arrived on this island court and crawled into Dusk Manor.

Too many thoughts fight for attention, and I struggle to grasp one long enough to focus as I stare at the scars covering me from head to toe. My ivory skin was once clear and shining with youth. Now, it is forever marred by the cage Tohminic kept me in.

His sneering face flashes across my mind, and the mere image of the High Lord of Summer sends waves of fury tearing through me. I curl my hands into fists, my short nails biting into the soft flesh of my palms. The scars on my legs, shaped like the flames stitched into the lace of that ridiculous gown he had me wear, are stark reminders of his power.

The fire magic of Summer that is etched into my skin is a cruel reminder of all I endured, and the nightmares of their necromancy power still haunt my nights. A grid of crosses and lines covers my arms and shoulders, reminding me of the iron burning my flesh for nine moons. The white lines remind me of why we are at war.

The High Lord of Dusk died and the veil blanketing this island fell, revealing the peaceful court to the rest of Radelea. Father, in his quest to claim the inhabited island as his own, demanded I find a mate to cement such a claim with an alliance.

What a foolish reason to incite war.

If males did not believe we females to be beneath them, none of this would have happened. I would not bear the scars of my past, Father would not have lost his mind to madness, and Fayeth — a fresh wave of anger courses through me when I think of Father's mate — would not have fled Autumn and given Tohminic every secret belonging to my home court.

I understand why Rennyn begged for our aid. Although, that does not mean I have changed my mind and agreed to form such an alliance. His shock at my words was clear in his golden-brown eyes, but I cannot find it within myself to sympathise with his pain. After enduring the torture, the threats, and the red staining my hands, I'm in utter disbelief he would dare to come to the Dusk Court and ask for our help. Despite that, I wonder if I made the right choice.

I twist my body around, looking into the mirror over my shoulder to inspect my back. It is the only part of me unmarred by my time in Summer. I drag my long copper hair to the side, revealing the curve of my shoulders and the scars forming a grid over my flesh.

The sigh that flutters past my lips is harsh and filled with hatred. Hatred at Tohminic and his court, hatred at the vicissitudes of my life, and hatred at myself. These scars are not only a reminder of my torture, but a reminder of my guilt. My hands are red, red, red and these scars are my punishment.

Nikolai, the Summer fae in the rotunda, and the Dusk fae who fought for my freedom. All those who died because of me or my actions. I'm responsible for it all.

A sharp knock at my door rips me from my thoughts, and I turn just as Vander lets himself into my bedchamber.

Vander pauses on the threshold, his silver eyes growing wide when he takes in my lack of attire. "Shit. Sorry, Princess." He turns away. "There's a messenger downstairs for you."

Given I arrived in this court in nothing but scraps of lace and shredded silk, I am surprised he feels the need to look away. I'm surprised he is respectful enough to do so. The move does little to soothe me. It does nothing but reinforce his claim of disinterest.

"You have seen it before. You should not feel embarrassed." I settle the lilac sleeves back onto my shoulders. "Did you accept the message?"

"He won't give it to me," he growls.

"Why ever not?" I look over my shoulder at him. "I am covered. You may turn around."

His face is a mask of calm when he turns. "He's from the Autumn Court."

Ice races through my veins, freezing me in place. Fayeth severed the mate bond she shared with my father. His broken mind makes me certain it was not he who sent the messenger. Given the last words I spoke to my brother, I would be surprised if Rennyn bothered to contact me, too. There is no one else from my home court who would bother with me.

"I do not think I can read it," I say as I follow him into the hallway.

He runs a hand over the stubble lining his chin, his tawny skin catching the light. "It's been fifteen days since Rennyn delivered Solana and begged for an alliance. Surely you can hear what he has to say?"

Fifteen days is not long enough to forget Autumn refused to rescue me from Summer's clutches. Fifteen days is not long enough to forget Rennyn only came to us for aid because his mother gave Summer everything the fire fae need to lay claim to the Autumn Court.

Downstairs, the messenger is waiting with a scroll gripped in his hand as if he fears losing it. The familiar caress of Autumn magic envelops me as I step into the brisk morning air; a melodic purring fills my ears, and the thick aroma of tilled dirt invades my nose. The animalistic and earth magic overwhelms my senses.

He bows. "Well met, Princess Bria. I've a message from High Lord Rennyn."

"Do not call me that. Here, I'm just Bria." I hold out my hand for the scroll, pushing down the sting of pain that surges forth at the mention of my brother's new title. He would still be a prince if Fayeth had not severed her mate bond with Father and fled for the Summer Court.

The moment the messenger places the parchment in my waiting palm, I pass it to Vander. The messenger balks and stutters a pathetic explanation about how Rennyn does not wish for anyone other than me to read the note.

"Thank you. You may leave."

"I'm to await your reply." His muddy brown eyes narrow as Vander cuts through the wax seal holding the scroll closed.

Vander's eyes dart back and forth across the long, looping letters, the crease pinching his brow and growing more pronounced the longer he reads. After a tense moment, he looks me in the eye, his silver clashing with my emerald. "Rennyn has requested your presence in the Autumn Court. Apparently, he has information that might cause you to reconsider an alliance."

"What information?"

"It doesn't say. He'll explain everything upon your arrival." He scratches a hand over his cropped black hair and faces the messenger. "Did your High Lord mention *when* he wants us there?"

The messenger dips his chin. "He's prepared a feast for tonight."

"Tonight?" My brows shoot up. He has not given us much time to consider.

When he returned my gorgeous mare, Solana, as a sign of good will and asked us to help his court, I was furious. The rage coursing through me did not allow room for sympathy or understanding. It did not allow me to consider that Rennyn is my brother and he needed my help. Though we do not share the same mother, he is still my blood. And I would very much like to know *why* he sent that ogre to attack me in the southern forest.

"It's up to you," says Vander. "The Dusk Court supports you no matter your choice."

"I appreciate that. I think…" My mind spins, and my heart desperately wants me to say no. But I'm no better than he is if I decline the invitation. "I think I should go."

It would be a pleasant change to wear clothes of my own for once, instead of relying on Wyn to source gowns for me. I could use the opportunity to retrieve my belongings, making my chamber at Dusk Manor my own at last.

"That's not the answer I was expecting." Vander smothers his surprise and flicks his eyes to the sky. "You don't go alone. We have time to prepare."

I dip my chin in thanks, then turn to the messenger. "We will arrive in time for the feast."

My eyes do not stray from the messenger as he turns and walks down the hill, heading for the forest that curls around the base. It is the same hill I dragged myself up after Wyn helped me escape Summer. The same hill I forced myself to climb without aid, believing the Mother Star was testing me.

I look at her now, where she rises to her zenith in a slow arc. The sun gleams today, but the scorching heat of Summer is missing. Instead, the cool lick of the Dusk Court smothers her blazing strength, and the gentle breeze brings the scents of lavender and orange rather than salt and flat bread.

I close my eyes against the Mother Star's light. *This is not the Summer Court. I am safe. I am in Dusk. He cannot harm me here.* My fingers twitch, searching for the abused branch of she-oak Torin gave me that night. The night I could see nothing but red.

Red, red, red.

Crimson still haunts my soul. Perhaps it always will.

"Are you okay?" Vander asks.

Vander is as astute as they come; there is no point hiding my pain from him. Still, I force my eyes to open and force the single word, red, to the back of my mind, where it will wait until I'm asleep to torment me some more.

"I'm fine. This is the first time I have laid eyes on the hill since arriving at Dusk Manor. It... brings back memories."

Memories of the pain, the mental torment, and the fear.

Memories of guilt and regret.

And a single good memory of the High Lord of Dusk on his knees, crawling beside me. *I'm not alone.*

He wraps an arm around my waist and turns us towards the manor. "You already conquered that hill, Princess. Move to the next one and flatten that, too."

He does not mean to speak of the literal hill, but the way I conquered my fear that night, the way I earned my freedom. Although I'm not sure I can emerge victorious after tackling the next hills of guilt, regret, and forgiveness. And it seems I will climb the hill of forgiveness sooner than I thought.

Vander removes his guiding arm the moment we are inside, walking ahead of me until we are in the upstairs apartment we share with his sister and his second.

We find Wyn and Torin in the bright dining room — I still marvel at the kitchen being within view, and how the three

Dusk fae cook for themselves — sitting at the wooden table. They take up one small corner of the large piece that ten fae could sit around with room to spare.

"Who's up for a feast?" asks Vander, sinking into the seat beside Torin.

Torin looks up from his ceramic mug. *Yet another design in Dusk that I have not seen before.* "Who are we hosting?"

"No one," says Vander, helping himself to a slice of Wyn's toasted rye. "We're the guests."

I sit beside Wyn, the view of the distant western ocean glittering through the many windows. Beyond the sparkling aquamarine, the dove grey mountains of the Night Islands claw for the sky. *Night is closer to Dusk than I first thought — it would take only hours to sail to the closest island from our western shore.*

Wyn's silken hair falls over her shoulder as she leans across the table and snatches the slice of toast back. "There's more in the oven. Where are we going?" Her silver eyes hold a hint of curiosity. "To seek allies?"

She looks so alike her younger brother that it startles me sometimes. They have the same light brown skin, the same ebony hair, and hold the same tension to their silver eyes. Today is no different, with the creases lining her eyes mirroring those on Vander's face.

"To pay Tohminic of Summer a visit?" asks Torin, his tone hopeful as he cracks his knuckles. His long blonde hair is loose today and hides the sharp angles of his cheekbones while making his already dark eyes seem like endless pits of black. "I've been waiting many moons for this day."

Vander sighs and stalks to the kitchen, returning moments later with a tray of steaming toasted bread. "The High Lord of Autumn has summoned us to his court."

Wyn freezes. "Why?"

"They have summoned *me*," I say, accepting a slice of toast. "But I appreciate you all coming with me."

Vander slathers some kind of blended peanut spread I'm not brave enough to taste on his toast. "No idea. Rennyn's note said he'll tell us once we're there."

The conversation continues to revolve around Rennyn and the Autumn Court while we eat, and despite the topic, I smile. The breakfasts I shared with my so-called family were always tense and awkward. This is how a family should behave.

The three Dusk fae have an easy, joking banter between them, and share the responsibilities of cooking and cleaning. As High Lord, Vander should be exempt from such a task as scrubbing dishes, but he slides on rubber gloves and an apron after the meal, happy to do his part.

Torin leans against the bench, watching rather than helping. "So, Bria, are you nervous about returning home? It's been, what, a month?" I'm still getting used to the word the Dusk fae use for an entire moon phase.

I set the baking tray down a little harder than I intend to. "Forty moons." Forty moons since I saw my home, my father, my court. Too many moons of torment and of red.

"Shall I teach that brother of yours a lesson?" Torin asks, bumping me with his hip. "I'd be more than happy to educate him on how to treat family."

He has changed into his leathers since breaking his fast, and the black fabric hugs every curve of his muscular body. Vander and Wyn will do the same, as well as carry an array of weapons for the trip into Autumn.

I eye Torin's leathers, counting twelve blades sheathed on his body — one on each thigh and arm, and three on either side of his torso, and two short swords crossed over his back. "You are over-armed for this. How about a deal?"

He arches an eyebrow, an eager glint shimmering in his onyx eyes. "I love a good deal. Enlighten me."

"You are not to harm a single Autumn fae unless they attack first. If you keep your blades to yourself, I will go with you on that date you keep pestering me about."

Vander tenses at the large sink.

Torin contemplates for a moment, his eyes flicking to his High Lord. "Deal."

I return to drying the dishes, my stomach turning to lead. If I had hoped Vander would say something about the date, I was so very wrong. He is supposed to be my pretend mate.

My mind is a mess of contradictions throughout the rest of the day. My thoughts swing from *this is the right thing to do* to *I should not do this* like a pendulum. By the time I am waiting in front of Dusk Manor with Wyn, Vander, and Torin, I'm still not certain entering Autumn's land will be good for me... or anyone.

Chapter 2

T HE MOTHER STAR SINKS beyond the horizon, casting the island of Dusk in an amber glow that distorts the senses. Much like the Dusk fae and their illusion magic, the time between the day's light and the moon's hours is mysterious. The light bends in such a way that anything could lurk in the shadows of the pines and she-oaks.

"It's time," says Wyn, adjusting the bangle that curls around her wrist. I have never asked her why she wears it. It feels too intrusive, given she twists it whenever she is nervous or angry.

She turns to me, those steel eyes creased with concern. "You're sure about this?"

I smooth the silk of my gown and grip the she-oak branch tighter. "I am as ready as I could hope to be."

Tonight's gown is simple, yet brazen enough that I know Rennyn will hate it. The emerald silk matches my eyes, making them seem brighter than normal, and that is where the decorum ends. The sleeves are nothing more than ribbons that cross over my back in place of my usual corset and the flowing skirt skates across my thighs, revealing the pale ivory of my legs. It is why I chose a gown that exposes my arms and legs.

The flame and cross scars are visible in the Mother Star's dying light. Though I hate my scars with every fibre of my being, they remind me of all I survived; they will keep me grounded while I struggle to recall why I despise my brother with such intensity. They will show Rennyn just what I endured in the Summer Court and remind him he could have prevented my torture.

I clasp a travelling cloak around my shoulders and move to stand between Torin and Vander, their magic cocooning me. Torin's whisper of wind flutters through my copper hair, the tingle of his memory stealing magic shooting along my palms. Vander's caress of cool air tracks across my nape while the calm warmth of his illusion power fills my every sense with the thought of home.

My magic swirls within me as if to remind me it is there. The metal bending power is a rare gift that is both feared and worshipped in the Autumn Court. It tastes of rust and screeches like the clashing of blades. As much as I try to draw the magical signature back into myself, I cannot. I have no control over my new power yet.

I'm determined to learn all there is about my magic, now I have it. After five and seventy years of thinking I could only wield the basics of folding and fae lights, I'm eager to begin training.

"Let's get going before he sends out a search party," says Torin, eyeing the darkness staining the sky in the east.

"I doubt he would do such a thing. He would assume I changed my mind and refused to meet with him," I say, gathering the magic of the realm and folding the Autumn Court towards me.

With one step, I leave the freedom of Dusk and enter the windy plains of Autumn. Long grass tickles my ankles as I continue to walk, closing the distance between me and the outpost while Vander, Torin, and Wyn fold into the court on either side of me. The wards crackle over my skin when I pass through them, an unwelcome reminder I'm no longer in the Dusk Court.

A mossy aroma blends with the crispness of ripe apples, and my heart clenches. There was a time when I would relish in the smell of my home court. Now, the apples and earth of Autumn make time feel as though it has slowed. A cold rush races through me and my shoulders curl forward.

The sentries in the outpost do not stop us as we pass under their watchful gazes and cross to the bridge of grass that leads to the gatehouse, but they grip their swords tighter, causing the weapons on their hips to gleam in the moon's light.

"Warm welcome," mutters Wyn.

Torin's eyes don't leave the two sentries, his head turning as we walk under the outpost until he is looking over his shoulder. "They blame us for their current circumstances."

Vander chuckles. "They only have themselves to blame."

The grass viaduct is usually empty of guards, so I am surprised to see them lining the long bridge, standing rigid at every gap in the crenelations. If Rennyn feels the need to station additional guards beyond the gatehouse, things must be worse than I first thought.

"So, how do we play this?" asks Torin, turning forward at last.

"We hear what he has to say and go from there," says Wyn.

Vander's magic churns. "Don't do anything to anger the guards. Send a whisper of wind through the castle and see what you can find out while Wyn and I lead the conversation with the High Lord."

"He is my brother," I say. "I think I should be the one leading the conversation. However, if you insist, I will not argue."

"I insist."

Wyn leans around her brother to look at me. "He's worried Rennyn will play on your connection to the court to get what he wants."

"I have no connection to this place." My tone is harsher than Wyn deserves. The Autumn Court was my home, yes. But that is where it ends.

My life here was nothing more than monotonous. I passed the days doing whatever Father ordered of me while wishing for a better life beyond the bailey walls. I was restless, weary, and a little jaded, and that was my downfall. If I had not wished for more excitement, Father would not have tried to claim the Dusk Court as his own. He would not have demanded I find a mate to strengthen alliances. I would never have met Tohminic of Summer. The only good memories to come from here are those of meeting Wyn and the others.

Beyond the gatehouse is much the same, with armoured guards patrolling both the outer bailey and the battlements surrounding. The inner bailey has twice as many guards. Both baileys, the courtyards that curl around the Autumn castle, are empty of fae other than those patrolling. Strange, given the time. There should be stalls bustling with activity. The metal forger should emit a bright glow and taint the air with the acrid scent of smoke. Fae should hurry from stall to stall, preparing for the next day by gathering supplies and placing orders.

This place is a shell of what it was mere moons ago.

A duo of guards — they are wearing their rarely seen armour — greet us at the doors and lead us into the castle I grew up in. I expect to see servants bustling about and lesser fae going about their nightly chores, but I see no one until we enter the vast dining hall.

Rennyn sits in Father's old seat at the head of the table with a spread of steaming food before him. He stands as we enter. "Welcome home, Bria."

"This is not my home. I'm of the Dusk Court now."

His golden-brown eyes narrow. "Blessed Mother Star, you even talk like them. Like the lesser fae."

"There is nothing *lesser* about contracting my words." I take the same seat I would have if this were still my home.

He runs a hand through his brown hair, freeing a curl. It falls over his forehead, and he brushes it aside with impatience. His hair is longer than I have ever seen it, a sure sign he is struggling to adapt to the role of High Lord.

"Well met," says Vander, taking the seat beside me and acting as a barrier between me and my brother. "I trust you're well?"

Rennyn lowers into his seat. "Well met. Had I known you would all come, I would have prepared beds." He turns to me. "Your chambers are as you left them."

"We're not staying," says Wyn.

Beside her, Torin is still. He cocks his head to the side as if listening to someone whispering in his ear. Perhaps his wind whispers are already reporting rumours from the lesser fae who staff the castle.

Rennyn's brows shoot up. "Oh?"

Already tired of the pleasantries, I load my plate with steaming buttery potatoes, crisp greens, and succulent slices of roasted beef. "No. We will return to the Dusk Court after I collect some of my things."

We have four Dusk fae arriving in an hour with cases.

"That is unfortunate," says Rennyn, following my lead and spearing a slice of beef with his fork. "I had hoped to speak with you in private, sister."

"Anything you say to her you can say to all of us," says Vander. I'm shocked by his stern tone. Shocked and thankful. "She's one of us now."

Before Rennyn can argue the point — he would be right to, given Vander and I are yet to announce him as the victor of Father's tournament to find me a mate — I stand and remove the travelling cloak, draping it over the back of the seat beside mine.

Rennyn freezes, his eyes growing wide as he sees the scars lining my arms for the first time. "Bria," he whispers. "Your arms."

I move around the table and slowly turn, gesturing to my legs. "My time in the Summer Court was not enjoyable. This is what you allowed, *brother*, what you could have prevented. This is why I declined an alliance when you visited Dusk." As I make my way back to my seat, I add, "I thought you should see them, so you realise my anger is not misplaced."

He pales. "Tohminic did that to you?"

I cannot look at him. "Yes. And Xaler, his selkie guard, and every member of his court who felt the need to poke and prod me with sticks and swords."

"He kept her in a fucking iron cage," growls Vander. The fork in his hand bends with the strength of his grip.

A glance at my brother, and I am delighted to see the colour drain from his face.

"I did not know," he breathes. "I am so sorry, Bria."

"It is done now." I collect my cutlery and slice into a potato. "I merely wished for you to understand."

"You warned Father time and again." Rennyn clips his words. I have never heard his tone so filled with anger.

Vander takes control of the conversation, steering it away from the past and to the future. "Your letter mentioned a bargain. You have something worth trading for our alliance?"

Rennyn shakes himself before recovering. "Yes. Though it is more for my sister than the rest of you."

"Before we go there," I say, setting my cutlery down and facing my brother. "There is something I have been wondering. Why did you send the ogre? After Tohminic had threatened me in the court gardens, the last thing I needed was to be attacked by that gruesome creature. Why?"

He shifts in his seat, his burgundy tunic pulling with the movement. "Mother wished to hasten your courtship. If you were scarred, she believed only Tohminic or Vander would have continued. I am sorry for agreeing with her plan."

How convenient Fayeth is not here to defend herself. A little too convenient, perhaps.

"And the parsley flowers in the Summer Lord's chambers?"

"Mother planted them there. It was she who poisoned Iker with hemlock."

Rennyn is being more forthcoming with information than I thought he would. It is a sure sign he is willing to negotiate. I let the subject drop before I push him too far and urge Vander to continue with his quest for information.

"What could you possibly have worth trading?" Vander asks. "We have everything we need in the Dusk Court. All you can offer us is land or your army, and judging by the guards stationed around this place, I'd say you're stretched pretty thin."

"Tohminic declared war on my court. He has since sent groups of both selkie and fae to attack my wards. No, I cannot spare the soldiers you need," says Rennyn. "What I offer is information."

We all turn to him, even Torin, who is supposed to be sending tendrils of wind through the castle and listening for secrets.

Rennyn ignores the others and focuses on me, his eyes dripping with apology and begging for my forgiveness. "If you agree to join forces, I will tell you who your mother is."

Ice runs through my veins. "You *know*? How could you keep this from me?"

"Mother and Father made me promise I would not tell you."

I push away from the table and stalk from the hall. A muted thud follows, the sound pleasingly similar to a fist smacking into a face.

"Bria, wait."

I spin towards Wyn, seeing Vander cradling his fist over her shoulder. Torin has Rennyn's arms behind his back. I guess I win that bet, then. The thought does little to calm me down.

"Are you okay?" Wyn asks, sparing a glance at her brother. "I can't begin to imagine what you're feeling."

She walks with me up the grand staircase towards the western wing as I try to explain. "My entire life is a lie. I always believed Father was the only one who knew my mother. Now I know not only did Fayeth know, but my brother, too." I shake my head, and a few strands of hair fall from the bun at my nape. "Perhaps everything I have ever known is a lie."

Wyn holds the door to my chambers open. "I will never lie to you. You have my word."

I offer her a sad smile. "And I believe you. Yet it does not take away the sting of betrayal I feel. Rennyn could have told me. He chose not to."

We work in silence for a time, filling the cases the Dusk fae delivered while we ate. I work on the jewellery and keepsakes while Wyn pulls gowns and cloaks from the armoire.

The silence becomes too much for Wyn, and she asks, "What are you going to do?"

"I do not know," I say, throwing a sparkling tiara atop a velvet cloak.

I have always longed to know my mother. There have been countless nights where I lie awake wondering who she is and what she is doing. So many of my dreams revolve around forming a bond with the female who birthed me. Yet... I cannot help but wonder if she thinks of me, too.

Of course, I know she is from the Spring Court thanks to my copper hair, and I think maybe that is enough. She has not tried to contact me in my five and seventy years, and that is telling.

"I do not wish to know her any longer," I say, surprised there is no sadness in my voice. "You, Torin, and Vander are my family now."

"Then let's tell your brother just where he can shove that slither of information." Her smile is devious.

Half an hour later, I'm standing among my Dusk friends in the Autumn Court's grand foyer staring Rennyn in the face and marvelling at the dried blood beneath his swollen nose. Vander defended my honour, which comes as a great surprise, and attacked a fellow High Lord. The consequences would be deadly if it were anyone other than Rennyn.

Wyn steps forward, her brows pinching and her mouth popping open.

I grip her by the elbow. "Allow me."

She smirks and waves a hand towards Rennyn and his four guards before stepping back beside Vander.

"You have decided?" Rennyn asks, his features harsh under the light shining from the few fae lights overhead.

I hesitate for a moment, my eyes dipping to the marble floor. A firm hand rests on my shoulder, giving me the strength and courage to look Rennyn in the eye and say, "With all due respect, you can shove your deal right up your arse."

He reels back. "Is that what they teach you in the Dusk Court? How to speak such filth? You have waited your whole life to know your mother. I can give you that."

"If you were a decent fae, and thought of family rather than status, you would have told me many moons ago. No, this is not a deal we are interested in. Goodbye, Rennyn."

When I turn, I'm surprised to see the hand on my shoulder belongs to Vander. His eyes twinkle with something I'm hesitant to believe is pride as he guides me through the large doors and into the inner bailey. There is a purple stain blooming on his left cheek, curtesy of the Autumn guards who rushed in to defend their High Lord, yet the pain does not seem to bother him when he smiles.

Wyn and Torin walk behind us, the latter sporting several bruises himself, and all I can think is how grateful I am for these three. Before meeting them, I would have given *anything* to know who my mother is. Now, I do not need to. Because what I said earlier is the truth. These three, however strange I may think them to be, are my family. They are my brothers and sister and parents and friends. They are everything I need.

Chapter 3

W E DO NOT SPEAK while we cross through the two baileys and under the portcullis. None of us utter a single word as we walk across the viaduct to the outpost, our steps slow and careful. It is not until we fold into the Dusk Court that the conversation flows.

"He deserved worse than that," says Wyn. She glances at the males. "How are you two feeling?"

"Better than I've felt in months," says Torin, his lips curling into a slow smile.

I cannot help but laugh. "You lost the bet."

His smile slips. "I didn't. He attacked first... with his words."

"You lost," growls Vander, taking the lead through the forest of pines and she-oaks that wraps around the coastline. "Bow out with grace."

"What are you all talking about?" asks Wyn, ducking under a low-hanging branch.

"I told Torin I would allow him to take me on a date if he refrained from fighting while in the Autumn Court." The relief that fills me is both unexpected and welcome. While Torin is beautiful and strong and brave, I'm not sure I could endure his joking nature if we were to mate.

He is all of those things, which should be enough. He would be the perfect mate. I know he would spend his days fighting to make me smile, defend me at every turn, and do whatever it takes to ensure my safety. Yet... Yet there is something inside me screaming he is not the one. He does not smell like home.

Wyn's eyes dart to her brother before she forces a smile. "Then I'm glad he held Rennyn's arms behind his back for two reasons. First, Rennyn deserved it after revealing he's always known who your mother is. Second, because no one should have to endure a date with Torin."

We break through the forest, and Dusk Manor shines like a beacon ahead. Its home atop the hill leaves the building exposed to the elements, yet the winds of Dusk seem to part and circle around the russet and iron-coloured bricks. The onyx tiles on the roof blend with the night sky, though during the day they are stark against the cerulean blue.

I love the manor. It is dark and mysterious. A welcome contrast to the beige and orange sandstone of Ad'Starrag, the Summer keep I detest.

"What's that supposed to mean?" Torin feigns shock.

"Enough," says Vander, as we navigate the twists and turns of the gravel path. "What did your whispers discover?"

In a blink, Torin's nature goes from joking to serious. "Rennyn wasn't lying when he said Tohminic was attacking his wards on the regular. Autumn has not seen more than three days of grace between attacks."

"No wonder he wants an alliance," says Wyn.

Vander pushes through the manor doors. "Have they lost fae?"

"Yes," says Torin. "Many."

I'm not sure how to feel about the knowledge. On one hand, the Autumn fae were once my denizens. On the other, none of them fought for me, none of them so much as batted an eye at my mistreatment. In fact, they taunted me themselves.

I tune out the rest of the conversation as we head to the third level apartment, my own problems rushing to the forefront of my mind. Have I done wrong in refusing to send aid to the Autumn Court, in sentencing them to a future of war and death? Perhaps I am no better than Rennyn and Father and Fayeth.

Guilt slams into me so hard I stagger on the spiral staircase.

"What's wrong?" asks Wyn from behind.

I brace a hand against the brick wall. "Father. I did not think to ask Rennyn if I could see him. He lost his mate and his mind, and I was too concerned for myself to wonder about him while we were in Autumn."

"Do you want to go back? I'll come with you."

Do I? Do I wish to see the pain and torment on Father's face? Losing your chosen mate is a destiny I would not wish on my worst enemy — even Tohminic and his sadistic ways do not deserve such a fate — and I'm not certain seeing Father in such a state would prove beneficial. Not to mention, if the blame for my circumstances does not fall on my own shoulders, it falls on his. I do not believe I can see him and hold myself back. Even with a tormented mind, Father deserves to hear my thoughts on his actions.

"No. I do not think it a good idea just yet." The smile that pulls at my lips is one of sadness. "I would not control myself.

I would not withhold my feelings. There will be time in the future to see him."

She dips her head. "It's your choice. Let me know when you're ready, and we'll go."

"Thank you," I say as we resume climbing the stairs.

Vander and Torin have already gathered around the dining table and have a length of parchment stretched out on the scarred wood. Torin mentions revealing something that is hidden, and both males scowl at the half-written letter while continuing their debate.

"I'd rather we keep that to ourselves for as long as possible," says Vander. "But without Autumn as allies, I don't think we have a choice."

"What do you mean?" I ask, approaching.

He spares me a glance. "Day and Dawn are hesitant to proclaim themselves as our allies. Jonik and Zentha both say they need more if they're to risk their courts."

"Is it not enough to see the proof of Tohminic's depravity?"

Torin shakes his head. "Jonik and his court have always been neutral, and Zentha and her Day Court are allies with Autumn. She wants something more concrete than torture before shifting alliances."

"It's understandable," says Wyn. "Has anyone told her of Kerym's fate? That Fayeth up and left him, giving Autumn's every defence to Summer?"

"Yes." Vander's voice is tight. "She's still not sure. Torin's right. We don't have a choice. Send a messenger and request their presence tomorrow."

I leave them to it, retiring to by bedchamber to pace. Politics is not my strong suit, and my mind is already too full of everything I have learned today.

Rennyn knows who my mother is. He has always known. Jonik, though he is responsible for leaving me alone in the forest bordering Summer and Day, is hesitant to join forces with Dusk. Zentha and her court, with their water magic and power to converse with spirits, were close with my father for many years and do not wish to tarnish his memory.

The Dawn Court's light and healing magic will be an advantage if war jeopardises Radelea's peace. Although, I'm determined to put an end to the fighting before it can begin.

Spring would be an ideal ally, too. Their nature and psychic powers would turn the tides of any war, though I'm hesitant to travel to the Court of Blooms to beg for their help.

The Winter Court would not do well against Summer. Their snow and ice magic proves useless against fire, and their shadow powers offer little reprieve from the scorching heat of the Mother Star. Every fae in Radelea knows that is why they are allies.

The Night Court, led by High Lady Maude, who has a grudge against the Dusk fae, would make good allies with their power over blood and bone and minds. It's a shame we cannot trust them as allies.

My thoughts churn faster and faster, and the walls seem to close in on me as I consider just how outnumbered we are with the threat of war on the horizon. I drag my eyes to the window, searching for an open space that will bring a sense of calm to my raging mind.

All I see is the western village in the distance. A village I have yet to explore.

It is the perfect way to take my mind off things.

I'm still wearing my travelling cloak; there is nothing to be done but sneak through the manor and into the crisp night air. A glance out my door and to the left tells me Vander, Wyn, and Torin are still bickering over the best wording of their letter. I sneak to the right and dash down the curling staircase to the ground floor.

Though Dusk Manor is open to all fae within the court, as well as the Ill-fated and their lavender-eyed leader, Nyree, the halls and rooms are quiet as I exit through the front doors.

Déjà vu threatens to bring me to my knees as I slink through the shadows. It was only two months ago I was sneaking from the Autumn castle to visit Nikolai at the docks in the village. Two months ago, sneaking from the castle was the most exciting thing in my life. Now, there is too much excitement and I resent the jaded crown I once wore.

At the base of the manor's hill, I duck into the safety of the she-oak forest, running my hands along the swaying branches to calm my racing heart. Sneaking from the manor is reckless. Anything could happen to me outside of the brick walls I call home.

Leaves rustle to my left, and I whip around, squinting. A glimmer of pearlescent hair flashes among the needle-thin branches, gone before I can determine who is hiding among the trees.

There is only one fae I know with hair such a colour, but she is at her Ill-fated home to the north-east, preparing her fae for the possibility of war. I shake the thought away. There is no chance Nyree would be here, in the forest at the base of Dusk Manor, spying. What could she gain from it?

The night is quiet as I turn right, taking the path those Dusk fae took when Vander and Wyn first brought me to their island court. The scent of pine and lavender fills forest, with a salty breeze drifting from the crashing ocean to the east and south. A myriad of greens and browns brings a sense of calm to my haunted soul, leaving no room for the crimson I so often think about to invade my thoughts.

I love it here. Truly. If not for the nature and scents, but for the serenity. It is seldom my mind is at ease these days. It is seldom I do not think of my crimson-stained hands and the guilt I carry for the lives lost.

Wyn is determined to believe I'm not to blame for those who died at Ad'Starrag when Vander and his court laid siege to the Summer keep. She claims the Dusk fae used their control of the wind to send those iron cannons back at Tohminic and his fire army. She says none who marched that night sustained injuries.

I believe her, but no one can argue Nikolai's death is anyone's fault but my own. From lover to undead guard, Nik's death will forever be a scar I carry. The crimson of his blood, dripping over the fish and rice I had yet to finish, will forever haunt my soul.

Red, red, red.

The word does not torment me as it once did, though there are moments when it surprises me with its ferocity. I may be in the bath, scrubbing the day's sweat from my body, and my mind will recall how hard I scrubbed my hands that night at Ad'Starrag. I could stand at the window in my bedchamber admiring the glittering ocean beyond the Dusk Court, and I will remember the way the Dawn Court ships lined the horizon, how the selkies dashed through the water towards them.

There is always something that causes my guilt to resurface, but here in the green and brown forest, there is nothing similar to Summer, nothing to remind me of the lives lost because of my actions. Here, my mind knows peace.

I am sad to leave the forest behind as the path twists to the west, though the feeling is fleeting. A slow smile builds. My breath hitches. I tilt my head as I take in the vast village before me. Bustling. It is the only word for it.

I have never seen a village so large, so bright, and so intriguing. The buildings are all made of the same brick as Dusk Manor, with the same dark roofs. The way they all match, with lights glittering from the panelled windows... Stories could be written about this village, images so carefully painted depicting the liveliness.

All worries and stress fade, replaced by awe as laughter and chatter drift towards me on the salty breeze. Other scents blend with the ocean's salt: ale, spiced meat, and something sweet like honey. I need to investigate those tantalising smells and explore the narrow streets.

I hold myself back to enjoy the moment. With the sea to the south, the forest at my back, and the view before me, this is a slither of peace I cannot find elsewhere.

Fae gather in a large space in the centre of the village, each of them gripping glasses filled with some kind of amber liquid — ale, I think. Every single one of them are lesser fae.

In the Autumn Court, my father would never have allowed them to gather like this. He would believe them to be conspiring against his title, and force them to retire for the night when the Mother Star dips beyond the horizon, their chores done until she rises once more.

Here, they have a life. Here, they have the freedom they deserve.

I sink to the ground, wrap my arms around my knees, and watch for a while. Two months ago, if anyone had told me there is such a place where lesser fae are *happy*, I would not have believed them. But as the fae in the village smile and laugh, flitting from one friend to another, that is the only word to make sense.

Somehow, Vander and Wyn have found the balance between leading these fae and befriending them. I have seen nothing of the like before, and I cannot help but marvel at the brilliance.

My heart sinks and my stomach clenches when a thought invades my peace. These fae may be happy, but the clashing of swords will haunt their lives soon enough. War will tear this moment from the world.

A sigh flutters through my lips as I stand and brush pine needles from my travelling cloak, intent on exploring as far as I can tonight. Leaves crunch from behind me when I take my first step towards the village.

"I didn't think you'd be the type to sneak out on your own," says Vander, stepping up beside me. "I figured you've had enough loneliness to last a lifetime."

"You gave me a fright." I unclench my hand from my chest and drop it to my side. "Why are you out here?"

He dips his chin. "I saw you sneak from your room and thought I should check that you're okay." He gestures to the village. "It's marvellous, isn't it? Would you care for a tour?"

I turn towards the glowing houses. "That is why I'm here. I wished to explore and take my mind off everything that happened in Autumn."

The walk from the forest edge to the village takes less time than I thought, and we are soon walking the cobbled streets between the brick buildings. We pass bakers and butchers and stores of every description, all closing for the night. The best by far is the clothing store, host to several styles I have yet to see.

"Where do the Dusk fae find such talent for clothing?" I wonder aloud. "I have never seen gowns with so little fabric."

His eyes brighten a little. "Would you hate me if I told you I can't say? Not until tomorrow, at least. You'll delight in the answer."

Curiosity burns through me, but I let it drop. I have not known Vander for long, though I know him well enough to understand he will not tell me what I wish to know if he deems me unworthy.

Every fae we pass, both high and lesser, acknowledges Vander in some way. Most of them bow their heads as a show of respect, some smile and wave, and some females stop in their tracks and dip into a curtsey. It is as if he is their friend rather than their High Lord.

As we wander along one of the residential streets, where fae lights entrapped in glass orbs atop metal poles light the way, I feel nothing but calm in Vander's company. Because he *crawled* for me. He got to his hands and knees and climbed that hill right alongside me. No matter the torment in my mind, I know Vander will always be there to help me through it. I know he will move realm and star if it ensured my freedom and safety.

It is no wonder I cannot stop thinking of his silver eyes and tawny skin when I'm alone in my chamber. It is no wonder a single thought of the male beside me chases away the red. When I think of him, I have something to hold on to. When I think of him, I am tethered to the here and now. I am grounded.

"We can thank my father for this village," he says as we approach a bustling square in the middle of the village. "It was the first thing we built after settling the veil over the island."

"I did not know that. It is certainly impressive."

He halts in his tracks. "Why do you speak so proper? You don't have to pretend here. You know that, right?"

"Excuse me?"

He runs a hand over the shadow of hair on his head. "The Autumn Court expects you to speak and act in a certain way. We don't bother with that here. Here, you can discover who you are beyond the tiaras, balls, and gowns."

"I'm not sure I understand." My eyes track over the laughing crowd in the village square. "I do not wish to be anyone other than Bria."

"That's my point," he says, gesturing for me to continue walking. "You're entire life has been determined by males of a higher social standing than you. Do you even know who you are beyond the title of High Lord's daughter?"

"I..." His question brings me up short. Not because he is being rude or cruel, but because he is right. I taught history to the younglings because Father ordered it, dressed in gowns every day because he expected me to, and never learned how to defend myself because the males in Autumn deemed it unnecessary. No one ever gave me a chance to discover who I am at my core. "No. I do not know who I am."

"I have an idea, if you'll allow it?"

We enter the large open space — though fae of every description bustle about, there are no ornaments or statues or guards like I am used to — to cheers from the revellers. The ruckus reminds me of the tavern in Autumn's western village, the one I would always yearn to enter and spend hours laughing with the anglers.

"High Lord Vander," the closest male shouts, "have you come for ale and dancing?"

He chuckles. "Not tonight."

"And who are you?" asks the male, his evergreen eyes assessing.

I curtsey. "Well met. I'm Bria Sutherland, formerly of the Autumn Court. Lovely to meet you."

"Why don't you join us for a drink?" He waves a hand in the air, calling over a female with wisps of wind for hair.

No one has seen the wind wraiths for millennia. Given the Dusk fae are wind wielders, I should not let the knowledge surprise me, but I'm beyond amazed to see one here, and startle at her glittering skin. It is as though she is made of nothing but an ocean breeze as she flits over to us with two mugs of ale in hands of flowing air.

She is there, but not. She is air with form as she hands both Vander and me an ale. Her voice is a whisper of breeze as she says, "Do enjoy, and call upon the wind should you need anything more." She turns to Vander. "Anything at all. Send my love to that delicious second of yours."

A shiver races down my spine at her words. Torin and a wraith? The Dusk Court is more... modern than I thought.

Vander thanks the wraith, named Alizeh, and the male who greeted us, then drags me to the side of the village square. Once we are under the safety of a striped awning, he says, "As I was saying, I have an idea."

I sip at the ale, the bitter liquid not at all to my taste. Of all the times I imagined joining the anglers for a drink on those nights I snuck away to see Nikolai, I never once thought I would not enjoy the taste of ale. I take my mind off my disappointment by urging Vander to explain his idea.

"You need to discover who you are away from titles and expectations." He sips at the ale, humming in approval. "If you have nothing to focus on other than what happened to you at Ad'Starrag, you'll never find the strength to move past it."

"What do you suggest?" I set my mug on a nearby barrel.

"First, you can't find yourself if you're unable to defend yourself. You have to train. You have unchecked magic roiling through you. I can feel the bitter tang of metal swirling and probing even now. It's imperative you get your powers under control. Second, you need to learn how to wield a weapon. Wyn said no one taught you how to fight?" I give a non-committal shrug, and he adds, "Torin and I will train you."

"And third?" I ask, growing more interested with every word.

"Once you have control of your magic, and you're able to fend off attacks on your own should it come to it, you need to find a hobby. You taught history in the Autumn Court, yes?"

"I did, but I would not say I enjoyed the subject. The students, yes, but I would rather read about events than teach them."

He nods. "We should be able to find something in the archives for you to do. There are scrolls that need translating from the ancient tongue, if you're able?"

All of a sudden, my life looks less bleak. With just a handful of words, Vander has filled me with hope. Hope for the future, hope for a life worth living, and hope that I will overcome the crimson haunting my mind. If I can focus on those texts he spoke of, there will be no room in my thoughts for anything else.

I can win the battle with my red demons.

And come out on top.

Chapter 4

"I'm not sure about this," I tell Wyn. My eyes track over my bedchamber as I look for an alternative to the gown she has me dressed in. "It reminds me of my nightgown."

Indeed, the minimal amount of white material falls to mid-thigh, and the only shaped section is the bust, which cups my breasts and is held up by straps the width of two fingers. I have never seen such a design. I'm wondering where the Dusk Court source such items of clothing, for every other court in Radelea prefers corsets and hooped skirts.

"Trust me," she says, circling me and nodding in approval, "you'll want something like this for what we're doing tonight."

"And you are certain you cannot tell me until we meet with Jonik and Zentha?"

"We've been over this."

I sigh and readjust my hair, moving it to the side so it falls over one shoulder. "Shall we head down?"

"I think we better. Everyone else will be there by now." She holds open the door and waves me out. "While we walk, you can tell me about your visit to the village last night."

"There is not much to tell. Vander gave me a tour, a wraith served us ale — which is disgusting, by the way — and we decided I need to train in both magic and fighting."

We descend the spiral staircase, Wyn at the rear. "You don't have to sneak out, Bria. This is not a prison. You're free to come and go as you please. All we ask is that you let us know when you're leaving."

My heart swells. This truly is freedom.

All I can do is thank her for her kindness and continue to the ground floor. Every window we pass offers me glimpses of the swollen moon high in the sky. It shines brighter than the stars, drawing the eye at every opportunity. I love it when the moon is full. The light shining on Radelea is like a fresh start, cleansing the realm of hatred and vileness.

I lead us through the middle level of Dusk Manor, where the living spaces and chapel take most of the space, along a narrow hallway with the guards' chambers on one side and a grand sitting room on the other, then into the archives.

The smell of ink and parchment tickles my senses, and my fingers itch to explore the shelves of books and scrolls. As much as I wish to begin my journey of the Dusk library, I will keep my word and refrain until I have mastered the metal bending magic swirling within me.

Wyn waves a lazy hand through the air mere moments before I step *into* a statue of a fae male wielding a miniature tornado in his palm. I know it is an illusion, but even with that knowledge, my mind rebels at the thought of colliding with solid stone.

On the other side, I knock on a wooden door that blends with the wall and wait for someone to grant Wyn and me access. For a moment, I wonder how to enter the room if no one is there to open the hidden door.

The thought slips away as we are let through, and I'm confronted with the same eight fae who were here the first time I graced the council with my presence. Vander, Zentha, Nyree, and Jonik are all seated around the long table, each of them assessing the map laid out on the wooden surface.

Standing beside the raised platform the table rests on, the Dawn triplets fidget. They whip their faces up in unison.

Larrad is the first to speak. "Bria, please accept my heartfelt apology for leaving you in that dreaded forest."

"And please accept my sorrow at what you endured after," says Ulakas.

Tasar says, "We three are beyond remorseful. Forgive us?"

Vander has told me I have plenty of hills to climb. I have yet to climb the steep mounds of guilt and regret, but this slanted hill of forgiveness is proving easy. I cannot help but smile at the triplets and their identical black hair and dark, almond-shaped eyes.

"You have my forgiveness, and an apology for my behaviour when we last met." I turn to the High Lord of Dawn, who is a mirror image of his sons. "As do you, Lord Jonik."

He bows his head. "I take it with thanks, though it is unnecessary."

The triplets take the three remaining seats on the other side of the table, sitting between their father and Vander. Wyn takes the seat beside her brother, which leaves me sitting between Torin and Nyree once more.

"Please," says Zentha once we are all settled, "tell us why you have called us back to Dusk Manor." She does not seem pleased to be here. I cannot blame her. Her son is due to cement his mate bond any day now, and planning for such a celebration takes a lot of time.

Torin leans forward, resting his forearms on the table. "Reconsider. Join forces with the Dusk Court. Tohminic has already attacked Autumn several times. We believe he will target us next. The moment he figures out how to get past our wards, he will come for us."

"I am sorry," says Jonik, "but we cannot risk the healers of Radelea without something more. We are a neutral court and we will remain that way."

Zentha's warm brown skin shimmers in the fae lights as she leans back in her chair, her tight coils shifting with the movement. Her honey-coloured eyes blaze as she says, "We cannot afford to anger Summer. It is a shame about Autumn, but we cannot help. We have told you this already."

"There is something else we can bring to the table," says Vander. His face falls, as if he had hoped more than anything it would not come to this.

Everyone quiets, all eyes on the High Lord of Dusk.

"For three hundred years, since the Night Court broke into many islands, the Dusk fae have hidden. You might wonder why. Why not declare ourselves all those years ago?" Vander's silver eyes seem to flare brighter as he meets the gaze of everyone here. "We were not worried about ourselves when we veiled this island, but the humans we protect."

I run through every word of every text I have ever read, trying to remember if I have heard such a term before. I come up empty.

"Humans." Everyone around the table, except the Dusk fae, utter the one word. Even Nyree looks surprised.

"What is a human?" asks Tasar.

"They are just like us," says Wyn. "Except unlike us, they don't have magic. We've protected the portal into the human realm for three hundred years. It's imperative the rest of Radelea don't discover it."

"Why?" asks Zentha. "If they are like us, why not amalgamate into our society?"

"Let us show you," says Vander. "Humans are not the only creatures within the realm. The land in which they dwell is called Earth, and it's rife with supernatural creatures."

"I refuse to go anywhere until you have told us more," says Ulakas. "What type of supernaturals? What *are* supernaturals?"

Vander stands and paces the length of the raised platform. "A supernatural is a being with power of any kind. We are fae. We are supernatural because we have enhanced senses and wield magic."

"Our senses are not unusual," says Zentha.

"I agree with Lady Zentha," says Jonik. His light brown skin shimmers with a sheen of sweat, revealing just how uneasy he is about the conversation and knowledge. "There is nothing unusual about us."

"But there is, according to the humans," says Wyn. She twirls her snake bangle.

Torin sighs. "Shifters are humans who can turn into animals. Witches are humans with the gift of brewing potions and casting spells through using herbs and such. Vampires are technically undead and drink the blood of humans to fuel their bodies. There are —"

"That is quite enough," says Zentha, the colour draining from her face.

I sit straighter, my eyes darting from fae to fae as they bicker. Jonik does not believe the supernaturals deserve our protection. Zentha is concerned the shifters and witches and vampires — I have never heard of these creatures, and I'm beyond intrigued — will prove troublesome. The triplets agree humans sound fragile, though are hesitant to interact with the other beings on Earth.

A whole other realm, just waiting to be explored. My leg twitches, as if I could just leap to my feet and enter this new world until my heart is full to bursting from exploring every nook and cranny.

"The humans will not attack you, and as far as we're aware, the other beings know nothing of us," says Wyn. Her tone is weary, as if she has endured this very conversation before. Perhaps she has. I can only imagine the reactions of everyone in Dusk when they discovered the portal to Earth.

"How many fae know of Earth's existence?" I ask, looking to Vander for the answer.

"Only those permitted entry to the war room."

"Can anyone access this place?"

He shakes his head. "It's warded against entry. Only those I allow in may knock on the door. If any fae tries to force entry without my permission, the timber will swallow their hand whole."

A shiver dances down my spine. That's not a fate I would enjoy. "I would very much like to visit Earth and see these humans for myself."

Vander smirks. "I thought you might." He turns his attention to Jonik and Zentha, where they sit at the opposite end of the table. "There's one other thing I should mention. The humans are nearing the end of their twentieth century. Their advancements... Without magic, they've found interesting ways of living. It'll be a shock at first."

"What *advancements*?" asks Larrad, leaning on the table.

It is Wyn who answers. "Technology. Electricity. Medicine. It seems magic has held us back."

I do not know any of those words, though they sound interesting. I lose the battle with my legs and stand. "When do we go?"

"All this time," breathes Nyree from beside me. Her lavender eyes narrow. "All this time, you've kept it from me, from the Ill-fated. Have you ever trusted us?"

"We're trusting you now," says Vander. "If everyone could step off the platform, please."

The Day and Dawn fae look like they would rather be anywhere else as we all follow his command and stand against the far wall, with Vander and Wyn remaining by the platform. They use their air magic to remove the table and chairs, setting them all to the side. Next, they roll the large, faded rug and place it against the wall.

Nyree gasps, but clenches her jaw when I look at her. Her pearl-coloured hair glimmers in a rainbow of colours, and I'm reminded of the flash of pearl I saw in the forest last night. I had all but forgotten about it with the war meeting and the tour of the village with Vander. Now I wonder if information such as this is what she was after, if discovering what Dusk is hiding was her mission in spying from the safety of the she-oaks.

I follow her line of sight to a hatch on the floor. It is just large enough for a single fae body to fit through. It creaks as Vander lifts the wooden board, revealing a dark tunnel that disappears beneath Dusk Manor. "The drop is not far. After you, Wyn."

Wyn steps over the dark hole and falls. Her ebony hair whips around her face as she disappears into the darkness. A thud. Then, "All clear."

Vander's eyes meet mine, but I shake my head. If I can wait until everyone else has descended, I can tell Vander what I saw in the forest. I do not trust Nyree. He and the others need to know she's up to something.

While the triplets descend into the tunnel, I wonder whether my history has made me paranoid, whether my time in the Summer Court makes me see threats when there are none.

Jonik follows his sons.

I wonder if Nyree was simply out for a walk and I'm mistaken.

Zentha drops.

Nyree could very well have been gathering branches, much like I do. I ache for the she-oak branch I left in my chamber. I do not handle confusion and contrasting thoughts with ease.

Nyree follows Zentha, and I think about keeping the information to myself. But what if I'm right, and she *was* spying or gathering information? It would be wrong to keep it to myself.

Torin offers help me down, but I decline, my mind made up at last. I'm going to tell Vander, and if he believes Nyree is to be trusted, I will leave it at that. At least I will have done everything I can to prevent anything from happening to the Dusk Court. My negligence will get no one harmed. My negligence will not add to the red staining my hands.

Torin shrugs and jumps down, and I'm alone with the High Lord at last.

His magic wraps around me, noticeable now it's just the two of us. It caresses my arms like a loving touch, the tickle of air both soothing and exciting. The mingling aromas of the freshest of breezes, the ripest of apples, and the warmth of a summer's eve surround me. It is the forest cedars and the salt of the beach. It is many things. Many, and one.

Vander smells like home.

I have thought it before, but my mind did not put the pieces together. There is a reason something as simple as scent would bring me such comfort, yet I cannot quite recall what that reason is.

"Are you ready?" he asks, stepping closer as if pulled towards me by the very gravity that grounds us.

Vander's eyes dart to my mouth when I graze my teeth over my bottom lip, suddenly nervous. I take a step closer, not knowing how my voice will travel to the party waiting below. "Last night, when I was walking through the forest, I saw Nyree. I think she was spying on the manor."

His brow lowers. "Are you certain that's what you saw?"

I remember the flash of pearl-like hair. "Yes."

"She has been a member of my court for three hundred years. If she wanted to betray us, she would have done it by now."

"Perhaps she has been waiting for the right moment." The words leave my mouth, but my mind is wondering how Vander and I got to be so close.

"I trust her."

"But you have not trusted her with this," I say, gesturing to the open hatch. "Surely there's a reason for that."

He lifts a hand as if to touch me, but he stops himself. "I will talk to her if it makes you feel better."

"That's all I ask." I turn and jump into the dark hole before he can change his mind. The ground is closer than I thought, and my knees crumple with the impact. I shout a shaky, "All clear," then scuttle to the side.

The cavern is spacious, the hewn walls curved and dripping water. The only fae to remain is Wyn.

She raises her eyebrows at me. "Why are you so flushed?" Vander lands beside me with a grace I do not possess, and Wyn shakes her head. "Never mind." There's a small smile playing on her lips I cannot make heads nor tails of.

"The others have gone ahead?" Vander asks, straightening his black jacket. It's yet another style I have not seen; I'm now left wondering if the Dusk Court source their clothes from Earth.

"Torin has taken them to the portal," says Wyn. "What took you two so long?"

He leans closer, whispering, "Nyree was in the forest last night, watching the manor from afar. Keep an eye on her."

Wyn frowns. "She's not going to do anything after we took the Ill-fated in and gave them a home when Lady Maude wouldn't. She was probably just out for a walk."

"I thought I could trust Father and Rennyn, and look where that got me," I mutter. It's the first time I have so much as thought such a thing, and the surprise on Vander's and Wyn's faces echoes my own. I shrug. "Trust is not everything. It's important, yes, but often it's placed in the wrong hands."

"They didn't deserve your trust," Vander growls.

Wyn's eyes flick back and forth between us as if watching an enthralling stage play in the village theatre — one of the more exciting places Vander showed me last night. She knows something I do not, and I intend to figure out just what that is. Her words from Ad'Starrag echo in my mind. *There's something you should know. I haven't mentioned it to Vander yet, but I believe you...* Tohminic cut her words short when he wheeled our cages to the battlements for the first time.

Vander takes the lead, leaving Wyn and me to trail behind in the narrow corridor that heads... south, I think.

I link my arm through hers and drag her closer. "Back in Ad'Starrag, before they took us to the battlements, you were trying to tell me something. What was it?"

Her face screws in confusion before she masks all emotion. "Not now. Later." When I do not let go of her arm, she sighs. "When we're alone, I promise."

It's enough for now. I let the subject drop and focus on our surroundings as we approach the group waiting for us. There's a shimmering curtain of water behind them, a gleaming waterfall that crashes to the ground without sound and without dampening the surrounding rock. There's no puddle of water, no hole above where the water has come from. It is a waterfall without a beginning or an end.

Vander steps up to the rainbow of colours. "All you have to do is step through the veil. The human city on the other side is called Melbourne. It's the second largest in the country of Australia."

"You speak in riddles," says Jonik.

"Australia is the equivalent of Radelea," says Torin. "You could compare each state and territory, of which there are eight, with each of our courts. Then there are the cities, which are larger than ours in both size and height."

"Height?" asks Zentha, her dark brows rising. "Whatever do you mean?"

"You'll see," says Torin, a knowing smirk tilting his full lips.

"Enough waiting around," says Larrad, moving closer to the veil. "I will go first."

Vander steps in front of him. "Wait by the brick wall once you step through. There is something we have to do before any humans see us."

This time, I do not wait for the others to step through. I bounce from foot to foot while the triplets enter the human realm, and my racing pulse fills me with a buzzing energy. The moment Tasar disappears beyond the trickle of colours, I move forward. "I cannot wait any longer."

Vander takes my hand. Warmth spreads from the contact. "Best not to do it alone the first time."

"You allowed the Dawn triplets to go through alone."

"Yes, but they need something to temper their attitudes a little. Though they're quieter than they were at the breakfast feast in the Autumn Court." The one where Fayeth poisoned Iker, whatever her reasons.

We both turn to face the mirage of colours — green flashes to blue, which flashes to red, and thank the Mother Star, a bright purple soon replaces the crimson — and step forward. The void pulls at me in a way that reminds me of stepping through the fold. My skin feels too tight and too loose simultaneously, my breaths seize in my chest, and my limbs lock. All I know is darkness and the feel of Vander's hand wrapped around mine.

It's over before I can panic, and I'm soon standing in a dark alleyway beside a tall building. I look up and up... and up some more. "That is most definitely the largest building I have seen. It must be at least eighty long swords tall."

"Two sixty-five, including the antenna," says Vander. "Two twenty-two to the top of the brick."

"Antenna?" asks Larrad, looking a little green. "Do you mean the long thing at the very top?"

Vander nods. "They use it for electrical signals and transmitting or something."

A human, a real-life *human*, walks past the entrance to the alley we are standing in. The male looks just like the males in Radelea, though he wears a strange set of smart-looking clothes. And the tips of his ears are *rounded*.

My eyes grow wide, and I trace the tip of my pointed ears with my free hand. "I did not know our ears were so different." I have never thought twice about my ears. How else are the humans different?

"A mark of our species," says Vander, his tone bordering unimpressed. Once everyone has gathered in the alleyway, he asks for quiet before saying, "I ask that you mask your ears. The humans know we're not from Earth, but they don't know the extent of our powers or where we're from."

"How?" asks Zentha. "We do not possess the power to change our bodies. Unless you wish for us to cover them with hair?"

"On Earth, and only on Earth, the Mother Star grants us an extra power," says Vander, his eyes gleaming as if he has waited eons to tell us this. "We call it a glamour." He spends several moments describing how to draw power from our well of magic and coat our ears with it, using sheer will to make them appear round at the tips.

It's a simple magic, like fae lights and folding, and I cast the glamour with the ease of a master wielder. I can only hope learning how to control my metal bending gift comes to me with the same instinct.

Once we no longer have the pointed ears that reveal our species, we walk through the busy streets of the human city. I thought the Dusk village was bustling, but it has nothing on this.

Most of the buildings tower over us, and I marvel at the ingenuity of constructing something so grand and intimidating, but mostly, I watch the humans. They are an odd bunch, that is certain. The females wear clothes that are either too tight or too loose, some of them in all black with silver studs on every surface. I do not see many gowns, but a lot of slacks and something Wyn calls double denim. The males are just as confusing with their baggy shirts open over baggy T-shirts, some with chains dangling from their hips.

My mind spins as Wyn and Torin explain the details to the group. T-shirts and jeans and poking metal through your skin... I would never imagine such a world to exist. And their music. Their music has *words*. Lyrics, Torin calls them. I am beyond stunned when we pass a music store and the words of a song filter into the street. A female sings about zombies, whatever they are, in a cool voice that sends a shiver down my spine and makes my hairs stand on end.

What intrigues me the most, and causes envy to burn through me, is the *electricity*. The humans do not use fae lights, but have switches for lights that hang from the ceiling. It's... amazing and frightening and awe-inspiring. They have cars and airplanes and trams, and it's all too much after an hour. There's too much to see, too much to digest.

We make our way back to the portal, Jonik and Zentha both agreeing this place needs protecting at all costs. The humans are vulnerable, and if we can save them from a shred of pain, it's our duty to do so.

Chapter 5

IT HAS BEEN FOURTEEN moons since Vander revealed the human realm to us. During that time, I have done little other than explore the Dusk Court. I have wandered through the southern forest, hiked the rolling hills in the centre of the island, and visited the western village many times. I even spent a day in the north, where a larger village rests by the sea, and met the younglings at the academy. My fingers itched to explore the academy archives, but I refrained from so much as stepping foot in the enormous chamber.

I have my first lesson in combat today, and if all goes well, I may visit the manor archives tonight. If only Wyn had not forced me to wear leathers for today's training, the day would be almost perfect.

I gather the offending fabric from my bed and hold it up. There does not look to be enough material to cover my whole body, and I cannot make out the direction in which it goes. It takes longer than it should for me to realise I'm *not* holding pants and a top. The darned thing is one piece.

"What if I need to relieve my bladder?" I wonder out loud.

"Trust me," says Wyn, letting herself into my chamber. "When you're fighting for your life, relieving yourself will be the last thing on your mind. Do you need some help?"

"Please. I do not know where to start with this thing." I hand her the intimidating outfit and strip off my gown.

She orders me to step into two — too small, I cannot possibly fit — holes in the leather. Then she drags the cold fabric up my body. Every slither of skin feels as if Wyn is forcing it into a vice and squeezing with all her might, but the discomfort only lasts a heartbeat before fading to a feeling of security and support.

We somehow slide my arms into the full-length sleeves, and Wyn is buckling the straps at my ribs in no time. There is minimal chance of me buckling those on my own, being too far to the side for me to reach. I would never have guessed the buckles were to be in the front, though now I have leather cupping my breasts, I can see that it makes sense. Every curve, every dip and swell. It's all on show.

"Test it out," says Wyn, nodding as she takes in every piece of leather from my wrists to the neat line across my ankles.

I stretch my arms up and around, holding them behind me to test the limits of the leathers. Next, I lunge forwards with my legs stretched far apart. The suit is more accommodating than I thought and does not hinder my movements. In fact, I may be more agile and flexible, if that is possible.

I turn to her with a smile. "It's marvellous. Though I'm not sure how I feel about being so restricted."

"Covered," she says. "Covered, not restricted. This is your first time wearing pants? Ever?"

I nod and bend to collect the leather knee-high boots from the floor. "Father never allowed me to wear them, even while riding. He claims it's unbecoming of a female."

She snorts. "Males are fools. The lot of them."

Wyn leads the way through the manor, and I cannot help but wonder about the differences in our leathers. While mine are full length, with as much skin covered as possible, hers are without sleeves, showing the light brown skin of her arms in all their muscular glory. Hers also have large pockets low on her thighs, bulging with... Well, I do not know what's in them.

I am all buckles and sheathes. She is smooth leather and defined muscle.

While Wyn leads me to the outdoor training grounds, she says, "We sent word of your mate bond with Vander to all who need to know."

I stop short. "Was it necessary? Every High Lord and Lady knows what I went through with Tohminic. They would understand if I did not choose a mate."

"If we want allies in this war, we need to act as they expect."

I sigh, knowing she's right. "You could have waited until after we visit the Day Court. Elmon and Kyra are cementing their mate bond in two days. We leave tomorrow."

"The mating of Zentha's son is irrelevant," she says, throwing me a glare. "It's already been too long since you left the Summer Court."

"But I will have to pretend," I whine. "I dislike lying."

"Lying just might save your life one day."

We cannot say more on the matter, not with Torin and Vander waiting for us in the dirt training oval a mere five sword lengths away.

Torin whistles long and low. "Damn. If I had known you'd look *this* good in leathers, I would have demanded you try them on sooner."

Vander turns slowly and drags his eyes over my black attire before forcing them away.

Warmth creeps over my cheeks.

"Stop it, Torin," says Wyn, "or I'll put you on your arse again."

"Again?" His dark eyes crinkle at the sides.

She smiles. "Yes, again. Your defeat was astounding last time we sparred."

They continue their jesting as they move to the far side of the enormous field, Torin's howling laugh floating back on the breeze.

"He's right, you know." I turn to Vander with my eyebrows raised. He runs a hand over his head, his full-length leathers — they are like mine, with straps and sheathes lining his arms and legs, but with extra padding on the shoulders — creaking a little with the move. "The leathers suit you."

I lower my gaze. "Thank you."

He heaves a large sack into the middle of the field, settling it between us. Whatever is inside clangs and rattles. "Tell me what's in the sack."

I jerk my eyes to his, emerald clashing with silver. "I cannot possibly."

"You're a metal bender. You most certainly *can*. Look within yourself to find the same well of magic you accessed when you glamoured your ears in the human realm and tease that power from its confines. It helps if you think of it as tangible."

Using a glamour on Earth helped me to realise my magic rests within my mind, accessible through a kind of hatch at the top as it awaits my command. It's like a chamber, where I only have to step through to find it.

"It is not within a well, but beneath a hatch, like the tunnel to the portal," I say, my voice strained with the effort of keeping a thought on the hatch while speaking. "Magic leaks from beneath it."

"That's your signature. If you imagine yourself locking the hatch, the signature should retreat into your magic room."

I open that hatch now, feeling the cold and harsh current of my power. It whips around in ribbons of gleaming silver, caressing my thoughts with the rust-scented edge of a blade. I'm confused by the feeling, confused about how I can somehow feel and smell something invisible, let alone know the shape in which it takes.

Vander's approach proves helpful when I imagine the ribbons of magic as tangible threads of silk and grip one with a thought. The ribbon crackles and thrashes and I lose my grip on the thread of power.

"It's too volatile," I say. "I cannot keep hold."

"You are the master. *Force* the magic to bend to your will. Without you, it would not exist." Vander is confident in his claim.

I'm not sure forcing it is the right way to go about it. What if those razor-sharp ribbons slice through my mind and I am left as a mere shell of myself, just like Father?

"Once you have a firm hold on the magic, send it to your palms. We'll go from there."

I gulp and close my eyes, hoping it will help, then descend the hatch into the chamber once more. The ribbons are moving faster now, no longer flowing like water but jerking abruptly as if they know I'm trying to control them. I grab hold of the closest one and wrap my thoughts around it. It thrashes and stings, and I lose my grip yet again.

The following hour is much the same, and by the end, I'm sweating and my leathers are uncomfortable. The best I can manage is eight and fifty heartbeats of holding one ribbon, though Vander does not seem perturbed.

"You'll get the hang of it," he says, moving the unused sack to the side. "It's a matter of knowing you're in control of the power, not the other way around. You've spent your entire life thinking you can't wield, and subconsciously, you think that still applies. Once you realise you're a true fae with magic and strength, the magic will bend to your will. Have you locked the hatch?"

I scramble to slam the invisible hatch closed and slide a bar through the lock, shutting out the metal bending power that's writhing with anger. "Done. Can you feel my signature?"

"Not anymore. There was a moment earlier when I thought you were going to strangle me with it."

"My magic is... angry."

He frowns. "You're angry. Your magic is you, remember?"

"Thank you for today. I appreciate your help."

"We're not done," he says, sinking into a defensive stance. "Take my axe from me. Only once you hold it in your palms will I let you leave."

The groan that slips free is harsh. "I'm tired."

He straightens. "And you'll be tired during a fight to the death. You'll be tired when Summer fae are swinging swords at your head and poking tridents at your stomach. You won't give up then. I won't let you give up now. Stamina, Princess." He sinks into the defensive position once more. "Attack me."

"I do not know how."

"I can't train you unless I know what I'm working with," he growls. "Attack."

I lunge, my left hand groping for the axe dangling from his hip. It's a pointless endeavour. He twists away at the last moment, and my fingers close over thin air. I try kicking to my right and grabbing from my left, but he sees that coming, too.

On and on it goes. My useless attempts at stealing his battle axe are laughable. Vander is quick and reads my moves before I'm not sure I have even made them.

After the sixth failed attempt, he beings to taunt me. "There are no guards here to protect you. No one but you and your own strength and determination. Fight. Get the axe."

A memory flickers at his words, something about the guards and being alone. I shove it aside and kick out. I miss his knees by too far. It's pathetic. I'm pathetic.

"If you can't get the axe, you'll learn just how cruel I can be in my teachings." Though Vander's words are not the same, all I hear is Tohminic's threat.

War is not kind. You will learn just how cruel it can be soon enough. Red flashes in my mind, and a scream tears at my throat as I throw my entire body at Vander. I'm not fighting for the axe anymore. I'm back in the Summer Court, fighting for my life and my freedom.

"Your leathers are nothing but a façade," he says, angling his body away. "There's no discipline, no strength. There's only desperation. I'll take great pleasure in honing your skills."

He means his words to both taunt and please, to urge me to fight harder. Again, I only hear Tohminic. From the forest, when he killed my guards and captured me and Wyn, and then from the rotunda when he was choking Chlora with his cock. He told me then that he would take great pleasure in torturing Nikolai.

Nikolai, who died because of my actions. His blood is on my hands.

His blood is *red, red, red*.

Somehow, I land a punch to Vander's chest. Tohminic's face swims in my mind. The mouse-brown hair, the yellow eyes, and the constant sneer replace Vander's softer features. Tears race down my cheeks as I slam my fist into his chest once more. Again and again.

Red is all I see. It's all I think as I continue to pound my fists into Vander's torso. Over and over and over, I smack my hands against his leathers. I do not notice the firm chest beneath; I do not notice Vander's hands in the air, raised in surrender, or the understanding on his face, or the casual stance he takes. I do not notice Wyn and Torin shouting at me from the side.

"Red." My fist meets his stomach. "Red." My palm stings when I slap his cheek. "Red, red, red." Ribs, arm, collarbone.

Strong arms wrap around my waist and haul me backwards. Torin's words are harsh in my ear. "That's enough, Bria. Calm down."

My chest heaves and I stop fighting against his hold when reality slams into me. I force my body to go limp and force my mind to shove the image of Tohminic's taunting face away.

"I am sorry. So sorry." I repeat the words over and over, as if every time I say it is for every punch I landed on Vander.

"Let her go," growls Vander. "Do you really think restraining her is what she needs?"

Torin releases me at once, followed by an apology of his own.

I sink to my knees, the tears still flowing unbidden.

Vander crouches before me. "We have a lot of work to do. Your methods are choppy and inconsistent. Your face betrays your every thought. There's no discipline, and no control."

My eyes trace his features, and I wince at the reddened mark on his cheek. "You are not angry I attacked you?"

A bemused look crosses his face. "It was kind of the point. Next time we meet, we'll start with the basics."

Chapter 6

Aғᴛᴇʀ ᴡᴇᴀʀɪɴɢ ᴍʏ ғɪɢʜᴛɪɴɢ leathers yesterday, today's flowing mustard-yellow skirt makes me feel exposed and the white corset feels all wrong, although I do like the yellow flower pattern of the tight bodice. The gown is a necessity. If we are to protect the human realm, we must not give the rest of the courts reason to believe Dusk is anything more than another court in Radelea. We must make them believe we follow the same rules, wear the same clothes, and act the same way.

I understand why Wyn was always so frustrated by Autumn's customs.

After one last look in the free-standing mirror, I decide the messy braid draped over my shoulder is good enough and head off in search of the others. We are supposed to be leaving for the Day Court at any moment, and I have to say I'm eager for tomorrow's event.

Elmon and Kyra's mating ceremony will bring a ray of light to a world of darkness and crimson. Zentha's son has always been friendly towards me, unlike most other high fae, and he deserves every shred of happiness this realm offers. Especially with war hanging over us like a dark cloud.

Low voices reach me the moment I open my bedchamber door, drifting from the dining room to my left. I pause just beyond the doorway.

"They taught her nothing," growls Vander. "She can't even block an attack."

He's talking about our early morning training session, where he had me on my back more times than I could count. He's not wrong to say I cannot do so much as block. My attempts at dodging his advances were more laughable than my attempts to steal his axe yesterday.

"I'll never understand why," says Torin.

Wyn scoffs. "It's because Kerym didn't want her to fight back."

"You don't think it's because she's —"

I step into the hallway, and Vander snaps his mouth closed. I do not know what he was about to say, and I do not care to find out. It is enough that I spent the first years of my life without magic or training. There's not a bone in my body that wishes to know why.

"Are you all ready to go?" I ask, pretending I did not hear the last part of their conversation. "Lady Zentha will expect us by now."

The males look dashing in their traditional clothing. Torin's suede tailcoat and vest are both such a dark brown they are almost black, and make his eyes seem like endless pits of swirling darkness.

Vander is handsome in a striped tailcoat of azure and cobalt blues. The beige pants hug his muscular thighs, and the leather of his riding boots shines from being polished earlier today.

When I look at Wyn, I almost choke on my saliva. It is clear the peasant-style gown is not from Radelea, though it still fits the style perfectly. The sage-green skirt has frills upon frills and matches the black waist-cincher and white bust. She is a sight to behold, and I envy her beauty.

"We might as well head off," says Wyn, standing from the dining table.

"We sent our cases ahead, so we'll fold to the docks and take a boat from there," says Torin. "Zentha has the entire island warded against folding since Tohminic declared himself their enemy."

"Smart," says Vander. "But annoying for us."

The manor is empty as we make our way to the front doors, all Dusk fae having been ordered to either remain in their homes while we are gone, or to guard and sentry stations. Vander does not wish to take any risks where his denizens are concerned. It would be just like Tohminic to attack while most of the nobles of Radelea are in the Day Court.

Thankfully, he and his Summer fae are not welcome at the mating ceremony. Neither are the fae of the Night Islands nor the Winter Court, because of their long-standing alliance with Summer. Three of Radelea's courts, cast out from noble society.

The day is cooler, the heat of high summer fading at last. There is no breeze to speak of, and the leaves of my favourite trees are still. It's the first time since I came to Dusk they have been so. I quite prefer it this way.

Vander takes my hand once we step onto the fine grains of sand at the edge of the forest, his magic wrapping around me in soft whispers. The potent scent of cedars and salt fills my nose, calming the racing of my heart.

Dusk is my haven. The she-oaks in the southern forest are a grounding force, and I do not wish to leave the safety of the island. Though I know no harm will come to me in the Day Court now Zentha has agreed to an alliance, I cannot prevent the trickle of fear thrumming through my veins.

We step through the void of time and space, leaving the sandy shore behind and landing on a wooden dock, where hundreds of ships and rowboats bob in the ocean to the east. Large pots line the gleaming timber, the bell-shaped flowers of lily of the valley bright against the terracotta. The smell is wonderful: crisp and watery, yet soft and welcoming.

"Well met," says a bronze-skinned male at the end of the docks. "We're very pleased you could join us on such a joyous occasion."

Beyond the dock master and restless ships, the Day Court's castle draws my eye. The island is only as large as the scattered homes lining the side of a low mountain and the gorgeous building sitting at the apex. The castle claws for the sky, many ivory spires piercing the lapis lazuli.

It has been thirty years since I entered the Day Court. As a youngling, I enjoyed the array of spices, the enticing scents, and the altogether exciting culture of Zentha's court. I suppose I will still enjoy those things.

We load onto the nearest boat. The small wooden vessel does not seem able to carry too many fae, and I wonder if it's on purpose. Without access to the larger ships farther out to sea, any army wishing to storm the Day castle are forced to take small boats. Zentha's guards would see them before they drew too close. It's the perfect defence. Perhaps the civil war between Day and Dawn benefited Zentha more than I thought.

"We call the island Warakoris," says the dock master as he grips the oars, merely to give his hands something to do. The cool splash of his water magic writhes around us as he propels us over the ocean. "It means spirit song. You'll feel spirits within the halls of the castle, but they shan't harm you. Sometimes they sing a lament during the night. It's the most beautiful sound I've heard." He continues to detail his favourite aspects of the Day Court as he rows us across the calm water.

By the time we come to a stop at the base of Warakoris, I know more about the dock master than I think is necessary. With his constant chatter and the roiling memory of when I fell overboard the night the Dusk Court's veil fell for the last time, the trip from shore to shore is uncomfortable. It's with relief that I step from the boat and onto solid ground.

"It's a direct path up the mountain. Start climbing." The dock master is too eager for this part. I track my eyes over the tight turns of the path — the only way into the castle at the top — and understand why he's smiling.

It's steep.

"Thank you for bringing us across," says Wyn, eyeing the winding path, too. Like me, she does not look happy to spend the better part of the morning hiking in a gown. But her face changes as she looks to her brother and his second, a slow smile pulling at the corner of her lips.

Vander surprises me by wrapping his arms around my waist. "Bury your face. Best you don't see."

"What are you going to do?" I do not know what he's planning, but from the look on his face, it's something I will not appreciate, so I follow his instructions and press my face to the curve of his neck, breathing in his homely scent.

One moment my feet are flat on the ground, and the next, they are touching *nothing*. A scream builds in my throat and I scramble to stamp it down, knowing Vander will not appreciate such a shrill sound so close to his ear. Like with the teacup ride at Rennyn's born day fair, my stomach abandons me in favour of the ground's safety.

I chance a look down and immediately wish I had not opened my eyes. A faint shimmer of solid air curls around Vander's boots, churning and sparkling as it lifts us higher and higher. The dock master is a mere speck of navy-blue below, watching us with his hand covering his eyes to shield out the Mother Star's brightness.

"While we're alone." His voice does not so much as hint that he's using magic. "I'd like to discuss what's expected of us here."

"We are to be loving mates. It's a show for the sake of Rennyn and High Lady Nyana of Spring, so rumour will spread that our word is true." I gulp. "Everyone will know Tohminic has no claim to me."

"Yes, but do you know what that involves?"

I fight to calm my racing heart — from both the dizzying height and the thought of how I'm to act while here — by taking a deep breath. "Newly mated couples are... They..." I cannot get the words out. Another deep breath, and I try again. "Their desire for one another is insatiable."

"I realise it isn't fair to you. For that, I'm sorry. But when Torin heard whispers that Tohminic intended to force your return to Summer with claims of you choosing him as your mate, I had to act. I couldn't let you go back there."

I startle at the news. "Why did you keep this from me?"

My head jostles with his shrug. "You have enough to deal with."

"He intended to do that? He would have sent word claiming you abducted me?"

"Yes." He's quiet for a moment as we rise, and does not speak again until we are moving forwards instead of up. "Torin's whispers are frighteningly accurate. They heard Tohminic going into great detail about the night you mated."

Bile burns the back of my throat and my fists clench around the soft fabric of Vander's tailcoat as memories of Tohminic and Chlora invade my mind. "I would never."

"I know. You understand why I was forced to announce our mating?"

"I understand, and I thank you."

"Good, because we've arrived." He sets me on a paved ground, and though we are no longer airborne, I think my stomach is still way down at the docks.

This close, the Day castle is enormous. Larger than Ad'Starrag in both width and height, with too many ivory towers to count and bright coloured curtains hanging from every glassless window.

Pots of every colour line the courtyard Vander has taken us to, the bright flowers either blooming hibiscus, azalea, or a strange flower that looks like the paw of some long-footed creature. The tangy smell of spices wafts from an open-air market down the mountain, not quite strong enough to overpower the freshness of the flowers.

Torin and Wyn land beside us, both raising their eyebrows at me.

I realise I still have my arms wrapped around Vander's neck, and though he does not seem to mind the proximity, I jerk my hands apart and step back. I miss his warmth even when the feel of him still lingers on my skin, and my traitorous mind fights to come up with a reason we should be so far apart.

Perhaps when he crawled for me, my subconscious decided Vander is worth the time and effort of courting. When he allowed me to pummel his chest with my fists, when he saved me from the ogre, when he stood up for me against Father and Fayeth... I think of those occasions often, and the knowledge he's not interested in love sends sadness crashing through me. If he were... Oh, if he were, I would be vying for his attention every day.

But I must put those feelings aside for the good of the world. War is brewing, and there is no time for courting or intimacy. The tingle in my core begs to differ, growing weaker now that I'm not so close to Vander.

"Well met, Dusk fae," says High Lady Zentha as she hurries down the entrance stairs. "You all look well considering the climb."

"Well met, Lady Zentha. We didn't take the path, but flew," says Vander.

"Flew?"

Wyn smiles. "Air wielders."

Zentha's gown of shimmering gold compliments her bright eyes, reminding me of the gown Kyra wore to Rennyn's born day ball. It's of a design I'm familiar with, yet have not worn myself. The skirt is one layer of material rather than many and flows around Zentha's legs.

Thank the Mother Star we will not have to wear hoops here.

"Vander and Torin," says Zentha, "Elmon is waiting for you in the northern courtyard. He wishes to take you through the garrison and discuss the use of our army in your plight. It is straight through the grand foyer. Wyn and darling Bria, I thought you might appreciate iced tea on the balcony."

Tawny skin and silver eyes obscure my vision before I can so much as thank Zentha for her hospitality. My eyes dart to the soft curves of Vander's lips as he wets them with a flick of his tongue.

"I hate to be away from you," he says, his voice rough.

Zentha is our ally and knows our mate bond is a ruse. Her denizens, however, do not. Even in friendly company, we must act as though newly mated.

"And I you. Do not let Elmon bore you with talk of war and politics."

He curls an arm around my waist and pulls me against him. Our bodies fit against one another as if made to be joined for all eternity. Every hard muscle, every inhale, I feel it all. My breaths become pants of yearning and desire, and I struggle to drag my eyes from those glorious lips to the gleaming silver of his eyes.

"I will miss you while you are gone," I whisper.

I gasp in surprise when those lips I so admire collide with mine, and the entire world slips away in the mere heartbeat it takes for me to realise he's kissing me. Vander Theron of Dusk is kissing *me*, Bria of no court.

The kiss lasts nowhere near long enough, and his fingers tense on my waist as he pulls away, as if his very being detests the distance between us. "And I will miss you, Princess."

"I thought we were not to call her that?" Zentha wonders aloud.

Wyn snorts. "Van is the exception, apparently."

My mind is dizzy as I watch the High Lord walk away. Everything from the shadow of hair atop his head to the way his pants pull against his rear when he walks snags my attention. I'm so lost in the image of him that Wyn has to pull me away by the elbow.

"I am offended you did not confide in me," says Zentha as she leads us up stone stairs that twist around the exterior of her castle home.

"We sent word of our bond," I say, fighting the urge to look to my right, where there is nothing to prevent my fall.

"Indeed, along with a warning that your mating is a ruse." She throws a knowing look over her shoulder. "I once told you your spirit soared being so near the Dusk island, but how it sings in his presence, Bria. If I did not know any better, I would think the two of you truly mated."

If my hand was anywhere other than planted against the stone wall, I would topple backwards. As it is, my heart is in my throat and my feet refuse to move. "Do you mean truly, as in our bond is not a lie? Or do you mean true mates?"

"Both," says Zentha with a shrug. She turns to face Wyn and me, her honey eyes assessing Wyn's aura. "Your spirit sighs in relief."

I whip my face to Wyn. "What is she talking about?"

"Back at Ad'Starrag" — a shiver prickles my spine at the mention of the Summer Court's keep — "when we were in the iron cages, there was something I was trying to tell you. Remember?"

And I questioned her about it in the tunnels to the portal, but Vander was right there. She said she would explain everything later. She never did.

"Does he know?" I ask. Wyn shakes her head, and I turn to Zentha. "Are you sure?"

"The Mother Star has not blessed Radelea with true mates for millennia. I will need to check some facts later, but I am quite certain."

"May I assist?"

Her head tilts to the side as she considers for a moment. "I seldom allow fae from other courts into my archives, but I can make an exception for you, dear. The stars know I have always had a soft spot for you."

Indeed, Zentha has always been kind to me, even after Fayeth demanded Day's High Lady treat me as she would a lesser fae. When I was three and thirty, Zentha was visiting Autumn to discuss trade arrangements, and refused to so much as acknowledge Father's mate for the rest of our stay.

We continue the climb to the balcony in silence, though my mind is buzzing. If Zentha's claim proves true, and Vander is my true mate, everything will make much more sense. How I yearned to be near the island when it appeared, how calm blankets me in his presence, and how he has always fought for me. Blessed Mother Star, he *crawled* for me. I should have suspected as much then.

Not a single mated pair in Radelea are true mates, and I know little about the phenomenon. What knowledge I have is mere speculation. If Zentha has texts on the subject, I want to read them. I *need* to read them.

The balcony at the top of Zentha's home is large enough to hold fifty fae should the High Lady wish it. Made of smooth ivory stone, the open ledge is sturdy. The Day fae have decorated it with their favoured colourful banners and pots, and I feel like I have wandered into a rainbow.

There is a small table set for five, the metal having been painted a lovely canary yellow. Atop the round table, cakes and other sweet treats shine in the light of day. A crystal carafe of iced tea drips condensation onto the table, and my mouth waters at the sight of the chilled drink.

"There you are," says a voice from the adjoining archway.

I turn towards them, smiling as Jonik's niece, Xaria, and Kyra, Zentha's daughter-in-law to be, join us. "Well met, Xaria and Kyra. I hope you are well."

Kyra smiles. "I am to mate with my beloved tomorrow. I am very well."

The morning passes in a blur of sweet pastries, gossip, and laughs. It's the first instance of interacting with a group of females I have enjoyed. By the end, I see myself sitting with these same four time and again, forming friendships that will last the test of time.

Chapter 7

Thε Day Court archives are in the centre of Warako-ris. Literally. They are deep underground at the base of the mountain. We descend in a wooden cage that makes me clammy with unease, though the fae guiding us to the bottom with a thick rope seems unperturbed by the confines and darkness.

Fae lights do little to light the way as we step from the lift and into the damp air of the tunnel, but Zentha knows this place as well as she knows the back of her hand. We enter the archives within heartbeats.

My hair brushes the curved and uneven stone ceiling, the solid timber shelves jut out from the right wall, the tomes sitting atop just waiting to be read, and the fae lights shine brighter without the dampness of the tunnel to smother them, illuminating the archives with amber light. Though not as large as the archives in Autumn, these shelves are fuller; there are so many scrolls and leather-bound tomes I do not know where to begin.

"The texts on mate bonds are just through here," says Zentha, gesturing to the second to last shelf. "I am certain we have an account from High Lord Taurid, the first Day fae to find his true mate. She was a Winter fae, if I remember correctly." There's a flash of something in her eyes, which she smothers before I can put a name to it.

"Why do you not allow others down here?" I ask, pausing to read the title of a thick book: *The Wonders of Wielding Water*.

"This is my private collection. We have public archives on the mainland, north of the forest village." She runs a finger along the scrolls as she wanders down an aisle, the beige dust stark against her warm brown skin. "Here it is." She slides a large scroll from the shelf and unfurls it.

"What does it say?" I ask the moment she begins to read.

She smirks and reads out loud, translating from the ancient tongue. "It is not love that brings true mates together, but equality, strength, and complement. Where one of the pair is hard, the other is soft. Where one is unforgiving, the other is merciful. To reject the bond is to forsake the Mother Star herself, and to disregard her power is to acknowledge you do not belong to this world."

"I have not heard of a truly mated pair who rejected the bond."

"Neither have I," she murmurs, her eyes darting from side to side as she continues to read.

A tight scroll bound in leather demands my attention, and I slide it from its home on the shelf. "Do you mind?"

"Not at all. Read whatever interests you." She's so enraptured by what she's reading, it's likely she has no clue which scroll I have selected. Her eyes do not stray from the angular writing of the text.

What I read is an academic piece on chosen mates. There are details on how to cement the bond by making your vows as the

Mother Star rises, about the benefits of such a connection, and what will happen if you ever reject the tether binding you to your mate.

"Zentha, did you know this?" I wait until she drags her eyes from the text on true mates before reading from the scroll in my hands. "If a chosen mate rejects what the Mother has blessed them with, she will curse them with irrationality and loneliness. While the fae responsible for severing the bond will never find such happiness again, the rejected party may overcome the madness of heartbreak through finding their true mate. Only the bond of destiny, blessed by the Mother Star, holds power enough to mend a broken mind."

"How fascinating," says Zentha, stepping closer and reading over my shoulder. "Poor Kerym may very well live through the madness. I had forgotten this scroll existed."

"What are the chances of finding his true mate?"

Her face falls. "There are millions of fae in Radelea. I would say our chances are slim, though it is worth a try. I miss my old friend. Did you know we were in love during our youngling years?"

I lower the scroll. "No, I did not." I briefly wonder if that has anything to do with Father's love of plum wine.

Her full lips stretch with a wistful smile. "Yes. But my father thought an alliance with Winter would suit him better. My mate and I had a long engagement, and when the time came at last to perform the ceremony, Kerym travelled with me. Blessed Mother Star, that must have been some seventy years ago."

"You never speak of your mate."

Her smile turns sad. "Elmon's father does not cope well in social situations. He... I do not believe he is quite himself of late. Sometimes he thinks he is still in the Winter Court, or he will forget our son exists."

I grip her hand. "How difficult that must be for all of you. I am so very sorry."

"It is the hand I have been served, and I will continue to be grateful for the life I have. Now, would you like to hear what I have read here?" She holds up the forgotten scroll.

"Very much."

"I will explain as we ascend." She rolls the scroll and ties it off with the thin leather strap before leading the way back through the archives. "Lord Taurid believed true mates were a gift from the Mother Star, that she does not bring them together because their spirits complement one another. He called them twin souls and does not believe true mates are a bond of love."

"Then what, if not love?"

"This is where Lord Taurid is using guess work. He thought each individual's soul to be incomplete, that finding your true mate makes you whole. Consider the Dawn triplets. They are three individuals, yet are entirely the same. Love for twin souls is a bonus, not an expectation."

"I do not understand," I say as we step onto the lift. The Day male closes the wooden gate before beginning to heave us up by pulling the rope. "True mates do not sound like mates at all."

"They are not. Long ago, when the Mother Star shone her first golden rays on the darkened land, twin souls were the leaders of each court. Back then, it was believed their personalities bounced off one another with such perfection, they could rule with both fairness and discipline. Their souls are... How do I phrase this without scaring you?"

I huff a laugh. "It's too late for that."

"Then I will just say it. If you and the High Lord are twin souls, you *need* one another. Your soul is not complete without him."

"My soul is split?"

"Yes. He holds the other half. The Mother Star will fight to bring you both together, believing you to be essential to the betterment of Radelea. Have you noticed unusual urges to be near him or his sister?"

It all makes sense now. Why I feel so close to Wyn, why I have always felt that burning desire to be in the Dusk Court, and why Vander seems to understand my every thought and desire.

"And completing the bond?"

"It will complete itself. A true bond is not something you can avoid. Knowing the soul of the other, knowing their pain and fears, as well as risking yourself for them, will strengthen your bond. I cannot say how long it will take to be complete, only that it *will*."

We reach the top of the lift shaft, and the male opens the gate to a room hidden in Zentha's ground floor chambers.

I step from the wooden cage and ask, "Am I expected to live life without love?"

Zentha frowns. "What do you mean?"

"I mean, the bond of twin souls is not one of love but necessity. Vander does not desire love or anything of the kind. If he is my true mate, I shall never experience love."

"You may, with time. There is one more thing you should know before you leave."

"Yes?" I ask, stepping into the bright hallway.

"Once the bond is complete, your soul becomes whole. You must never reject it, for severing the tether that binds you severs your soul from your body."

Chapter 8

I TWIRL IN FRONT of the mirror and admire how the moonlight shines off the diamonds in my gown. The onyx lace is a wonderful choice and allows the diamonds to stand out more than they would with any other colour. It's a sleeveless piece, though there are loops of lace that drape around my upper arms, like the sleeves have fallen from their place on my shoulders.

The bust is all lace and diamond in a sweetheart plunge that compliments my curves. The bodice fades at the waist, replaced by a sheer and glittering skirt that trails along the floor as I walk hand in hand with Vander to the main courtyard.

Wyn and Torin walk behind us, both of them dashing in their formal clothes. Torin's vest is black with a shimmering blue design, and the sleeves of his white shirt are crisp. It's the most well-dressed I have seen him.

Wyn is nothing short of beautiful in her silver gown. The corset-style strapless bodice hugs her torso and plumes to a glittering skirt from the waist. She sparkles as she walks, and the slit that reaches her hip reveals her long, tawny leg with every step.

Vander is a work of art. His obsidian vest is simple, yet suits him perfectly. The black shirt beneath hugs the bulging muscles of his arms to denote his strength. Together, we are a pair who represent the darkness and the stars we so love. Onyx, obsidian, sparkles. Darkness with specks of light.

Like my life.

We arrive in the courtyard — it's lined with multi-coloured banners that flutter in the warm breeze — to a crowd of excited fae all dressed in magnificent gowns or handsome tailcoats. There is a friendly, eager air about the space, and I smile along with revellers.

I dip my chin to High Lord Jonik as we pass him, his mate, Leilani, and the triplets, but we do not pause to converse. The alliance Dusk shares with Dawn will remain secret for as long as we can hide the information.

Elmon and Kyra are greeting guests at the far side of the courtyard, where they must remain until the Mother Star rises. Only then will the ceremony begin. The moment the bond forms, the newly mated couple will disappear into their shared chambers and cement their bond the traditional way. Through intimacy.

Servers twist around those gathered, carrying platters of chilled wine and miniature feasts designed for eating while socialising. Zentha is chatting with High Lady Nyana of Spring — I yearn to speak with her and ask her what she knows of my mother — both females smiling. Wyn and Torin disappear into the crowd when a group of five Day fae set their instruments on a temporary stage in the corner.

It's only the beginning of the long night, and I am already bursting with happiness.

The music begins before we can greet anyone, and Vander pulls me to the dancefloor without hesitation. His arms circle my waist, pulling me tight against him as he bends to my ear and whispers, "You look stunning tonight, Princess."

Heat crawls up my chest. "As do you, My Lord."

With our bodies pressed so close together, I can smell his distinct homely scent. I inhale deeply, relishing in the cedar and crisp air, then press my hand against his chest to feel the steady beat of his heart as he twirls me around the other fae. I look into those glorious eyes, wondering if I'm destined for a lifetime of loneliness, or whether he would fall in love with me if given the chance and time.

His voice is gravelly as he tells me he would give every coin to his name to know what I am thinking.

We change direction, twirling the other way with dizzying speed. "I was thinking about the walk we took through the Autumn gardens and what you told me that day."

His brow creases for a moment before smoothing. "That I'm not interested in finding love."

"Yes." My skirt swishes around my ankles, caressing my skin with kisses of gossamer and diamond. "And I was wondering two things, if you would allow me to ask them?"

His cheek grazes mine as he gives me the go ahead to ask my questions. To the outside, we must look like any other mated pair, with our heads so close together and nothing between our bodies. The closeness of Vander brings a delicious heat to my core that I fight hard to take no notice of.

"First, why? Why do you shy away from love?"

His hand slides lower, his smallest finger grazing the curve of my buttocks. "If I tell you this, swear not to say anything after. I don't want to know your reaction."

"You have my word." My hand finds its way to his nape, the spiky hair at the back of his head prickling my forefinger.

"Losing Father was difficult. Not because my only parent left this world, though that is a part of it, but because I was the one to do it. His struggle…" He gulps. "Father begged and begged. At first, I refused, but it was the compassionate thing to do. I have since learned this life takes more than it gives, and I'm not prepared to suffer more loss than I need to. Maybe it's selfish, I don't know, but there you have it."

I cannot even imagine the strength it would have taken to end Lord Connak's life. While escaping Ad'Starrag, I fell to pieces knowing those Summer fae were dying at my hand, and they were my enemies and captors. To take the life of a fae close to you, someone you have spent your life loving… It's unimaginable.

His hesitation makes sense to me now, and though I am not sure spending your life without love is the right way to live, I understand. Perhaps it's too soon for him to tell, or perhaps he's still blinded by grief, but I need to know.

"Will you ever change your mind?" I whisper, flattening my palm against the back of his head.

He sighs. "If I'm to answer right now? No."

My stomach sinks to the stone ground, even as my heart flutters at his proximity. Surely Zentha is mistaken and Vander is not my twin soul. The Mother Star would not hand me a life with a male uninterested in love. I do not deserve such a fate.

I'm about to tell him about the twin souls Zentha spoke of when Torin interrupts our dance. He looks frantic, and his dark eyes are wide as he pulls us apart. Pink colours his bronze cheeks, as if he's been running in circles trying to find us.

"What's wrong?" Vander asks, his hand groping for an axe that is not there. "Is it Wyn?"

"Wyn's fine. It's the court. Something's wrong at home," says Torin in a rush. "The wind whispers of the undead."

"We must go. Now." My frantic eyes search for Zentha in the crowd.

"Get Wyn and meet us at the docks. Send your whispers to the other Dusk fae here and order them home with our cases," Vander tells his second.

Torin rushes off, slipping between a Spring fae and a male from Day.

Vander grabs my hand and pulls me in the other direction. We make quick work of the dancefloor, twisting and sliding around the revellers and appearing as though nothing is amiss. The music builds to its crescendo just as we step from the smooth stone onto a raised section of the courtyard, and I cannot help but think the musicians are watching us and playing their tunes to suit the increasing panic in my eyes.

Because it can be nothing but panic burning through my veins. Undead in the Dusk Court? Torin did not mention where the undead are gathered, or how many. The Summer Court — for it cannot be anyone but the necromancers — could have ordered the soulless bodies they command to attack Dusk Manor, the village, or Mother Star forbid, the academy.

My new home is under attack and I'm not there to help. Instead of protecting Dusk, I have been dancing and thinking of Vander's body pressed against me. I have been having fun.

Fae turn with wide eyes as Vander shoves past them, dragging me behind with a tight grip on my hand.

"Lord Vander," says Zentha's calm voice from the left. "I sensed your urgency. What is it?"

I almost collide with Vander's back when he comes to an abrupt stop. The tension is clear when he says, "I'm afraid we must go, Lady Zentha. Undead are attacking my court."

"Then why are you wasting time with formalities?" she asks. "By all means, go. Write and tell me about it. I will explain to Elmon and Kyra, as well as offer them your best wishes."

"We wish we could stay, Lady Zentha. Please give the mates my love," I say as Vander drags me away. My gown catches on the occasional loose stone or finds itself trapped beneath the feet of the closest careless fae. I hike it up with my free hand.

He tugs harder on my arm, and I spin around and race forwards as we head in a direction I have not yet explored. We slip through a narrow alley at the side of the courtyard and dash between the stone walls towards...

"No."

Vander stops at the edge of a sheer cliff. "Do you trust me?"

"I..." I search his eyes. "Yes. I trust you with my life." The moment the words slip past my lips, I know them to be true. He has fought for me more than any other fae in Radelea. He, of all the fae I had hoped would, saved me from Ad'Starrag. Then he damn well crawled for me.

"Look over the edge." His voice is tight, and I remember from the teacup ride that he's not fond of heights.

I glance at the cliff, then flick wide eyes back to him. "I'm not sure I'm able."

He raises his eyebrows. "We don't have time for this. Look over the edge."

I wipe my sweating palms on the skirt of my gown and step forward. The hairs on my nape prickle as I look to the docks below. Far, far below. We have to be higher than those buildings in the human realm.

"Look at me." I do, and his face is set in stone. "I won't drop you. We won't fall to our deaths. You trust me."

I nod along with his words. "I trust you, but I'm closing my eyes."

He holds his arms wide, and I step into his embrace as if it's a learned move from years of doing exactly this. Wrapping my arms around his neck feels natural, as does the fit of his body against mine. He orders me to wrap my legs around his waist, and I have to say, the feel of his manhood pressed against my aching core is one of the more exciting things I have experienced in recent days. Even with the threat of a long drop to the docks sending tingles of fear crashing through me, my body reacts to Vander, sending delicious waves of lust from head to toe.

He clears his throat. "Hold tight."

It's the only warning he offers before he takes several steps back, then sprints for the edge of the cliff. I tighten my hold on my wrists and lock my ankles into place as I'm jostled from his movements. The friction is all-consuming.

Then he jumps.

Wind whistles as it tears at my hair and clothes, all but drowned out by the sound of my pulse rushing in my ears. This is freedom. I'm weightless, with not a care in the world... other than landing, of course. The rasp of breath that pulls at my tight throat is muted, but loud enough for Vander to hear.

He wraps his arms around my waist and holds tight for a mere moment before letting go again. Our descent slows, the howl of the wind decreasing to a reasonable level before decreasing once more to a whisper.

A rough jolt, and we land on the docks with a thud. The move causes me to grind against him, and I know in that moment that if we were not racing to defend our home, I would beg him to consider finding a private chamber. I'm a female with needs, and the near constant ache low in my stomach demands to be soothed.

"You can let go now."

I clear my throat, embarrassed at where my mind has taken me, and unhook my ankles. Sliding down Vander's body does little to soothe the raging fire within. I avert my eyes and thank him for not killing us.

"My pleasure. The dock master's waiting."

There's a hint of curiosity in his tone, but given what we are about to face, neither of us will probe into the mess of my thoughts. I must be broken if I'm thinking about intimacy in the face of a battle with the undead.

The rowboat rocks from side to side as I step in and take the middle seat. Torin and Wyn are already on board at the rear, both of them strapping weapons to their bodies.

The moment Vander sits, the dock master sends us hurtling over the water. His magic is restless and frantic as he pushes us through the gently lapping waves; he knows the urgency in which we need to get beyond the wards. I feel for him, having to leave the celebrations to row us to sea so we can fold Dusk towards us.

I count my heartbeats to calm myself, only reaching two and twenty when the magic of the wards washes over me. Cold, like the depths of the ocean, and raging like the waves far out at sea. Salt and the bitter tang of lemon coats my tongue.

"This's where I'll leave you," says the dock master the moment the magic fades. "I wish you luck and pray for the Mother Star's mercy."

"Thanks," says Wyn, before disappearing.

Torin follows close behind.

Vander reaches back, and I take his hand, following the unspoken deal we seem to have. Perhaps the need to protect me stems from the twin souls we share. Whatever the reason, I do not complain. The realm wraps around us as Vander steps through the fold, and within a heartbeat, the soft sands of the Dusk Court replace the gentle swaying of the ocean.

The screams reach my ears first. My blood turns to ice as my stomach drops. Sweat beads on my forehead. The sound haunts my nights, it blends with crimson and torments my mind, an echo of the pain I endured at Ad'Starrag.

The screams mirror those of my own all those moons ago. No one will endure the pain I did, not when I can prevent it. There's not a single fae who deserves such a fate. I race for the village, towards the screams and cries, ignoring the shouts of Vander, Wyn, and Torin.

She-oak branches tear at my arms and face as I race along the worn path. Birds chirp as they wake, and I note the lightening of the sky in the east as I cast a glance over my shoulder to check the others are coming. Three blurs of black race after me.

I skid to a stop at the edge of the forest and assess the mayhem below. Fae run from buildings, shielding babes from forceful blasts of wind and ripples of illusion magic. Males drag their mates behind them, seeking shelter away from the dozen undead in the village square.

The undead grope for whoever they can, their teeth snapping as if they intend to eat whichever fae is unlucky enough to fall victim to the corpses' plans.

Anger, hot and consuming, flushes through my body like lava. Those are innocent fae. My entire body tenses as an undead grabs hold of a female and tears into her neck with frightening strength. My magic churns in the vault I keep it in, bashing at the hatch with a force that steals my breath. The metal bending powers are sharp and cold as ice, but beneath the comfort of that is something else entirely. Something… calm and soft, yet dominating and coarse.

The three Dusk fae tear past me, Wyn shouting an order to stay where I am.

The foreignness of the calm yet dominating magic distracts me enough that I assess it with interest. There's something familiar about the feeling. The scent of musk overwhelms my senses, and the feel of fur trickles over my knuckles. Pain cracks through my mind, and my vision flickers as I grab hold of the amber threads, ignoring the silver of my metal bending power.

The distant image of the village disappears, and I'm aware of my body sagging to the sandy ground as I look down at the mayhem from above. I stretch my wings and angle to the left, banking in a wide circle around the chaotic scene.

Instinct rules my every move as my mind wraps around that of a hawk. The wind rustles the brown feathers of my spread wings as I dip lower. My eyesight is sharper than ever, picking apart the tiny details in a heartbeat. From the glistening saliva on the teeth of an undead to the beads of sweat on a fleeing fae, I see everything. Even specks of dust churning in the predawn light.

I open my beak wide and let out a piercing cry as Vander and the others enter the fray of bodies below. My talons sink into the ceramic tiles of a roof when I come to land, my balance steadier in this form than my fae body. I tilt my head to the side, watching the battle below.

Gusts of air whip through the village centre, chased by the flash of metal as daggers fly and swords arc. The undead grope for anyone and anything, sinking their glistening teeth into skin the moment they find what they are looking for.

It's disgusting. Horrible.

Tohminic will pay for this. I will make certain of it.

I watch as Vander binds a decapitated undead with threads of solid air, and my poor little bird heart stutters. He wears a stained sailing smock, with tan pants and leather boots I know too well. And the head he carries... The undead is Nikolai.

I had thought Tohminic to be merciful in releasing Nikolai's body from his necromancy magic. I was so very wrong. He was merely waiting for the right time to shock me with my former lover and guard.

Wyn races to Vander and says something to the High Lord. He frowns at Nikolai's headless body before nodding.

Wyn dashes back into the fray of fae and undead, swinging her daggers in wild arcs.

Torin fights beside her, his short swords cutting through limbs as if they are nothing more than butter.

Wind wielders send dead bodies hurtling through the air. Undead crash into buildings. Alizeh, the wind wraith I met when Vander and I toured the village, cackles as she blasts through bodies.

Her words reach me on my rooftop perch. "You do not come into *my* home and cause destruction. You will feel the wrath of the wind for what you have done. Thirty dead in the time it takes the sun to rise."

How she continues to speak through her screams, while using her powers to shred through the undead, is beyond me.

When there are but two undead remaining — one of them missing the better part of their right leg — I decide it's time I return to my body. As Torin and Wyn gather anything flammable they can find amongst the destruction, I look inside my mind and search for the hatch that holds my magic.

It's easy, given I'm still *me*, although I am within the body of another. It strikes me that I'm a tier one animalist with the rare ability to control the bodies of animals and access their instincts, stronger than Rennyn and Father combined. I do not believe the tiered system of strengths to be a good one, however I relish in the thought of telling my brother I rank above him.

I focus on the threads of amber and seek the one that smells of the metal bending magic and lavender from the oil I used in my bath yesterday. A gasp fills my lungs with a blissful sea breeze when my soul races back to my body. Between one blink of my hawk eyes and a beat of my fae heart, I change from bird to female.

I do not waste time, but leap to my feet and race for the village, my mind a mess of revelations, relief, and the remnants of fear. By the time I reach my friends, Torin and Wyn have lit a raging fire and Vander is collecting the undead bodies that are strewn around the open space.

Tears track down my cheeks as I watch Vander lift Nikolai's body with his air magic and place him on top of the others, the amber and gold flames sparking and flickering around him. They are tears of relief, for I'm glad Nikolai's soul can rest at long last.

When he moves to shift the next body, my mouth runs dry. The light brown hair, bright hazel eyes, and the bronze of her skin. Just as I knew the headless undead to be Nikolai, I know who this is.

I grab hold of Vander's arm, preventing him from adding her to the pile of writhing bodies. "That's Fayeth, my father's mate and Rennyn's mother."

"Are you sure?" he asks, lowing Fayeth's body to the ground, away from the fire. She writhes in the binds of his dense air, hissing an animalistic sound no fae should ever make.

"I would bet my life on it." Although Father's mate was never kind to me, she was a constant in the Autumn Court. Tears build in my eyes. "It's not right for us to burn her, Vander. The farewell belongs to Rennyn."

His eyes blaze, the amber of the fire flickering in their silver glow. "You're right. It's the virtuous thing to do. We'll go now, before the necromancy magic wears off. Let Rennyn see for himself where lies and betrayal get you. He wasn't in the Day Court, did you realise?"

I blink back the tears, refusing to shed a single one for the female who spent her life tormenting me. "That's not quite what I meant. A son should have the chance to farewell his mother upon her untimely death." I take in the settling mayhem around us. "Do you not wish to remain here with your denizens and help them?"

"Torin and Wyn can stay. They'll make do without us."

We leave Fayeth to the side of the village square with strict instructions to the butcher, whose store is undamaged, that no one is to move her to the raging fire. Black plumes of smoke curl to the sky, stark against the golden glow of the rising sun.

Dusk fae who live above their stores open the doors of their businesses, checking the danger has passed before stepping into the morning light. The togetherness of the Dusk Court takes me by surprise. This would never have happened in Autumn, where the fae would all remain safely beyond their doors and leave the cleaning to whoever was unfortunate enough to be there when the undead attacked.

Alizeh blows past us in the form of a gust of wind, chuckling as she feeds on the remnants of air magic rippling through the village. There is no better place for a wraith, a wind creature who feeds on the very element that forms her.

As we approach the others on the eastern side of the square, Vander says, "This is your fight. You tell them."

"You want me to take control? To have a say?"

His answer is simple. "Of course."

Torin and Wyn turn at our approach, both of them looking as though they have just stepped out of bed a little ruffled, but otherwise unharmed.

"We just received reports from Day and Dawn," says Torin. "Both courts fended off similar attacks this morning. Zentha has postponed Elmon and Kyra's mating ceremony."

"That's terrible," I say, feeling their loss to my core. To think you're about to tie your life to another, only to have it snatched away by a vengeful Summer fae, is heartbreaking. "But how did he know?"

Vander's face whips to me. "What do you mean?"

My brow pinches. "Surely you understand this was not random? Attacking the Dusk Court while we're in Day, and the same for Dawn, too. Then sending undead to the Day Court while they have Elmon's mating as a distraction." I look each of them in the eye. "Seems a little too lucky for Tohminic, I think."

"Say what you mean to say," says Vander, his tone rough with anger.

I look to only him as I say, "He knew. He knew we would be in Day, which can only mean one thing. There's a traitor among us."

Wyn scoffs. "We trust every fae in our court."

"Then tell me where Nyree of the Ill-fated is." I raise my brows in question. "Why isn't she here defending her court?"

"We've been through this," says Vander. "We trust her."

"I do not." I turn away, unwilling to see the frustration on their faces. My eyes land on Fayeth's still trashing body, and I steer the conversation back to the reason for us meeting. I do not look back as I say, "Vander and I are going to the Autumn Court. You two are to remain here and deal with all this." I wave a hand over the general destruction of our village.

Torin chuckles. "Too much for you, is it?"

"Shut up," growls Vander. His patience is wearing thinner with every beat of his heart. "Do you not recognise her?"

Wyn and Torin drag their eyes to where Vander points, to where I'm still staring.

Torin does not recognise Fayeth, but Wyn whispers an expletive my father would loathe to hear.

"We will return her to Autumn, so Rennyn may farewell his mother," I say.

"Stop at the manor and change first," says Wyn. "A ball gown isn't appropriate for what you're leaving to do. Good luck." She turns away, marching towards Alizeh, who is trying to antagonise a female into using her magic.

"Send word if anything happens," Vander says before guiding me away.

We're quiet while we pass fae dragging large lengths of timber from one side of the village square to the other, quiet as we observe five males working together to find the parents of a babe, and quiet as we slip through the last street and into the forest.

That's when I can no longer hold it in. "Vander?"

He hums to let me know he's listening.

"Something happened while you were all fighting the undead. Something... Well, it's a good thing, I suppose."

His steps falter. "You don't seem sure about that."

"I'm an animalist."

He turns towards me, slowing his steps until we're walking side by side. "Explain."

"I was angry about the attack. All I could think and feel was how the fae in the village are innocent and do not deserve to be dragged into our fight. Something inside me snapped. One moment I was watching everything unfold from the forest, and the next, I was in the body of a hawk, circling the battle from the sky."

"Interesting. You have both fields of magic that stem from the Autumn Court, yet nothing from your mother's side. It gives us insight into her family."

"How so?" I ask, Dusk Manor coming into view.

"The weaker the magic, the less likely their offspring will inherit it. Your father is a strong fae with tier two animalist powers —"

"He's a tier one, actually. Though he cannot control animals, only see through their eyes and plant seeds of thought. Rennyn is a tier two and can control creatures from afar, and does not have insight into their minds and instincts. I can do everything. Flying was as natural to me as walking."

We crest the hill, and Vander holds the manor door open for me to enter. "Both threads of your magic are rare. Do they feel different in the room in your mind?"

"Of course," I say, leading the way up the stairs. "They both feel how a magic signature does. One is sharp and bitter, the other is soft yet coarse. The metal bending magic is silver and the animalistic powers amber."

"Dress in your leathers. We'll continue this conversation on the way to Autumn."

Chapter 9

I CANNOT REACH THE buttons of my gown, so I cut it off using the dagger I borrowed from Wyn. I will not wear it again, not now it is stained with the memory of stolen mate bonds and attacks from the undead. It's a shame that such a beautiful gown has gone to waste.

Pulling on my leathers is more difficult than I imagined it would be on my own, but I get there in the end... after a lot of huffing and swearing that does not help matters at all. I even buckle all but two of the straps at my ribs.

Vander's timing is immaculate. A knock sounds at the door just as I'm struggling to buckle the next strap. "Come in." My voice is strained with my body contorted as I try to thread the leather through the metal clasp.

"Do you need a hand?" he asks, his voice laced with humour. "I didn't think bodies could bend in such a way."

"Quit teasing and help me," I say, straightening and moving my arms out of the way to make it easier for him.

"Wyn didn't think this through when she had it made, did she?" His knuckles graze my ribs as he deftly threads the leather strap and pulls it taut. "It's not possible for you to do this yourself."

"Perhaps she intended for me to need help."

I feel the huff of breath from his laugh against my neck. "How are things going with Torin? Has he convinced you to go on that date yet?"

"Honestly, I think that was more to annoy the both of us. I have caught him waggling his eyebrows while we train."

He moves to the top buckle, and this time his knuckles graze the side of my breast. I suck in a breath as warmth spreads from the contact, sizzling through me like wildfire. He does not comment on Torin's antics, but focuses on keeping his knuckles away from my body.

"There you go," he says, stepping back as if I'm a barrel of boiling oil waiting to explode. "We should get going. I'm feeling the strain of keeping Fayeth bound."

I slide Wyn's dagger into the sheath at my thigh and accept another from Vander, which I sheath on the other leg. "Why do we need to be in our leathers for this?"

"We can't take any chances now," he says as we move through the manor. "Another attack could come at any moment, and we were too restricted in our formal clothes. Not to mention the lack of weapons we had in our arsenal. This morning was the worst possible time for an attack."

"Likely why he chose now." This time, I hold door open for Vander. "As much as I hate to admit it, Tohminic has the mind for war. We will need to be alert from now on. Perhaps strengthen the wards."

"It's an idea worth looking into. It's been decades since we assessed the ward stones."

I almost trip over my feet. "Stones? The wards are not blankets of magic cast by the High Lord or Lady?"

He frowns as we enter the bordering forest, both of us ignoring the thrashing Fayeth behind us. "No one's ever told you how they work?"

"No. It was deemed inappropriate for the High Lord's daughter." One of the many things Father kept from me. I wonder what else I do not know that I should.

In all my learnings, I never read of the wards or their makers. I was never allowed to read about casting or shielding, let alone how to defend myself if I needed to. It's as if Father and Fayeth *wished* for me to be useless, to rely on stronger fae than I.

"Strong fae can imbue objects with their magic. If cast right, and under the right circumstances, that magic can form a kind of dome around places. That's a very basic summary, but you get the gist of it," says Vander, holding the branch of a she-oak aside while I pass.

The day is already beginning to take its toll on me. We did not sleep, instead celebrating the joining of Elmon and Kyra until late, then we rushed off to fight the undead, with members of Day and Dawn doing the same in their courts. I have not slept since the night before last, and I'm a little more than weary. And when I'm running on mere crumbs of energy, my nightmares take advantage.

I snap a branch from the she-oak and caress the needle-like leaves. With so much happening of late, I'm not sure I can withstand what's still to come.

Vander continues his explanation as we exit onto the sandy shore. "We place the ward stones in secure locations around anywhere we need to ward, and the magic from each stone connects, forming a larger dome than a single stone allows."

"It sounds very complex," I say, taking his offered hand.

He does not alter his stride as the void wraps around us and we step from the Dusk Court into Autumn.

Fayeth is still hissing, dragged behind us by invisible threads of air magic. She hisses harder when Autumn's familiar scent envelops us. It's as if she knows where we are, as if she has *thoughts* of her own, though she has clearly left this world.

We fold in farther from the Autumn castle than we would on a normal occasion. It is a clear sign Vander's magic is reaching its limit. I do not mind the walk, especially after everything that has happened. It gives me time to think and consider.

I inspect the hatch in my mind, ensuring it's locked tight and neither magical signature is leaking through. I'm not ready for Rennyn to know of my magic and comment on the miraculous revelation, though I believe he knows more than he lets on.

Every fae in Radelea is born with magic. It's a fact known by all. No one our history has developed powers later in life. This is something I have been working through over the past days, yet I have not given myself the freedom to consider it further like I am now.

There is only one reason my powers would appear out of nowhere. Someone put a block on my magic when I was a babe. I'm certain it was Father. It could be no one else.

As we near the outpost of Autumn's castle, I'm left wondering *why*. Why would he leave me all but defenceless against this harsh life? The only reason I can think of is so I do not uncover my mother's identity. Meaning she is a noble, high fae, or someone just as important to our society.

I'm pulled from my thoughts when we reach the outpost, the two sentries above shouting for us to wait. Their hurried footsteps echo from the weather-worn ladder, their rushed words garbled and too quiet for me to hear.

The look I offer Vander is one of confusion. They did not treat us as enemies when we last walked through the outpost. What has changed? I look behind me, to a thrashing and hissing Fayeth, and understand why the sentries are so red-faced and enraged as they aim their swords at our chests.

The tip of a sword to presses against my leathers as I step forward. "I'm Bria Sutherland, and you *will* permit me entry."

"Our High Lord has better things to do than entertain his errant sister," says the male on the left. "Leave the Lady and be gone."

Although I do not know how to use them, I palm my daggers. I have spent five and seventy years being talked down to. No longer.

"Let me through or pay the price. The choice is yours."

"We take our orders from High Lord Rennyn." The guards are too stubborn for their own good.

I catch Vander's eye, and he shrugs as if to tell me I'm on my own. There's a telling strain around his eyes and in the slight downturn of his lips. He will collapse if he does not free Fayeth from his magical hold soon. If the twin soul bond was complete, I could mind link with him and ask his thoughts on revealing my metal bending magic to get out of this nuisance.

I decide before I can think it through. I rip open the magic blocking hatch, but only long enough to wrap a single thought around a ribbon of silver, drag it from the depths of the chamber in my mind, and then I slam the hatch closed once more, sealing away the force and signature of my magic. Revealing one of my gifts is enough.

I guide the ribbon of magic through my body until my every nerve is tingling with power. The sharp tang of metal fills the air as the magic gathers in my palms and cools my hands. The metal of the guards' swords shines bright, and I focus on the blades with everything I have. Intending to curl the weapons in on themselves, I picture the moment the blades bend.

They both explode into thousands of glittering pieces.

A grimace pulls at my bottom lip, revealing a row of crooked ivory teeth. "I guess I need more practice."

"I'd say that's a fair assessment," says Vander.

The guards shout and leap out of the way, clearing the path for us to push through. Fayeth thrashes harder than ever as we step onto the spongy grass of the viaduct.

A guard calls after us, but neither of us offer him so much as a look back.

The sentries at the gatehouse, perhaps having seen the destruction I caused at the outpost, do not prevent our entry, and we pass into the outer bailey without issue.

"What has happened?" I ask no one in particular.

"I have no clue," Vander answers, his tone tight.

The outer bailey, the large courtyard that surrounds the inner bailey and the castle, is teeming with fae. Males, gripping their hands to wounds and moaning. Females, dashing about with strips of white cloth and bowls of water. Weapons, discarded. Armour stained with red. There's so much red here. It dribbles through fingers, spreads over cloth, and drips from weapons and armour.

Red, red, red.

My breaths come in harsh pants and sweat beads on my forehead as my feet stop obeying my command to move. I cannot drag my eyes from the closest female who's wringing a crimson-stained cloth. The dark pink water runs down her bare arms to her elbows, dripping to the dirt where a large puddle of ruby awaits.

Vander places a hand on my lower back. "Breathe through it, Princess. You're stronger than this."

"I'm not," I whisper, my head moving from side to side without my commanding it to. "I'm not strong enough."

"Your brother needs you."

Four words. Four simple words that should not mean as much as they do after everything Rennyn has done. It's all I need to shake away the demons clawing at my thoughts, trying to find a foothold.

I nod. "Yes. He needs me."

Rennyn, he needs to burn his mother. He needs to say farewell. His needs are more important than my spiralling thoughts. I shove them into the darkest recesses of my mind, where not even my subconscious will find them.

I make my feet move again, taking one step after the other, and letting my body adjust to the ebbing moroseness. We pass too many injured to count as we walk through the outer bailey, too many panicked females trying to help, and too many faces screwed in pain.

"Where are the healers?" I ask as we enter the quieter, though still chaotic, inner bailey.

"Jonik has pulled all his healers from every court except ours" — my heart does a little flip at the collective — "and Day. It's a war tactic."

"And a way to anger anyone who is still deciding who to align themselves with. Spring, Night, Winter… They are undecided."

"High Lady Maude won't pledge an allegiance to us." He steps aside as a male leads an injured horse into the outer bailey. Thankfully, the beast's gaping wound will heal. Coming back to my side, Vander adds, "When we split from Night three hundred years ago, she swore to never lend us aid, even if the realm depended on it."

My eyes flick to the stables out of habit, finding Solana's empty stall beside that of the High Lord's stallion. Ames is in his stall, thrashing his head from side to side and snapping his teeth at the stable hand. His onyx coat gleams with sweat.

"Seems drastic," I tell Vander, though I'm not invested in the conversation any longer.

Rennyn, dressed in full regalia and armour, marches from the stables, growling orders to three nobles who struggle to keep up with his long strides. His golden-brown eyes find me in the crowd, widening a little before landing on his mother behind me.

Reality crashes into me with the force of a tidal wave. I'm no better than Tohminic and his fiery court if I refuse to help the Autumn fae in their time of need, I'm no better than Father withholding truths when it suits me, and I cannot, in good conscience, decline an alliance with my half-brother.

"Vander," I say, as Rennyn alters his path to head straight for me.

"I know. Do what you think is right."

Rennyn orders the three nobles away, and they each cast furtive glances in my direction before scurrying into the castle.

Vander steps forward, angling his body so he's shielding me when Rennyn gets close. "That's close enough," he says, resting his hand on his axe.

"How?" Rennyn asks, without tearing his gaze from his mother.

I push Vander aside so I can see Ren properly. "There was an attack on one of our villages. Undead. She was among them. I thought..." Emotion clogs my throat, and I clear it away. Now is not the time to show weakness. "I thought it was the right thing to do to bring her here, so you may say goodbye and burn her yourself."

He closes his eyes and breathes deep through his nose. "I had hoped Tohminic would spare her, given the information she handed him."

"We haven't assessed her body for wounds. If you wish to know how she died, I suggest you do so now. I can't hold her much longer," says Vander. "My magic is waning."

"Very well." Ren signals for two guards to approach. "Please, come inside. Seems we have a lot to discuss."

"Thank you, Ren," I say, pouring as much appreciation into the words as possible.

Last we were here, Vander punched him and I told him to shove his deal where the Mother Star cannot shine. Now, we have shown up with his dead mother amidst the healing after a battle of some kind. He has every right to despise us. Yet, here he is, welcoming us to his home.

The guards cuff Fayeth's wrists and ankles with strange metal contraptions that are tethered by a thick chain. Then they put a collar around her neck and thread the long chain through, linking her arms, legs, and head together.

It's... horrible. Heartbreaking.

"You can release her, Lord Vander," says a guard. "We've got her."

Vander groans when he sucks his magic back into himself, freeing Fayeth from the air binding her. He staggers a little, and I know we will not have the strength to fold home anytime soon.

I take his hand, giving him something less obvious to rely on in front of the Autumn fae hurrying about. His warmth engulfs my hand and trails up my arm, taking residence in my chest. If I had known something as simple as holding hands would elicit such a reaction, I would have spent my days searching for anyone willing to thread their fingers through mine.

We follow Rennyn and the guards, who drag a resigned Fayeth, into the castle I once called home, our hands never slackening. Vander's steps are slow, as if lifting the bonds took the last of his energy.

The guards peel away in the entrance hall, heading towards a hidden, rickety stairwell that leads to the underground dungeons. The entire time I lived here, I refused to think of the rock walls deep below the castle, refused to acknowledge the horror that lurks within the stone.

Rennyn leads us to the sitting room — the very room where I told Father I would no longer endure his punishment, the punishment for straying outside his mate bond and bringing me into the world — and gestures for everyone to sit. He leans against the open fireplace; the flames cast long shadows over his already harsh features.

He drags a hand down his face. "This is not how I envisioned my first moons as High Lord."

"And you think this is how *I* saw my life?" snaps Vander, sinking into the sofa and dragging me down with him. "My father dies, and I'm forced to reveal my court to the entire realm. I'm shunned, laughed at, and ignored. Now, we're at war for little reason more than a claim to a female."

I squeeze his hand, acknowledging his defence of me in front of Rennyn. "We have all endured hardships in recent times. It's not a competition."

"You're right," says Vander. He turns to Rennyn. "What happened here?"

Ren straightens. "Not here. The villages. We have been fending off attacks since Bria fled the Summer Court."

"Both villages?" I ask.

Ren's eyes skate over my body. "The leathers do not suit you, sister." He turns back to Vander. "Tohminic has been sending drafts of selkies to the east. Last night, he sent a horde of undead to the western docks. We were fighting from both sides."

"You can speak to your sister as you would to me. Times are changing. Best you change with them rather than be left behind." Vander's tone is commanding, strong, in complete contrast to the exhaustion plaguing him.

"How often?" I adjust my position when Vander leans to the side.

"Every two moons," says Rennyn, peeling away from the fire and sinking into one of the cushioned chairs. "It is constant. We barely recover from one attack before fending off another."

"Why?"

He arches an eyebrow at me. "Why what?"

"Why is he attacking? It cannot be because I escaped. That had nothing to do with you." I narrow my eyes, showing my displeasure at being forgotten. "What have you done?"

Vander finds it within himself to straighten. "He sent undead to my village. My second believes there is another wave coming. Summer attacking the Dusk Court makes sense, given your sister is one of us now." Rennyn flinches, but Vander ignores it. "She's right. There has to be another reason he's so insistent on causing you pain."

Rennyn throws his hands in the air. They slap back to his thighs with a thud. "Fine. He wants his mother back."

"You still have her?" I shout, jerking to my feet. "What's wrong with you? Just give her back."

Ren's jaw is tight. "Not until he agrees Autumn is not his enemy."

Air whistles through my nostrils. "You're as stubborn as Father. Look where that got him. Give Yaryn back to her son, or lose this court forever. He will not rest until he gets what he wants. Give her back, and Dusk will ally with you."

I had intended to offer an alliance regardless, but using Tohminic's mother sweetens the deal for me. If the High Lord of Summer has no qualm with Autumn, he has no reason to attack. If we keep our alliance secret, Autumn will be safe.

"I will consider it." He stands.

It's clear he's about to dismiss us, so I rush to ask, "How's Father?"

"I had assumed you would rather not know. Would you like to see him?"

"No. I'm not ready for that yet. I just wish to know of his health and mind, if you would be so kind as to enlighten me."

He runs a hand through his hair. It's flattened by the metal helmet he wore to battle, and the move makes strands stand on edge, making him look a little... ruthless. "Most days, he is lucid enough to understand what has happened. Today will be difficult for him, watching his mate burn."

"Ex-mate," says Vander. "She severed the bond from the self-ishness of her own heart. You are old enough to acknowledge your mother's shortcomings."

"Age has little to do with it."

"I beg to differ. Only a babe would blindly defend their mother's actions."

Before the two males can come to blows — the Mother Star knows Vander cannot handle it right now — I drag Vander to his feet and thank Rennyn for his time, adding, "I'm sorry for Fayeth. It's no secret we did not get along, but there's not a single fae in Radelea who deserves such a fate. Except perhaps Tohminic."

"You will hear from me soon," is all Rennyn says as we exit the castle.

Vander does not deteriorate as we walk through the inner and outer bailey, does not grow more fatigued when we cross the viaduct. Though he is not worse, he's no better, either.

It's up to me to get us back to Dusk. Me and my unpredictable magic. I take note of the shards of metal beside the outpost and smile. I could not have done even that at the last full moon.

Outside Autumn's wards, Vander pulls me to a stop. "I will guide, but I need to use your magic. Have you ever read of magical conduits?"

"No."

He explains how it works, and I agree to try. Though I have limited control over my powers, we have little other choice unless we wish to walk and sail.

I place my hands on either side of his face and rest my forehead against his. He mirrors my actions. It's startling in its intimacy, but when I open the hatch to my magic, the thought is gone before it takes hold.

Silver and amber threads of ribbon flow through me, spreading warmth and cold as they find the connection between us. The magic seeps from my hands and forehead into Vander's, where he gathers it with the remnants of his own.

Together, we step from Autumn and into Dusk. As we do, a niggling in the back of my mind takes form, a bone-weary exhaustion and incessant worry replacing the wonder of my own emotions.

Chapter 10

I T HAS BEEN EIGHT and twenty moons since Tohminic sent the undead to attack the village. Eight and twenty moons since Vander's emotions settled in the back of my mind. To feel remnants of his every feeling was disconcerting to begin with. Now, I delight in knowing him better.

He has not indicated the phenomenon works both ways. Perhaps he feels the happiness swelling within me now, as I sit with Wyn on the grass beside the stables, watching as Solana shows off to the other horses in the fenced arena. We are both in our leathers, ready for yet another training session after having run for far too long.

I set the water skin aside and recline on the soft grass, resting on my elbows. "Why must we spend hours running every morning? My legs feel as if my bones have turned to liquid."

Wyn snorts. "It builds stamina and strength. You'd be surprised how much a battle takes out of you, always swinging a weapon and dodging attacks. Endurance helps. Still no word from your brother?"

"No. Though Torin says the Autumn Court has faced fifteen attacks since we last spoke. I do not know what's keeping him from reaching a decision."

"Might have something to do with Vander smashing his knuckles into his face while Torin held him back."

It's my turn to snort. "You may be right."

We sit in silence for a moment, still catching our breath as we watch the horses. In the time since the village attack, I have been dedicating every spare moment to honing my animalistic magic. It comes naturally to me, and I'm pleased with my progress. It makes me feel better about not being able to control the metal bending power.

Solana trots around the arena as if she owns the entire court, tossing her mane and nickering. The other horses roll their eyes at her performance.

I wish my life was as simple as hers. She has not a care in the world, while nightly terrors and the constant wondering of when Tohminic will next send a horde of undead to torment us both play on my mind at all times.

"Bria? Can I ask you something?"

I hum, closing my eyes and enjoying how the Mother Star's morning light warms my face.

"Why haven't you told Vander about your twin souls?"

A sigh slides past my lips. I made the mistake of telling Wyn everything when I returned from the Autumn Court. She's been pestering me to tell Vander ever since.

"I'm not telling you to do it... this time. It's just that I want to understand why you haven't."

I sit up, resting my elbows on my bent knees. "There has not been a time that felt right, and I do not think he would react well to the news. The longer I wait, the more hesitant I am to tell him, thinking he will be angry I kept it from him for so long. I'm nervous."

"It's more than that." She slides a dagger from its sheath and a leather strap from one of her many pockets. "Don't get angry, but I think you're falling in love with him. I've seen the way you act around him, and I know you told Torin to back off with the flirting when you declined his offer for yet another date."

"I do not know what you mean."

"Oh, come on. We're friends. You can tell me anything."

She has proven that time and again. I know her words to be true, yet I fear admitting the truth to her will gain me little more than embarrassment. But what kind of friend would I be if I did not confide in the only female to offer me something as sacred as friendship?

"Fine. Yes, I am falling in love with him. Are you happy?"

She nudges me with her elbow before continuing to run the leather over her dagger. "That wasn't so difficult, was it? Why haven't you said anything?"

I shrug, then rip a handful of grass and tear the blades into miniscule pieces. "He does not feel as I do. He never will."

"Never say never." She stands and pockets her leather and dagger before offering me a hand to help me to my feet.

I'm pleased to note I only stagger a little. "I'm not so daft I do not see it, Wyn. He once told me he's not interested in love." I watch Vander and Torin as they approach from the manor. "My heart just needs time to forget how it feels for him."

"Ready for another round, Wyn?" Torin calls as the males descend the slope. "Or are you too sore from your run?"

Wyn laughs. "Yesterday was a one off, Wind Whisperer. Prepare to have your arse kicked." She places a hand on each of my shoulders. "Fight for him. He's worth it."

I'm disappointed to see Nyree trailing behind the males, dressed in casual clothes. At least she does not intend to take part today. Eight moons ago, she involved herself in my training and left me with bruises and a dislocated elbow. It still aches.

Vander assesses me, his silver eyes trailing from head to toe as if looking for injury. "How was your run?"

"Tiring," I say, joining him on the way to the training field and ignoring the leader of the Ill-fated. As much as he and Wyn and Torin claim she's trustworthy, I do not buy it. She has yet to give us a reason for her absence when the undead attacked.

"You need more practice. Maybe we should add a night run, too?"

I groan. "I would rather not."

"Would you rather be unable to outrun an undead?" asks Nyree from behind.

I ignore her, but Vander tells her to keep her snide remarks to herself.

We enter the dirt field we use for combat and magic duels, and I chant a mantra in my mind. *I am safe. Tohminic is not here. This is not a real fight.* The words help keep my emotions under control, though I still slip from time to time. The worst was when I thought Vander intended to choke me — just as Tohminic did that day in the Autumn gardens before an ogre attacked me in the forest — and I punched him square in the nose. I think it's still a little crooked. Van does not seem to mind.

Vander. Using a shortened version of his name only leads to false hope. It only makes our relationship seem friendlier than it is. It's difficult not to fall into the trap of shortened names and contracted words. I do not wish to lose myself entirely, although I think it's inevitable. Sometimes I wonder if it would be such a bad thing for me to become someone else. Other times, I fear losing myself to the new female emerging.

The training session is much the same as it always is. I punch and jab and duck under Vander's outstretched arms. I believe I'm getting faster and able to see some attacks coming now, though Nyree disagrees.

She comments from the sidelines every so often. "This is pointless. We're wasting our time teaching her. She'll never be more than a burden."

At least her goading gives me something to focus on. It's easier to block out the echoes of Tohminic's words when hers are so clear.

At one point, I make the mistake of glaring in her direction after twisting away from a kidney jab. Vander's fist smacks into the side of my skull, sending stars scattering across my vision.

"Don't ever let yourself get distracted." He uses my moment of astonishment to kick my legs out from under me, and I crash to the ground, hard. He pins my arms beside my head, dipping his face low. "Distractions lead to mistakes, and mistakes cost lives."

I pant beneath him, my head throbbing in time with the rapid beat of my heart. I forget how many nights I have tossed and turned, imagining Vander looming over me as he is now. Although those fantasies do not come with pain.

He presses harder on my wrists when I fight to free myself from his hold, smiling as if he has not a care in the world. "Earn your freedom." They are an echo of the words I spoke the day I came to Dusk.

I thrash harder, but it does not take me long to realise I will not gain freedom with my arms. Considering my torso pinned beneath him, I know that part of my body is useless. I have the freedom to move them, but the angle of my splayed legs is disadvantageous. Unless...

It's my turn to smile. I raise my head, my lips skimming the shell of his ear as I repeat the words he's always drumming into me in a whisper, "Never let your guard down. Assess every scenario and ensure you're aware of every move your combatant can make."

I'm pleased to see his frown when I pull back.

Then I move.

I twist my hips a little to the left, giving myself enough purchase against the dirt to wrap my legs around his waist and draw him close. My traitorous body wants to delight in the feel of his bulge against my folds, but I push the knowledge aside and focus on my next move. Using the purchase I created, I twist to the right with enough force to flip Vander onto his back, then unsheathe a dagger and press it to his throat.

"You forgot about my legs." My smile is wide as I lean forward, making sure he hears every word. Again, I ignore the friction between my thighs. "Such a novice mistake for a male such as yourself. Oh, and... I win."

It's the first time I have taken the High Lord by surprise, and I have to say, I rather enjoy the elation of winning.

"Get a room, you two," Torin shouts from the side.

I turn to him, still smiling. "I won!"

In my peripheral, I see Nyree scowl and stalk away. It only makes me grin wider.

"We're done for today. Good work," says Vander from beneath me with pride in his tone. We never train my magic while Nyree is here, and I wonder if the Dusk fae trust the Ill-fated as much as they claim.

My mood remains elated as we leave the training field. Vander and Torin have some kind of meeting with a few store owners in the village, so they do not return to the manor.

But Wyn remembers an appointment in the northern village — something about her hair and sword pins — and rushes off before she misses her opportunity.

For the first time in many moons, I'm alone. I decide to take a bath and relax while the upstairs apartment is empty. It's rare any of us have time to enjoy such a luxury as soaking in scented water.

While the tub fills with steaming water, I add drops of oil that smell of sweet orange and lavender, and cannot help but remember the feel of Vander between my legs. A deep ache throbs in my core, and I clench my thighs.

My grip loosens and the vial slips, oil sloshing over the rim and coating my hand. I set the vial aside and wipe my hand on my naked body, my heated skin reacting to my touch and the slide of my fingers against my torso. I close my eyes and slide my hand lower, the image of Vander's silver eyes and cunning smile filling my mind. The echo of his comforting weight settles over me like a blanket as my fingers dip between my legs and brush against my clitoris.

A gasp pulls from my throat and I jerk my eyes open. Heat crawls over my cheeks as I take in the room, hoping no one has dared to enter while I was distracted. I slip into the water to hide my shame, to hide the glistening oil on my thighs. The heated water does little to soothe the building desire. I snatch the washcloth from the table beside the tub and scrub my skin with rough strokes to distract myself.

All I can think of is Vander's rough strokes if we were ever to be together.

I groan and close my eyes, resting my head against the edge of the tub. The water is warm, but I find no reprieve from the ache building low in my belly. Why must the Mother Star torture me with this on top of everything else I have endured?

Wyn's words from our trip through the Summer Court echo in my mind: *"You've never given yourself an orgasm? Try it one day, Bria. You might just enjoy yourself."*

She does not find shame in touching herself.

Why should I?

This burning need inside me will not just go away because I want it to. It's insistent, it's… commanding. I fear if I do not put out the flames, they will consume me altogether.

These feelings cannot be entirely my own. I have never felt such an overwhelming need to relieve the ache, not in all my five and seventy years. When I look into the recess of my mind where Vander's emotions run rampant, I can hold myself back no longer.

He's just as affected as I am. Desire, burning and raging through him. There is no other explanation for what I feel from his end.

My eyes close and my hand trails down my stomach, still slippery with oil, and slides between my thighs before I can stop myself. Whether or not he wants to admit it, Vander is riddled with lust. Lust for me. The realisation spurs my fingers into action, and I slide two along the length of my folds, feeling the slickness gathering.

The moment I tease my swollen clit, my toes curl and my free hand grips the edge of the tub. That same throbbing ache blazes into an inferno of scorching fire, claiming my every sense as my fingers move in frenzied circles.

I spread my legs wider, the wildfire building too hot, too fast. Vander's emotions flare along with my own, doubling the ecstasy coursing through me. He is all I can see, all I can smell and taste as I continue to work myself into a crazed state of bliss. Vander, who crawled for me. Vander, the High Lord who cares more for his denizens than himself, the male who has taught me to defend myself and brought me back from the brink of giving up.

My core tightens to the point of pain — Vander's emotions follow suit, a desire like he has never felt before crashing through him as he realises he's feeling *my* ecstasy as well as his own — and I flick my clitoris faster, determined to dive into the depths of untold pleasure.

I cry out as an orgasm tears through me, and black encroaches on the sides of my vision. Although the intensity of the fire ebbs, it's like a yawn that does not have the desired effect, and you yawn again and again just to find release. I will not dampen these flames on my own. It's impossible when what I need is Vander.

Chapter 11

"Hi, beautiful." I keep my voice soft so I do not wake the other horses. "Let's go for a ride."

Solana nibbles at my open palm, then pushes it aside and turns her face away. It's as if she's excited I am here but just remembered she's mad that I have not come to see her as often as I should.

"I know, and I'm sorry. That's why Wyn and I are here. The forest stretches along the southern beaches, and I thought you would like to run through the water." Her ears twitch. I smile. "And there's a grove of apple trees at the western edge."

She snorts and offers me her jowls to pat.

I slide open the bolt that keeps the door to her stall closed and grip her reins in my hand before leading her through the stables and into the crisp morning air, where the stable hand is waiting with her saddle.

"What took you so long?" asks Wyn through a yawn.

"She's mad at me." I tie the reins around a wooden post. "It's been too long since we went for a ride." That's the reason I gave Wyn for dragging her out of bed at the rise of the Mother Star.

I do not wish to be caught alone with Vander after my bath yesterday, though I want to talk to Wyn about it. I went to great lengths last night to avoid him when he was near, even demanding he allow me access to the archives on the grounds of winning my first sparring match. He agreed, and I remained among the texts reading on how to strengthen wards until I was sure he would be retiring for the night.

"Such fickle creatures, aren't they?" Wyn eyes her mare with distrust. "She tried to bite me when I walked her from the stables."

"I do not think they appreciate the early start. I cannot say I enjoy it too much, either, but when else am I to find the time?"

Wyn arches an eyebrow. "After training?"

"They're ready," says the stable hand, offering me Solana's reins. "Remember to let them rest when they need it. It's been a while since either of them went farther than the field."

"Thank you," Wyn and I say concurrently.

He places a step beside each mare, guides us onto their backs — I have to say, I wish Father had allowed me to wear riding pants long ago, my leathers make riding such a breeze — then scurries back into the stables to wake and feed the other horses.

We take it steady down the sloping hill and through the pine and she-oak forest along the southern side of the manor, allowing the horses to warm and find their strides. Once we're on the water-logged sand of the beach, though, we give them a chance to stretch their legs.

Solana relishes in galloping over the firm sand, stretching her legs for the first time in... Blessed Mother Star, it has been close to three months since she ran like this.

I slow her to a trot when sweat glistens along her golden-brown coat and guide her into the shallow water of the sea. "How was that, my beauty?"

She nickers.

Wyn pulls up beside me, her long ebony braid beginning to fall free. "You're right. It's so freeing to ride. I should do it more often. Now, tell me the real reason for dragging me out of bed, and don't give me any of that nonsense about Solana needing to stretch her legs."

"Do you remember I told you the twin soul bond will strengthen over time?" She nods. I tuck a strand of copper behind my ear and continue. "It strengthened after Vander and I shared our magic to fold out of the Autumn Court."

"Why didn't you say?" There's hurt in her tone.

I wrap the leather reins around my hand, finding solace in a habit I could never break. "Honestly, I'm not sure. It feels kind of intimate, and it's an invasion of privacy. I can feel his emotions, and I think he can feel mine. Well, as of yesterday."

She faces me, letting her mare pick the path among the sand and rocks. "What happened yesterday?"

Heat crawls up my cheeks. "Remember what you told me when we stopped for luncheon in the Summer Court? The day Jonik ordered the triplets to return to Dawn."

Her brow furrows, and she looks out to sea while she tries to remember.

I graze my teeth along my bottom lip, waiting for the questions that are sure to follow when she realises what I'm talking about.

"Oh!" she gasps. "You gave yourself an orgasm? How was it? How did you do it? What does my brother have to do with this?"

I cannot help but cringe. "It's private, Wyn, but yes. Vander and I can feel each other's emotions. If he's hot or cold, I know. If he's in pain or glad or filled with rage, I know. After our training session yesterday, I was... flustered. I did not realise until I was in the tub that I was feeling his lust as well as my own. He did not notice the connection between us until I was on the brink of orgasm."

"He felt you come undone?"

"Yes." I nod. "I felt him, too."

She shouts a sound of disgust. "Too much information, Bria. Too much. So, what, you're avoiding him now?"

"I do not know how to broach the subject. Not that I want to. It's mortifying."

"You're embarrassed?" She rushes to grip the horn and pommel of the saddle when her mare takes it upon herself to leap over a rock the size of my head. "Why?"

The conversation remains on topic as we walk through the apple groves. Wyn pesters me for details as we take the western and northern paths back to the manor, and she demands to know every detail of our bond as we hand the mares over to the stable hand and flatten our hair.

"I don't understand," she says as we stretch before our pre-sparring run, "why you're embarrassed about it. Vander felt your orgasm. Most males would delight in that."

"He does not wish to be more than friends. I would be just as embarrassed if *you* felt my orgasm."

She cringes, and her arm falls to her side. "Point made. Though I still think you should use it to your advantage."

We start out at a jog, heading south for the forest, where we will travel east before looping back to the manor. The entire run will take an hour, half as long as our run yesterday.

"How?" I pant, hating running already. "How do I use it without seeming desperate?"

Breathlessness does not taint her voice as she says, "Males think about sex more than you think. He won't be able to stop thinking about it all day. Probably kept him awake last night. I'm sure I heard him tossing and turning."

I duck under a low-hanging pine branch. "That explains nothing."

"Make him remember how it felt," she says. "Trap him beneath you again, find ways to touch him, or draw attention to your stars-given gifts when he's looking."

"I cannot possibly."

"Use your body to get his attention, then ensnare him with your cleverness and bravery. He respects courage more than he'll admit."

"I'm the least courageous fae in Radelea."

She snorts and side-steps a boulder. "You found the courage to fight when you were on the brink of death in that fucking iron cage. You were brave enough to go on when your mind was trying to destroy you. I can list dozens of reasons why you're brave."

I have never thought of myself in such a way. Since escaping Ad'Starrag, I have assumed I was merely fighting to survive, not being brave. Any fae would do the same. True, it took courage to fight my inner demons — it *still* takes courage to fight them every damn day, to wake from the nightmares and decide to go on — and it took all my bravery to keep fighting that day in the water, when the selkies were coming for me and I believed the peace of drowning would serve me better than a world of pain and torment.

A gust of wind blows past us, a whisper tickling my ears. "Manor. Now." It's followed by a second, rougher gust. "Undead."

My wide eyes whip to Wyn. "Did you hear that?"

She's already running back the way we came.

I skid to a stop and spin, taking off again in the same breath. I run harder than I ever have during my morning runs with Wyn, pushing my body to its limit as I tear past she-oaks and pines. We knew another attack was on the horizon, but I did not consider where Tohminic would next target.

Dusk Manor. The place I have called home since escaping the Summer Court, the solace among heartache and anxiety, and the freedom I fought so very hard for. He will not take my home as well as my peace of mind. I will not allow it.

The hatch keeping my magic settled rips open with a single thought, and I bring my metal bending power to the surface. I do not consider the lack of control I have over the sharp ribbons and bring it to my palms as I sprint up the manor's hill — Wyn darts to the left, skirting around the outside.

When I reach the manor, I race to the right and catch a hand on the outside wall to slow myself down. The hessian sack Vander uses when we train is where he left it two days ago. I snatch it up and heave it over my shoulder before racing in the direction I saw Wyn head.

When I round the other side of the manor, Vander, Wyn, and Torin are each locked in a duel with an undead. Two more are trying to break through the wall, right where the war room must be. It can only mean one thing.

They're trying to reach the human realm.

I throw the sack on the ground, rip it open, and rods of different metals gleam in the light cast down by the Mother Star as they spill out. I pull on the threads of my magic, search for the bars of copper I know to be in the sack, and wrap ribbons of power around two of them.

The metal clangs as I drag the copper from the mess of atryxium, silver, and platinum, causing an undead to whip towards me. Their feet drag in the grass as they leave their companion in favour of hunting me. It's what I want, for just one of them to attack.

A pulse of worry niggles, and I send calming vibes back to Vander. *I have this,* I think towards him, though our bond is not strong enough to form a mental connection yet.

I place one of the copper bars at my feet and grip the other in both hands. My power crackles as I bring it to my palms, as if eager to be used as it was intended, and I realise my magic is not separate from my soul, but a part of the core of my being. I have been treating it as foreign when I should have been thinking of it as another limb. I have locked it down and feared the consequences of using it instead of delighting in its power.

With a grunt of effort, I push my intention into the magic, willing it to bend the copper into a curve. It does as I ask without resistance. When the copper is bent just enough, I drop it to the ground and pick up the next piece and do the same.

By the time I have both lengths of metal shaped, the first undead is upon me. I twist my upper body until the male is groping my shoulder and slam the copper onto his wrist. He does not notice the cool metal touching his skin, instead clawing at my chest with his other hand.

The second undead pauses her pounding against the brick wall and turns to look at me. She twists her neck too far to be possible and walks backwards towards me.

My fingers grip the male's free wrist tight and I drag it to the other arm, looping the copper around both wrists and using my magic to pull it tight. Next, I shove him with all my strength.

He hits the metal poles that serve as a railing outside the horse paddock — a new addition Torin installed one and ten moons ago. It takes all my concentration to soften the copper enough to weld it to the steel fence, then harden it once more until I have trapped the undead. Freeing the body from its confines is a problem I will deal with later.

I spin back to the second undead, wrongly guessing she is almost upon me. Instead, her gnarled hands close around Vander from behind and pull him back. My legs move faster than my mind, and I bend mid-step to pick up the next length of copper.

I reach Vander, who is struggling against two undead now, within three heartbeats, and swing the bar wide. It smacks into the female's head with a crack, distracting her just enough that she releases Vander. There is no chance of knocking her unconscious given she's already deceased, but it was worth a try.

Her nails scrape down my leathers when I'm too slow to loop the copper over her wrist, and her teeth come too close to the skin of my neck when I'm trapping her other wrist.

I recoil with a grimace. "Your breath is utterly offensive."

She only hisses and snaps her teeth.

I shove her backwards in response, curling my magic around her copper cuffs and sending it across the grass to the fence, where I weld it right beside the first. The two undead look an unsightly pair thrashing against the bands around their wrists, and their eyes are intent on me. It's unnerving.

"Creative," says Torin, moving to stand beside me. There's an undead female standing statue-still to his left, her mind lost to his Night magic. "Effective. I like it."

I offer him a bemused look. "There is little else I can do unless I slip into the body of a horse. But I'm reluctant to risk them."

He raises his palms. "I'm not mocking you. I'm impressed. More often than not, you shatter metal instead of bending it. How did you do it?"

"I decided my magic doesn't scare me anymore."

Chapter 12

AFTER FREEING THE TWO undead I trapped from their copper confines and leaving Wyn, Torin, and Vander to burn them, I head inside to triple check something I read in a scroll last night.

The archives are my favourite place in Dusk Manor. The walls are dark, like blackened steel, and the fae lights shining from the brass sconces cast an amber glow over the four rows of shelves cutting through the room. A large panel of glass runs the length of the northern wall, the view looking out towards the Spring Court in the distance.

There's a statue in the corner I know is a mere illusion and leads through to the war room the undead were trying to enter. I take the time to check that room, thinking it pointless since no one is in there to let me in, but deciding it's worth a look. At least I will know I tried.

Passing through the statue of the wind wielder is as easy as walking through air. It's the trick of the mind that makes me uneasy, and I tell myself the stone body will not trap me in its rocky cocoon.

Though I'm adamant no one will be in there, the wooden wall that serves as a door is ajar when I enter antechamber beyond the statue.

"Hello?" I call out as I push open the door with one hand. I step into the large hidden room. "Nyree? What are you doing in here?"

She startles and straightens from where she's leaning over the table, assessing the map of Radelea, its courts, and where known infantries and armadas are. She presses a hand to her leather-clad chest. "Bria, you scared me."

I do not enter the room fully. My trust for her is miniscule, and I do not wish to be trapped in a room with only one exit. I narrow my eyes. "What are you doing?"

"Oh, I was just thinking about our allies and where they are." Her pearlescent hair shines as she twists back to the table. "If Autumn refuses our deal, we'll be surrounded from south-east to north-west. We need an ally in Spring."

"You know there was another undead attack, right? At the manor."

She freezes. "No, I didn't. Is everyone okay?"

"There were only five of them, and we took care of it. It's funny how you never seem to be there when the attacks come." I step back into the antechamber. "I will leave you to your planning."

She turns back to the map as I leave, though it's clear she's not taking any of it in. I do not believe her reasons for being in the war room. As an Ill-fated, she does not belong to the Dusk Court, so why is she so concerned for our welfare?

I select a tome from the shelf in the archives without reading the title and find a hidden seat in the back, letting the book fall open to a random page. My eyes do not move across the words as they should, and I tilt my head, listening for Nyree's steps when she leaves at last.

The soft pad of her leather boots comes much later, when the Mother Star is well past her zenith. I can only assume she spent time in the human realm before deciding it's safe to leave the war room.

I make sure the coast is clear by poking my head around the nearest shelf before returning the book to its location, then moving through the archives to find the scroll from last night. Though as much as I search, I cannot find it.

It's not on the shelf I placed it on before retiring for the night, it's not on the floor beneath the table I used, and it's nowhere else within the archives. I'm certain I read a text on the wards of Dusk, where they are, and how to strengthen them. It was late, and my eyes were gritty with fatigue, but I'm certain.

Giving it up as a wasted effort, I head off in search of the female who cleans the lower floors of the manor, finding her in the ground floor kitchen scrubbing an already gleaming bench.

"Excuse me, but did you do any cleaning in the archives this morning?" I ask, leaning against the door frame.

"I did not. Why?"

"A scroll is missing."

She jerks upright, the scrubbing brush forgotten. "Impossible."

"I assure you, it's gone." My brow furrows. "Who else has been in there?"

"I cannot say for certain," she says, collecting the brush. "Leave it with me. I'll look into it, though if you could not find it, I assume it gone." She begins to scrub once more.

My thoughts are a mess of wondering where the scroll could be and trying to remember what I read last night as I take the stairs to the top-floor apartment. The text mentioned a conduit and there was something about the bones of an original fae, but other than that, I cannot be sure of what I read.

I have failed the Dusk Court. I should be someone they can rely on to defend them, someone they can trust. The first opportunity I have to show I'm reliable, and I blow it.

"What's up, Bria?" Torin asks as I enter the sitting room. He leans forward and rests his elbows on his knees. His face is slack, an air of fatigue wafting from him.

Wyn is in a patch of sun in the corner painting some kind of polish onto her toes, and Vander is sharpening his axe. Anyone would think the trio have just come from a day in the village, not a fight with five undead.

I sink into one of the plush chairs and run a hand down my face. "I was just in the archives searching for the text on strengthening wards but could not find it anywhere, though I know I read it just last night. How can it just disappear in a matter of hours?"

"Books aren't my forte," Torin says, leaning back again. "Why were you looking for it?"

I say my words to the three of them, but I face Vander when I say, "Because the undead are getting past our wards. We need to strengthen them, or they will succeed in entering the human realm next time they attack."

He frowns. "What's the human realm have to do with anything?"

"Did you not notice the section of wall they were clawing at?"

"We were too busy fighting them," says Torin, closing his eyes, a sure sign he's listening to the whispers in the wind.

"Well, I noticed. They were trying to get into the war room." I brush a strand of hair from my eyes. "Tohminic knows of the humans."

"It's our duty to protect them, Van," says Wyn, blowing gently on her toes.

"You're certain you read about it?" Vander asks me. I nod, and his face falls. "There's only one way we can retrieve the information if the book is gone. Allow a Night fae to look into your mind."

A shiver dances along my spine. I have not felt the mind magic of the Night fae before, though I have read it's somewhat... uncomfortable. "I will do it, if you think it will help."

He turns to Torin, who's eyes are still closed. "Would your mother be willing?"

He hums, his lips curling down. "It's been years since I last saw her. She could be dead for all I know."

"Torin." The single word, spoken in a stern voice, comes from Wyn.

He opens his eyes. "Yes, she would be willing. For a price."

⁕ ⁕ ⁕

"Are you sure about this?" I ask. The small rowboat rocks from side to side, the churning current crashing against the wooden hull. I eye the narrow corridor we're supposed to navigate and gulp. "It does not look safe."

A quick glance over my shoulder, and I'm both pleased and concerned the other boat is still there. The ivory rope pulls taut as it trails behind us, occupied by the five undead from this morning.

"We've done this plenty of times," says Torin.

"The elderly have *breathed* plenty of times, but when they grow to a certain age and their breaths become laboured and rattled, I'm sure they wonder why they cannot draw air into their lungs when they have spent their lives doing so with ease."

Wyn nudges me with her elbow. "You're rambling makes little sense, Bria."

"Are we sure this is the only way?"

"If we're to avoid detection, yes," says Wyn, removing her hand now that I'm no longer panicking. "High Lady Maude despises us, as you very well know. So much that she's prohib-ited all Dusk fae from entering her lands. This is the only path we can take where we'll remain unseen."

The sheer cliffs on either side of the sea corridor reach for the night sky, the twinkle of stars blocked out by their mammoth size. Somehow, the waters here are more dangerous than any-where else in Radelea. We call it the Deathly Rapids for a reason.

"Besides," says Torin, "Mother lives at the other end of the Rapids. This is both convenient and the fastest way to her home."

Vander continues to use his air magic to push the rowboat along, seemingly unbothered by the constant rocking. "Is she expecting us?"

"I sent a whisper," says Torin, resting his feet on the rickety seat beside me. He shrugs. "She'll know if she was listening."

We enter the corridor — the end of the churning sea tunnel is shrouded in darkness — and the boat lurches to the right. I squeal and grip the seat so hard my knuckles turn white. My breaths become harsher than the dark water below, and I do not think my body can handle the frights I'm forced to endure.

Darkness blankets us, becoming denser with every sigh of wind from Vander's hands. He has just taken over from Wyn, who guided us from the western shore of the Dusk Court to this spine-chilling tunnel. Though I'm not sure I can call it that, since there is nothing above us but the clear sky of the Night Islands.

The undead in the boat behind hiss and thuds come from their direction, as if they are trying to be free of the metal restraints I welded onto their ankles and wrists. It seems even those no longer living fear the Deathly Rapids.

Slithers of something sparkling dart through the water ahead, and I pray to the Mother Star whatever's down there remains so during my time here.

I keep one hand on the seat for balance and use the other to clench my travelling cloak tighter around my shoulders, offering an illusion of safety and warmth. It does little to fend off the icy chill in the air, less against the splash of cool water against my face.

Something slams against the left of the hull, and the little boat teeters too close to tipping for a moment before Wyn uses a blast of wind magic to straighten us. "Something doesn't want us here," she says through her pants.

"It seems rougher than normal," says Torin, sitting straighter and losing his carefree expression for once.

"I'm going to push it faster," says Vander. "The sooner we break through the Rapids, the better. I don't like the look of those fish."

Indeed, the glittering figures within the water are growing in number and size. They are forming some kind of ring around the boat, like they plan on surrounding us and then attacking.

"What are they?" I ask.

"Damned souls of the Night fae," says Torin. "Thirsty for blood to replace the magic they once controlled."

I close my eyes. The less I know and the less I see, the more likely I will get through this. The darkness of the Rapids is impenetrable this far in, and having my eyes open will do little other than cause more panic.

Every bump against the rowboat, every vicious wave that crashes up and over, and every damn beat of my dread-filled heart sends prickles of anxiety and fear along my skin. Goose-flesh pebbles my arms, notable even beneath my leathers, as the bow rears up before slamming back into the water. I can only hope the undead remain firmly in the boat we're towing. Otherwise, we visit Torin's mother with no trapped souls to offer as payment.

My hair sticks to my face as if glued, though I'm not brave enough to uncurl either hand to brush it away. I count my heartbeats, reaching seven and eighty before the roughest lurch yet causes the numbers to slip from my mind. Thankfully, the ordeal only lasts another few moments, and we are soon tying both rowboats to a barnacle-covered post along a rocky shore.

I have never been more thankful for solid earth in my life, and that's including the time I almost drowned after falling from Zentha's ship off the coast of Dusk.

Set into the jagged rock of a small island — this must be the island Maude deemed uninhabitable when the land broke apart — is a kind of hut I'm hesitant to call a house. It's small, only big enough for Torin's mother, and looks about ready to fall down with one of Vander's more powerful gusts of wind.

What a lonely life, living on a small island made of nothing but rock with only the sea creatures to keep you company, set away from the rest of your court because... A shudder runs down my spine as I remember why Maude banished Blodwen to this island. She takes pleasure in *feeding* off the tormented minds of others, even torturing fae for the desired effect.

"Mother." Torin's voice is tight as we make the short walk from the boats to her front door, where she is standing and watching us with curiosity.

"My darling son." Blodwen's dark eyes swirl with a kind of knowing that makes my skin crawl as she takes in first Vander, then Wyn, and me last. She licks her thin lips. "And you have brought friends."

Vander shields me with his body, though it's a pointless move when I'm about to allow her into my mind.

Torin does the same with Wyn. "We're here to ask for help. We brought payment." He gestures to the two rowboats. "Five undead, caught this morning."

She glances at the undead for a mere heartbeat before her haunting eyes fall on me once more. Her nostrils flare. "The fae are sufficiently tortured, my boy. Come in."

My entire being screams this is a bad idea. My skin prickles with fear as I cross the threshold into her dilapidated home, but I force my legs to move. The Dusk Court needs this. I need this.

Inside is just as run down as the exterior. The logs that form the outside wall continue to the interior, and a draft runs through the open hut, rustling the loose and drying hair around my face. There are no curtains framing the two small and yellowed windows, no rugs for warmth covering the uneven floorboards, and no items that make the space a home.

The thick layer of grime covering the window sills and the surface of the tall dresser makes me think Blodwen doesn't spend much time here, though the roaring fire and unmade bed prove otherwise.

I flinch when the door slams closed behind me, shutting out the light of the crescent moon — there's barely a slither of light after last night's new moon, but still I miss it — and blocking the sound of the waves crashing against the rocky shore.

"Why have you come?" Blodwen asks from beside me.

I had not realised she was so close, and I move to stand beside Vander while Torin explains.

"We're hoping you can help Bria recover some information she read in a text. In exchange for your aid and hospitality, you get all five of the undead outside."

My stomach churns. I don't like the idea of handing them over to Blodwen any more than I like the idea of her rummaging through my memories. They deserve to have their bodies burned and commended to the Mother Star.

But this is one of those deals that is both necessary and dreadful. I won't rest easy knowing what we have done, though I will be thankful for their sacrifice for the rest of my moons. The worst part of it all is their blood will join that of the fae injured at Ad'Starrag, the Summer fae from the rotunda, and Nikolai. My hands will be heavy with crimson, my soul haunted for eternity.

"I find your terms acceptable." Blodwen moves farther into the room, walking slower than the average fae. She limps a little, as if an old injury causes her pain. "What information are you seeking?"

"It's from a text I read last night about wards and how to strengthen them." I keep the unease I feel in her presence out of my voice. I'm beginning to understand why Torin stayed in Dusk with his father rather than fight alongside Blodwen in Night.

Blodwen smiles, revealing two rows of crooked and missing teeth. "Fresh. That is good. It will not hurt as much."

"As much?" My voice is small. I move even closer to Vander.

"Oh, yes. Retrieving memories is a nasty business."

Torin tenses. "You've never mentioned that before."

"You have not bothered to ask," she says. "Sit down, Bria of Autumn."

I sit on the dirty floor. "I hail from Dusk."

She lunges, gripping my face in her hands and pressing the tips of her gnarled fingers into my skull. "Keep still and keep silent."

Magic, grating and rough like a barbed stinger, rushes from her fingers into my mind, where it pokes every crevice and tightens around every bend of thought. Her presence is slick and cunning as she sorts through my memories as easy as turning the page of a freshly bound book.

My spine aches as my body contorts from the pain. The barbs of Blodwen's magic aren't gentle as they pinch and probe, they give no mind to comfort while they search for the information we need.

Training magic with Vander, running with Wyn, and joking with Torin. The shock at seeing Fayeth's undead body, Tohminic's hands around my throat in the Autumn gardens, and the ogre attack in the forest. Blodwen sorts through everything that is always in the forefront of my thoughts before delving deeper until she finds yesterday's memories.

She hums in amusement at the memory of yesterday's bath and tuts at Nyree's words from combat training. Then she finds the moment I read through the scroll. She lingers and allows me to read the slightly blurred text from my memory before focusing on a dark shadow in the corner, a shimmer of pearl catching the light.

She retreats from my mind as fast as she entered, leaving every thought sluggish and painful. "You have what you need?"

"Yes. Thank you." My voice is strained as I push myself from the floor and move to stand beside Vander, who has his fists clenched.

"Are you okay?" Wyn asks. The narrow slits of her silver eyes don't stray from Blodwen's smiling face.

"I'm fine."

"She is more than fine," says Blodwen. "I quite enjoyed the memory from your bath yesterday. Lord Vander, too, I believe."

Vander tenses.

"Thanks for your help, Mother," says Torin, grasping the tarnished handle and ripping open the door, saving me from sure embarrassment.

Blodwen frowns. "Before you rush to leave, Bria of Dusk, may I suggest you remove the cages within your mind and free what remains of your magic?"

"Whatever do you mean?"

Vander asks, "How many?"

Blodwen, seeming to delight in knowing something we don't, smiles a crooked smile. "There were once four, though you have broken two. To free what remains, you must face your fears and truly *need* that magic."

"Enough riddles," says Torin, stepping outside.

"Do come again, son. Leave the fae where they are. I will collect them when I am ready."

I push the image of what she's going to do to them from my mind and exit into the cool night air. It washes over me like a comforting blanket, soothing the frayed nerves and jumbled thoughts.

No one says anything until we are in the rowboat and far enough out to sea, there's no chance of Blodwen overhearing. I watch as the strange soul fish writhe. They're calm now they know we're leaving. Their glow is beckoning and beautiful in the night. I wonder what they look like during the daylight hours when the Mother Star shines her brightest and if the urge to dip my fingers into the water would be stronger.

Vander draws his magic back into himself, allowing the boat to bob on the water. "Four. It's unheard of."

"Unheard of?" Wyn scoffs. "It should be impossible. No wonder Kerym didn't want her training her powers. She's a force to be reckoned with."

"Every fae in Radelea would want her," says Torin. "They'd use her."

"It's imperative we keep this to ourselves," says Vander.

I let their words wash over me, let them sink in and take root. I have two more powers inside me. My mother is from the Spring Court; it's safe to say I wield both nature and psychic magic.

If I can get a handle on my powers once I free them from their cages, I might see the outcome of this war. I could see what we need to win. This could be a tremendous advantage for us.

I understand why Father kept this from me. Torin's right, if anyone finds out I'm a wielder of *four* powers, I will be hunted to the ends of the realm. It doesn't make the knowledge easier to swallow. He still lied by hiding an important part of my being from me. He caged it. It's unforgivable.

To spend a lifetime believing yourself unimportant, beneath society, and without magic, then to discover you're potentially the most powerful fae in the realm is... It's overwhelming and shocking, and if I'm being honest with myself, it's frightening.

Blodwen mentioned facing my fears to free the last two of my powers. My metal bending magic appeared when I was scared for my life on the Ad'Starrag battlements. Tohminic's knife was at my throat, and I was certain my blood would stain the sandstone walls of the keep. But I decided to fight. I faced my fear of failure and fought for my freedom.

The animalistic power broke through the cage in my mind when the undead were attacking the village. Again, I looked fear in the eye and acknowledged that Dusk is my home, that the fae there are innocent. I chose them, and in doing so I squashed my fear of not belonging.

I fear the Dullahan of Day and most spiders, although I don't think those are the kind of fears Blodwen spoke of. To break through the cages keeping my power at bay, I have to face something far more sinister. I have to face the fear of meeting my mother, of discovering her identity.

It's all that makes sense, given the two hidden powers come from her court. The Court of Blooms is a peaceful land for the most part, though something has always held me back from defying Father's rule and folding to Spring to demand my mother make herself known. Perhaps a part of me fears her rejection.

"Bria, for the love of the Mother Star, can you pay attention?" Wyn snaps.

I drag my eyes away from the water. "I'm sorry. My mind was elsewhere. What was it you said?"

A pulse of concern flitters from where Vander's emotions run rampant.

"Did we endure Blodwen for no reason, or did you get what we came for?" Wyn asks.

"I did. It won't be easy. Prepare for a rough few days."

Chapter 13

I T HAS BEEN THREE moons since I learned of the two other powers hidden inside me. Three moons of trying to force the cage in my mind to crack open and reveal my true nature. Three moons of preparing to gather what we need to strengthen our wards and protect the humans.

I don't think I have had a moment of peace in those three moons. We have been preparing non-stop. Vander has sent letters to every High Lord and Lady — except for Tohminic, of course — requesting permission to enter their lands. We have not told most of them the true nature of our visits, fearing the questions they would ask if they were to discover our need for stronger wards.

My leathers creak as I turn to face the Winter messenger, and my mouth hangs open in surprise as Tarathiel dips his chin in respect. I have not seen the male since he fled the Autumn Court after Tohminic's threat during my quest for a mate.

Tarathiel's skin is more translucent than I remember, almost glowing in the afternoon light as we stand at the front door of Dusk Manor. His veins pulse beneath his skin as he straightens. "An answer from High Lord Ruith for High Lord Vander."

The fae female behind him whips her ebony hair over one shoulder. "An answer from High Lady Maude."

"Two responses at once," says Wyn, nudging her brother with an elbow. "You must have done something right."

"I do not know Maude for her patience. She will want us in and out sooner rather than later," says Vander, accepting both scrolls at once. His silver eyes track over the first scroll, the glittering blue-white seal of Winter shining from the bottom. "Ruith has granted us permission to access his lands with the caveat we be gone before the moon rises. We risk our lives if we linger in the caves at night."

"Sounds fun," says Torin, the humour in his voice is clear. As is the eagerness.

A shiver tracks down my spine and disappears at my toes. The Caves of Apricity are deep below the Winter Court, beneath their largest village. While they're rife with atryxium, they're also more dangerous than anywhere in Radelea. With icicles larger than any male, creatures more beautiful than the most admired, and critters more cunning than the cleverest of high fae, the cave system is a place of nightmares.

"I thank your High Lord for his kindness and warning," says Vander, dismissing Tarathiel before reading over the note from Night's High Lady.

Tarathiel doesn't bother to look my way before turning and all but skipping down the hill and into the forest at the base. I cannot help but feel glad he bowed out of the courtship when he did. Life with the Winter fae would not have suited me.

"What does it say?" asks Wyn, peering over Vander's shoulder to read the note. She scoffs. "Permission granted for one hour tomorrow. That's impossible."

"Thank you for delivering the note," Vander says to the messenger. He rolls it into a tight scroll and tucks it into the pocket of his leather gambeson. "Offer Maude our thanks and assure her we'll stick to the time restraints."

"And of your reasons?" the messenger asks, her starlight eyes gleaming.

Vander's lips thin. "Our reasons are our own."

The messenger dips her chin and follows in Tarathiel's path without another word. Her hair shimmers for a moment but turns a flat black when a cloud moves in front of the Mother Star. It's kind of uncanny how it resembles my feelings.

After three moons of wondering if the other high fae will grant us access to their courts, they permit us entry at last. The thought is exciting, though my entire being rebels at the risks we are to take in order to protect the humans.

To strengthen our wards, we need an item from each court. Some of them are simple. A certain flower from Spring, a handful of sand from Summer, imbuing magic at the sun's rise in Dawn, and placing the artefact at the moon's rise in Dusk won't be all that difficult — unless Tohminic catches us on his land. Collecting a piece of spine from the Dullahan's whip, a finger bone from Baba Yaga's hut, and plucking a fresh harpy talon will all be more dangerous than anything I have done in this life.

"We leave in one hour." Vander's tone leaves no room for argument. "The other courts may send messengers at any moment, and we have no time to waste."

"That doesn't leave us with much time, Van. Do you think we're ready?" Wyn asks.

I don't miss the way she flicks her eyes towards me, and I cannot blame her for thinking I'm not ready to face the dangers in the Caves of Apricity. Especially after my abysmal effort at training this morning.

Five times. Vander had me on my back on the hard ground five times, all within mere heartbeats of beginning. The bruises will remain for hours.

"I will be okay." My tone holds more confidence than I feel. "I'm stronger now, and I can wield magic. If need be, I can hide and rely on a small animal."

They're my favourite to merge souls with. Their bodies can squeeze into the smallest of spaces, and they're easier to control from afar. Though with the field mice, I cannot say I enjoy the yearning for rotting food.

Wyn's face softens. "Of course you're okay. I'm just worried. You've been doing so well after everything you went through. I don't want to see you retreat back into yourself again."

"And I appreciate your concern." My smile is tight, but genuine. "If anything brings me down again, I know I can pull through it. I did it once before."

"She'll be fine," says Vander.

Torin jabs his elbow into my ribs. "Bria's the strongest female I've met. Except for you, of course," he adds when Wyn moves to kick his legs out from beneath him.

I do not believe my words to be false. Facing hardships will prove difficult, that much is true, but if anything happens, I have the strength to move past it. I'm still learning how to live with all that happened in the Summer Court, and that's the point. I'm learning. If I can learn to live with that, I can live with anything that comes my way. Besides, I have my found family now.

Vander disappears into the manor after casting one last glance at all of us. Torin follows, chatting excitedly about what's to come.

"This won't be like when I escaped Ad'Starrag," I say, determined to make Wyn believe I'm okay now we're alone. "I'm strong now and I can do this. Trust me, Wyn."

She links an arm through mine. "I trust you with my life. I just don't want to see you hurt."

Leaning close, I whisper, "Then you should not have encouraged me to pursue your brother."

"Oh, I wasn't wrong to do that. If you're to believe anything I say, believe that."

⁂

My heart stutters to a stop before beating so fast I can feel the pulse of it when I place my hand against my chest. The sight of the wooden rowboat brings a sheen of sweat across my forehead, the few strands of copper that have broken free of the tight braid cling to my face for dear life as if they can be saved from the churning sea that lies between the Dusk and Winter Courts.

"Quit panicking," says Torin. "We're not rowing across the strait. We're folding."

"Thank the Mother Star for that," I say, dropping my hand until it rests on the hilt of the dagger Vander gave me before we left.

My leathers feel tighter today. It's as if they, like me, fear the night we are walking into and are trying to warn me to return home and hide beneath the blankets on my bed. Or perhaps I have gained muscle, and they're fitting me just as they should. Perhaps I'm panicking for no reason.

We're walking into danger, yes, but with the five of us, we should be okay. I cast another furtive glance at Nyree, wondering yet again why she's here. Her long hair flutters in the wind as she stares at the curved land in the distance, and the blaze of the sinking Mother Star reflects a rainbow of colour in the pearlescent strands.

Vander adjusts the strap of his axe before taking my hand. "It's easier if we fold together. You've never been to the Caves of Apricity."

Torin, Wyn, and Nyree disappear in the blink of an eye, chased by a forceful gust of wind. While the day was calm, the evening has turned chaotic, with dark clouds swirling overhead and a blustering wind tearing at my face.

"I can fold on my own. Just because I have not been there does not mean I cannot step through the void successfully." I say the words, but I don't let go of his hand. In fact, I hold tighter. If even for a moment, I can enjoy the feel of his warmth seeping into my palm.

He turns to face me, those glorious eyes shining in the dying light. "I know you can, Princess. Allow me this. To know you're safe soothes my nerves."

"I —" Our eyes are still connected when he folds the slick stones of Winter towards us and we step off the sandy north-west shore of Dusk. His magic pulses around me, fresh and inviting as it caresses my every sense. It's a stark contrast to the bitter wind and frosty breath that clouds before me with every exhale.

My feet slide on the smooth stones even when I am not moving; the cold of night has brought a layer of slick ice to the southern shore of Winter, making our already dangerous mission perilous. I brave a glance to my left, where the icy water rushes for my feet, and step closer to the cliff face. "We're fools for doing this."

Vander releases my hand with a chuckle. "Sure steps. The caves are just ahead."

Torin takes the lead, picking a careful path along the slippery stones and keeping close to the cliff on our right. There's no hope of seeing the peak of such an enormous cliff, though I know the bustling city of Apricity rests on the icy slope at the top.

Wyn follows Torin. She uses her air magic to keep the lapping waves at bay and makes it to the cave's entrance with dry feet.

I try my hardest to follow in her steps, to place my feet where she did and avoid dealing with damp feet for what remains of this night, since we have decided to fold straight to the Night Islands from here to make our mission easier. The harpies wake with the moon, and the Winter caves are close to the northern island of Night, where the Harpy Barrens are. It makes sense to collect both relics at once, but means we're in for a long night.

I keep my eyes on the dense patch of darkness ahead. The entrance to the Caves of Apricity is all but hidden amongst the rough grey rock of the cliff, but there's one slither of darkness that is a little denser than the rest, and I know that to be the entrance only because it's where Wyn disappeared.

Most of the stones lining the beach are sturdy. There are some that shift beneath my weight, causing me to lose my balance with every other step. I make it to the cave slower than Torin and Wyn — much to Nyree's disgust, if her mumbles from behind me are anything to go by — and relief fills me when the ground is rough stone rather than slick rocks.

Inside would be pitch black if it weren't for the two fae lights hovering overhead. I throw an orb of my own into the air, where it joins the blueish light of Torin and the amber light of Wyn. The trio throw long shadows over the antechamber and reveal deep crevasses ahead and icicles growing larger the farther into the cave I look.

A bone-chilling chirp rings through the cave system. It bounces off the walls and sends a shiver of fear dancing along my spine. No one knows exactly what creatures dwell in these caves. No one can talk about it... if they ever find their way out of the labyrinth, that is.

Nyree steps up behind me and her arm brushes against my back.

I hold in the cringe of disgust and fight the urge to leap out of the way. If I so much as step forward, I risk falling into the first of many bottomless crevasses. "Please watch where you're stepping. It's a maze of holes in here."

"Sorry," she says, not bothering to hide the humour in her voice. "I didn't see you there."

"Any whispers, Torin?" Vander asks as he steps into the antechamber.

With the five of us in here and the irregular cracks across the ground, there's not much room to move. Torin stands beside one of the three tunnels with his head cocked to the side. He's listening for whispers of wind, trying to determine which fork in the road we should take.

I wish he would hurry. The Mother Star is almost touching the western horizon; night will soon fall. High Lord Ruith warned us of the dangers of remaining here after the sun's light has faded, and I intend to heed his warning.

"I can't hear where the atryxium is, but there's a polar bear down the right tunnel," says Torin. He closes his eyes and his brow dips as he concentrates harder.

My pulse races. Polar bears are vicious, especially if it's a mother with cubs. If Torin can't find the atryxium, and we are forced to investigate every tunnel, we risk being here at night and waking the bear. Both are not scenarios I wish to witness.

"We could scout from left to right and hope for the best," says Wyn.

"I'll take the left tunnel with Vander," says Nyree. "Wyn and Torin, stay together and take the centre fork. Bria can take the right since she can control the bear."

I close my eyes to her words. The others may not see what she's trying to do, but I do. My metal bending magic thrums through my veins of its own accord. It senses the atryxium, the strongest metal in all of Radelea. My body turns without my guiding it, and I take a step forward.

I'm jerked back by Vander's rough hands. "Blessed Mother Star, what are you doing?"

My eyes spring open. "The atryxium's down there." I point to the tunnel the bear is in. "My magic can feel it. *I* can feel it. It's not far down."

"You were just going to go in on your own?" asks Torin, his brow lifting.

"I... I don't know. The metal called to me. I just acted."

Vander keeps a tight grip on my wrist as he says, "Think before you act. Foolish actions will get you killed in here."

Chapter 14

A SWEET BUT SOUR odour filters through the tunnel, edged with a musty dampness that clings to my nostrils. The icicles overhead crack now and then, the sound louder than the boom of a hammer and anvil. I freeze each time the glistening spears threaten to impale us from above, but it's a pointless effort. If I needed to leap from harm's way, I would be unable.

The tunnel is narrow; I have to tuck my elbows close to my side as I navigate the passage behind Torin. If I don't, the stone will rub against my leathers and wear them away, then graze my skin. The only positive is how sure I am the vein of atryxium is down here. The farther we walk, the stronger the pull on my power becomes.

I'm struggling to rein in the pulsing magic. With every slow step I take, the tugging grows more insistent. With every breath of frigid air, the tighter I grit my teeth against the urge to run.

"How much farther?" Nyree does not keep her voice low, which is a necessity if we are to enter without waking the slumbering polar bear in the den ahead. "Night has almost fallen."

"How do you know?" I ask. There's no way she can tell night is blanketing the land from within these caves. The Mother

Star's glow has long since disappeared, and there are no openings that allow us a view of the sky.

"I am Night fae. The moon calls to me."

Of course. She wields the power to manipulate blood and bone and is a tier four mind reader — the lowest tier of mind magic — which enables her to read surface thoughts. The gooseflesh that prickles the hairs on my arms has nothing to do with the cold and everything to do with Nyree knowing my thoughts.

I make a mental note to keep anything private out of my thoughts when she's near. If she were to discover my feelings towards — No. I force myself to focus on my metal bending magic, reading how the ribbons of silver swell and dip in my mind.

A single thought opens the hatch that keeps my magic calm, and I coax a thread of power to my hands. Several veins of atryxium lie deep in the walls on either side of us, but it's not enough to strengthen the artefact we need to make. The blue-grey veins grow larger farther in, merging to three major arteries before gathering in a chamber to the left.

I advise the others of my findings with whispered words.

Torin swears under his breath. "That's where the bear is. This might prove more dangerous than we first thought."

"We'll be fine," says Vander.

Wyn, who is at the rear of our line, says, "I'll stand guard. I'm in no mood to fight a protective mother bear."

"We don't know it's a mother," I say, stepping over a fallen icicle.

Nyree scoffs. "Only the mothers den, Bria. You were born into the court of earth and animals. How do you not know this?"

I ignore her and return my attention to the atryxium. With any luck, we will stumble upon a larger vein of the metal and won't have to face the bear. Although, luck does not seem to be something I have much of in recent times.

I have angered the Mother Star somehow, and she has deemed me unworthy of a simple, happy life. Though I believe that with every fibre of my being, I will not stop fighting for the right to peace and simplicity. I will regain her favour one day... or die trying.

My attention is so focused on finding the most precious metal of our realm, I don't notice when Torin stops walking. I collide with his back and lose my balance, falling to the floor with a loud crash.

Nyree, either distracted like me or with cruel intention, steps on my hand before jerking back with a hiss of annoyance. "Blessed Mother Star. Get up, Bria." Her voice is too loud.

I silence her with a venomous look before accepting Torin's hand and allowing him to pull me to my feet. "You okay?" he asks, his dark eyes mere pits of shadow in these caves.

"Yes. Thank you. Why have we stopped?"

He gestures ahead with a casual wave of the arm. "We're here." A deep growl shakes the tunnel walls. "The bear knows it, too."

I shoot another glare at Nyree, expecting to see remorse pulling at her features. My eyes widen in surprise at her smile before narrowing in realisation. She spoke loudly on purpose, so I would have to use my magic to control the bear. It will both tire me and keep me from finding the atryxium.

"Do your thing, Princess." Vander pushes past Nyree to stand beside me. "Just tell me where to mine for the metal, then keep the bear from shredding me."

"You can't go in there alone." My heart beats faster at the thought, but all I feel from the High Lord is confidence and trust in my ability.

His eyes flick between mine. "We need to get this over with, and fast. We're risking the night creatures waking if we remain for too long. You won't let anything harm me."

I nod and my eyelids shutter closed, the glow of Vander's silver eyes imprinted in the darkness. The veins of atryxium dip low before pooling underground. It will be harder than Vander thinks to collect it. I tell him as much as well as where to dig.

Boots scrape against the stone floor, followed by a deafening roar that makes my ears ring. I don't need to open my eyes to know the males have entered the chamber ahead. Nyree's presence lingers beside me, and Wyn's beside her. Magic pulses from each of them: one calm and crisp, the other heated and menacing.

"Bria!" Torin shouts.

I rip open the hatch in my mind and free the amber ribbons that allow me to merge my soul with that of an animal. It's wild today, and I wonder if the strength of the beast determines the behaviour of my magic. The power caresses my thoughts as I allow the calm yet dominating magic to overwhelm my senses.

Musk and mildew invade my nose, cold hard rock presses against my palms, and the taste of stale breath fills my mouth.

One blink, and I'm looking through the eyes of the polar bear as she takes a menacing step towards Vander.

My soul wraps around the bear's and soothes her tension with gentle strokes. It does not take long for her to calm down and sit back on her haunches — leaning to the side to avoid compressing her swollen stomach. I send comforting words through her mind while watching Vander and Torin struggle to cut the atryxium.

The gleaming metal shines through dozens of cracks in the floor and looks to be a large plate of blue-grey. It's the strongest metal in Radelea, and I know the males will not make a dent in it without my help.

All it takes to make the bear drowsy is a single thought planted in the back of her mind. She curls around her stomach and rests her chin on one enormous paw, her eyes drooping.

I grab hold of my magic and drag my soul back to my body, which has sagged against the wall.

Wyn helps me to stand when my eyes flutter open. "What happened? You're supposed to be keeping the bear calm."

"She's asleep," I say, brushing dirt and sleet from my legs. "They need to be quiet or they'll wake her again. They can't get the atryxium without my magic. I had no choice."

Wyn urges me to go, adding, "We'll keep watch."

I dart around the corner and into the chamber, holding a finger to my lips with one hand and pointing to the bear with my other when the males look up. "You need my help."

I don't allow them time to argue, and grapple with several threads of silver magic before drawing them to my palms. The power pulses violently and shoots from my hands before smothering the entire plate of atryxium. A scream tears at my throat when a stab of pain shoots through both arms and settles in my skull, throbbing and prickling. I push the pain aside and command the power to fracture the metal, and piece by piece, I chip away at the dense atryxium.

My jaw aches from how hard I grit my teeth, and my legs grow too weak to hold my weight. I sink to the ground with a guttural roar and send another pulse of magic into the metal.

I have never given a thought to how difficult it would have been for Fylson to forge the sword I commissioned for Rennyn. My heart knows nothing but regret for not considering the consequences. Fylson's effort and pain add another layer of red to my hands, though it stings less than the rest of the crimson haunting my soul.

"That's enough," a low voice growls. Tender hands drag me towards a firm body. "Pull your magic back. Lock it away."

I inhale a ragged breath, my thoughts racing, and pry my eyes open. All I can see are the contours of Vander's chest and the rough stubble lining his chin. I tilt my head to the side, where Torin's collecting shards of gleaming metal and placing them in a leather rucksack. Beside him, Nyree has a satisfied look on her face as her eyes flit from male to male.

A bone-chilling chirp, the same as the sound I heard upon entering the Caves of Apricity, sounds from above, and I lift my face to the hewn ceiling. My blood turns to ice, colder than the frigid air of the caves, at the sight of thousands of beetles converging. If I did not already know them to be flesh-eating monsters, their barbed pincers would have sent prickles of fear through my veins.

A second chirp joins the first, followed by at least a hundred more. The sound is so loud, I cannot hear even my thoughts.

The moment the first beetle moves, the void closes around me. For a single heartbeat, I know nothing but darkness. All I can feel is Vander and his warmth. Then the scents of lavender and orange replace those of ice and stone, and my eyes adjust to the darkness of the Dusk Court.

Vander folded us to safety, leaving his sister, his second, and the leader of the Ill-fated behind.

"Take us back, Van!" I cry, shoving at his muscular chest. "We can't leave them there. We have to help."

"I admire your concern, but they're fine." His face is a mask of calm, as are his emotions, which flutter in the back of my mind.

A low chuckle pierces the night from behind, and I spin to see Torin's eyes watering with humour. "Were you really so worried about me that you're trying to fight *Vander* off?" He holds a hand to his chest. "How moving."

"I've changed my mind," I say. "We were right to leave *him* there."

Nyree appears beside Torin. I'm pleased she's no longer smiling. "We should head straight for the Night Islands. Wait much longer and the whole harpy population will be active. Our best chance to collect a fresh talon is before they wake."

I'm sure it's the smartest thing I have heard her say, and for the first time since meeting the Ill-fated female, I agree with her.

"Smart thinking. The sooner we collect the talon, the sooner I can go to bed," says Wyn, appearing beside Nyree.

"Your tolerance for late nights is not what it once was, sister," says Vander. He angles his body, so he's speaking to only me. "Are you up to it? We'll be okay without you if you need rest."

I send a wave of calm at him, showing him my energy levels are fine and using so much magic at once was a temporary drain. I watch as his face changes from concern and kindness to surprise and wonder. At least I know for sure he can feel my emotions just as I can feel his. There's no hiding from the twin soul bond we share. Not anymore. We will have to talk about it soon — it's a conversation I'm not looking forward to.

Vander's eyes shutter and he turns away with his lips pulled into a tight line. "We go now. She's fine." His magic engulfs me, and we step through the void without another word.

While Blodwen's hut is at the southern end of the Night Islands, the Harpy Barrens are at the north-western point, close to the Winter Court and shielded from the rest of Night by a mountain range that runs the length of the three largest islands.

A quick look around the arid plain and I'm certain we have folded to the right place. The magic in the air is different, threatening with an edge of hysteria, and the miasmic atmosphere is as intolerable as sulphur, likely because of the decaying carcasses spread over the hickory-coloured land.

The harpies rest on the greying branches of the dead and dying trees. Their silky feathers are all different: some brown and long, some black and stubby, and the rare russet or white. Although their feminine faces are peaceful in slumber, they will morph to anger and cruel intention upon waking. Their deadly talons are as large as my hand and gleam under the light cast from the rising moon. With the torso and face of a female and everything else resembling the foulest of eagles, the harpies are creatures that belong in nightmares.

The nearest, an enormous creature who would tower over Vander if they stood side by side, ruffles its feathers, and I know we are almost out of time.

I follow Vander's plan and dive into my animalistic power, pulling a ribbon of amber free, then wrapping it around my soul and sending the pulsing thread towards the closest harpy. Only to meet a solid wall.

"Oh, no." My mouth pops open as the ribbon and my soul return to their rightful body with a crack of pain. I face Vander with fear dripping in my eyes. "There's too much fae in them. They're more like us than we thought."

"You can't control them?"

I shake my head. "I cannot."

"You're drained from collecting the atryxium," says Nyree.

"It's not that," I snap. "There's nothing to send my soul into. They're not animals."

She raises her brow, and her eyes twinkle. "There's no need to use that tone when I was only making a suggestion."

"Torin," says Vander, ignoring the brewing tension, "we'll have to make this quick. I'll hold her while you collect the talon. Wyn, be prepared to hold the rest of them back with blasts of air. Nyree, keep your mind open to their intentions."

"What about me?" I ask, suddenly feeling like I should be doing something, if only to prove myself to the Ill-fated beside me.

"There's little you *can* do," he says. "Unless you think you can hold them back with weapons?"

I hang my head. "It's not likely."

"Don't worry, Bria, the rest of us will get it done. Just sit back and relax." Nyree rolls her shoulders. "It's what you do best, after all."

"You did more than enough in Winter," says Wyn. She flexes her fingers, and the crisp freshness of her magic surrounds me. Then she cracks her neck and trains her eyes on the harpies nearest to us, watching every twitch of a feather and every rise of a chest.

I draw my magic around me in preparation to fold home. If I can do nothing other than get us from this place to safety, I will fold better than any fae has before. I tuck a strand of copper behind my ear, grazing my fingers over the point to remind myself of how different we are from the humans. This is all for them, and if their safety means I feel inadequate for a moment, then so be it.

Torin frees his short sword from the sheath at his back and creeps closer to the harpy while Vander approaches from behind. The realisation of what they are about to do hits me with the force of one of Dusk's tornados.

I avert my eyes. It's not something I wish to witness.

The cool lick of Vander's wind brushes against my cheeks as he cocoons the harpy with a dense blanket of air. A spine-tingling screech and the clang of metal against splintering wood follows the move like an echo.

Nausea churns in my stomach and bile burns my throat, but I make myself watch Vander so I know when to grab him and fold to safety.

"They're waking," Wyn warns. A rush of wind drowns out her words.

The harpy screeches once more, the sound echoing around the arid plain. My ears ring with the sound of Torin's sword slicing through the claw of the harpy, and the scuff of his boots against the dead earth fills my ears.

"Got it!" he shouts.

I race for Vander with my hand outstretched, gripping the ends of his fingers and wrapping my magic around us. The void welcomes me like an old friend as I step from the brown dirt and onto a beach, the scents of Dusk replacing the tang of blood that was tainting the Barrens.

"Two down, four to go. Six if you include imbuing the artefacts and placing the ward," says Wyn, panting.

I frown at her. "Why are you so... sweaty?"

She looks at me as if I have lost my mind. "Didn't you notice I was holding thirty of them back that entire time?" She smirks and tilts her head towards Vander. "Or was your attention elsewhere?"

"Where to next?" I say a little too loud.

"Bed," says Torin, wiping blood from his fingers. "Then we start fresh tomorrow."

Chapter 15

THE SPRING COURT IS north of Dusk, and though our lands were once connected, the two could not be more different. While this island is all she-oaks and pines, sand and ocean, Spring is fields of wildflowers and petals the size of my face, billowing grasses of emerald green and fluttering butterflies I know to steer clear of.

They may look beautiful on the outside, but like any fae, their image is a trick. They're deadly when provoked — they consider something as simple as disrupting the air around them as a threat — using the fine powder on their wings to paralyse their targets.

"It's beautiful, isn't it." My words are more of a statement than a question. "The flowers are more aromatic than I thought they would be."

"Where are we supposed to find these flowers?" Nyree groans. It's not the first time she's expressed distaste for the Court of Blooms.

I arch an eyebrow. "There is beauty in nature. Do you not enjoy it?"

Ahead, where he walks beside Torin, Vander's head tilts to the side. It's clear he's listening for Nyree's response, perhaps wondering if she and I will come to verbal blows again. It would be the fifth time this morning if we do, and I cannot blame him for tiring of the bickering.

I'm tired of it, too.

"No," she says, her tone harsh. "I believe all Spring fae to be glorified gardeners."

"And their psychic magic?"

"Parlour tricks. Akin to a jester."

I make sure my thoughts are loud when I think she's a jerk. She's only saying such petty things because my mother is a Spring fae.

Before leaving Dusk this morning I made sure we were going nowhere near Spring's bustling centre, a crystal palace shaped like a spear of foxglove with vines of blossoms creeping up the walls. I feel bad that Wyn's approaching High Lady Nyana on her own to plead for an alliance in the war, but I'm not ready to stumble upon my birth mother. Not today.

A dense forest emerges in the distance, and the glittering lake to its right brings a kind of unease to my stomach. It's our destination. The blue mock lotus, the flower we're searching for, grows along the shores of lakes. There is only one lake in Spring, and it marks the edge of Nyana's palace. It's too close for comfort.

Snapdragon flowers grow in abundance in these fields, and I brush my fingers over the petals when I walk past, feeling the silky texture and relishing in the touch of nature. It helps to calm my racing heart and soothe the nerves of being so close to my mother, whoever she may be. I keep my eyes trained on the sparkle of water and don't let them wander farther east, where the palace shines like a beacon.

We continue heading towards the lake, taking the time to walk around a flight of blue and black butterflies that flutter around a patch of snapdragons. Their peach and pink flowers are gorgeous in the weak light, with beads of morning dew still clinging to the petals. It is beautiful here. Peaceful. Peaceful, but deadly.

As we close the distance, the blue mock lotus flowers come into view. Their glowing petals shine brighter than the Mother Star in the morning, though I know their beauty to be a lure. When prepared correctly, the nectar gathered in the flower's bowl makes a fae weak, as if the nectar drains the energy from our bodies. It can paralyse when dried into a powder.

"Tread carefully," says Torin, slowing his steps until we're walking in a tight group. "We don't want to disrupt anything here. I don't fancy having a prune for a hand."

"We should have folded," I say. "It would have saved a lot of time. We still have to steal a piece of spine from the Dullahan and sand from Summer. Not that Tohminic gave us permission." I aim the last of my words at Vander.

He shrugs. "I didn't ask. His answer would have been no, then he would have added patrols to his border. If we enter across the Autumn border, there's a chance the guards won't catch us. We'll be in and out before anyone knows we're there."

"Rennyn hasn't given us his reply," I remind him. It has been four days since we sent the messenger requesting access to his lands, and we have heard nothing from Autumn's High

Lord. I'm beginning to wonder if he's ignoring us on purpose. Strange, since we offered him the alliance he begged for.

"We couldn't risk folding," Vander adds. "If we step on the flowers..."

"I don't think it works that way. The nectar cannot seep through our boots." I'm sure of my words, but there's still a hint of hesitation. Shrivelled feet isn't something I would wish for.

"There's Wyn. She doesn't look happy," says Nyree from beside me.

I follow her line of sight, spotting Wyn waiting for us at the edge of the lake, a glowing blue flower gripped in her gloved hand. Nyree's right. The scowl on Wyn's face is clear even from here.

Our walk is brisk but careful as we meet Wyn halfway. The moment we're within hearing range, she launches into a tale of supercilious Spring fae and orange-haired bitches. Apparently, Nyana refused to meet with Wyn, and the guards escorted Wyn from the flowering castle without so much as a 'Well met' from their High Lady.

Vander sighs. "We'll make do without them. There will come a time when Nyana cannot remain neutral in this war. Soon enough, we'll all be targets of Tohminic and his rage."

After a quick trip back to the Dusk Court to store the blue mock with the harpy talon and atryxium, we fold straight to the border of Summer and Day. The forest is rife with small creatures and bushes of both edible and poisonous berries, though we're not here for either of those.

We're here for the Dullahan. To steal a fragment from his spine whip.

The stories that plagued my nights as a youngling flash across my mind. Tales of a fearful creature who wanders through Day's forest listening to the whispers of any who dare move close to his den, listening for your name so he may use it to claim your life.

I have always been afraid of the headless rider and his skeletal horse, but more so of his whip, which I always have believed resembles a spine. Now that we're here to collect a piece of that spine, I know those rumours to be true. It makes the stories I grew up with more horrible.

"Remember not to mention anyone by name," I say as we pass the first trees of the forest and step onto Day territory. "Don't look the beast in the eyes, for doing so incites his wrath. He will wield his whip and gouge your eyes out the moment you dare to meet his gaze."

"You put too much trust in bedtime stories," says Nyree.

"Or maybe I put in just enough," I hiss.

Wyn sighs. "She's right —"

"Thank you," says Nyree.

"I didn't mean you," says Wyn, rolling her eyes. "We need to be careful. Not only are we walking into his den, but we're on the border of Summer's land. Right where Tohminic and that arsehole Xaler kidnapped me and Bria."

Just the mention of Summer's selkie leader sends a rush of ice crackling through my veins and dread settling in my stomach.

He was here when we were taken to the Summer Court, he delivered me to Tohminic's rooms each night where I witnessed the brutal love between him, Chlora, and any other female he wished for, and he took me on a tour of their land in that damned iron cage.

I wipe my clammy hands on my leathers and push every thought of Xaler and Tohminic from my mind. If I dwell on the past now, I risk this entire mission. Not to mention, Nyree is likely listening to my thoughts.

We pass the place where the Dawn messenger met us, where the triplets abandoned me. The deep grooves in the ground, made from wagons being pulled during wet days, lead us to the same clearing we camped in that night. I'm surprised to see our tents still here, stained with dirt and with weeds beginning to claim the canvas for themselves. Our cases remain, still filled with useless gowns and silly jewels that mean nothing. I had wondered what happened to them. There is no relief at uncovering the mystery. There is nothing but sadness.

Along with the cases and tents, the three skeletons belonging to my two guards and the stable hand mark this as a place of horror. Though hungry creatures have taken many of the bones, I know the bodies belong to the three fae. The memory of their screams haunts me still.

Red, red, red.

Their blood is on my hands, too.

There was a time when I thought the eerily perfect circle of pines was the perfect place to hide from the Dullahan, but I was wrong to hide from him then. I should have ensured the likes of Tohminic of the Summer Court could not find me.

I cannot force my eyes to move from the three skeletons, and I cannot think past the events of that night. If I had just run like I had planned. If I had just folded to Spring and taken Wyn with me... The stable hand. The two guards. They died because of me. They died *for* me.

My hands clench and slacken, as if the simple move will rinse the crimson from my palms. I'm distantly aware of voices beside me, but I cannot focus on the words. All I can remember is the taunt of Tohminic's voice. *I will take my revenge in any way I see fit. Welcome to your new life. War is not kind, Bria. You will learn just how cruel it can be soon enough.*

My new life of red. That is what he meant.

Silver blazes before me, twin orbs glistening in the dim light of the forest. "Breathe, Princess. Breathe, and remember yourself. You did not harm the fae. You got out." Vander grips my upper arms, squeezing to the point of pain. "You. Got. Out."

"I got out," I repeat in a whisper. "I'm not responsible."

Do I believe that, though? Do I believe none of this is my fault? I don't know anymore, not after seeing the bones of my guards. My head shakes in answer to my own question, and my throat tightens. I'm so heavy I could sink into the ground, so numb a whisper of breeze could blow me away. I cannot look into his eyes any longer and drop my gaze to my hands.

He crooks a finger under my chin and lifts my face until our eyes connect once more. "I don't know how, but I can feel everything you're feeling. You're mistaken. You're not to blame for this. What do you need to get past this right now? Do you want me to crawl with you? I have done it before, and I'll do it again. Do you want me to carry you? I'm happy to shoulder your burden."

"I..." I blink back the tears that threaten to fall. He's right, of course. His words remind me I'm no longer in this alone. He will crawl if I ask him to, and he will carry me if I so much as stumble.

The humans can't flee if the rest of Radelea discovers their existence. They have no way to defend themselves if our war should breach their realm. I have to be strong, if not for me, then for them.

Besides, I cannot hide my emotions from Vander even if I wanted to. There's no point in lying, no point saying I'm fine. He will know the truth, regardless of how much confidence I put in my words.

"Turn me so I'm not facing them," I whisper. "Then lead me from this clearing. I cannot force myself to look away, but with your help, I can push it to the back of my mind, for now."

He follows my order without question and steers me through the clearing until we're among the denser pines and no longer beside the canvas tents and tormenting bones.

The trees are restless here. The branches sway, but not in time with the gentle breeze. Their song is damning, urgent, as if nature itself is warning us to turn back. It's all I need to know we have found the den of the Dullahan.

And he has found us.

Hooves clack against the ground before a wide sequoia. The tree, which is at least one hundred long swords high, forms a natural arch with its exposed roots. The trunk is like a cavern, smothered in the shadow cast from the beast standing guard at the den's entrance.

My eyes travel from the ivory hooves of a horse over the skeletal body and come to rest on the decaying chest of the Dullahan. I refuse to make them travel higher to see if he's truly headless, but make them remain on the whip curled at his side.

Bone white.

Jagged.

The bone whip is as lethal as the stories say.

All thoughts of red and Xaler and Tohminic flee my mind, replaced by the bone-chilling fear of my nightmares come to life.

"He's carrying his head," says Torin in disgust as he pulls both short swords free. "No one look into his eyes."

"Thanks. I wouldn't have known not to if you didn't say," says Wyn, moving to the left with careful feet.

"I'll distract him while you collect the spine, Van," says Torin. He tosses one of his swords in the air and catches it again before throwing it at the Dullahan. It hits the skeletal horse in the chest. "I got the talon. It's only fair."

The horse rears back, then stamps its hooves on the ground with a chilling thud. The Dullahan roars in anger, his whip cracking as he uncurls it with a flick of his wrist.

A gust of wind blows from Wyn's direction. It distracts the Dullahan, but not long enough for him to take his eyes from Vander, who he's singled out.

Nyree stands immobile beside me. We already decided she's our last defence should things not go in our favour; her bone magic can control the Dullahan's horse if need be.

The whip slices through the air with a sharp whistle, but Vander is too fast for the Dullahan and throws his axe with more precision than any male could possess. The blade pins the end of the whip to the sequoia, and Vander darts forward, dodges the trampling hooves, and uses his dagger to sever the sharp tip of the spine. He yanks his axe free of the towering tree, spins, and races towards me, his face a mask of determination.

Behind him, the raging Dullahan screams and wields his whip once more.

My feet slam against the forest floor as I fight to reach Vander before the whip does. My twin braids smack against my shoulders and back as I run, and I cannot help but wonder if the gentle thud is a warning.

The Dullahan's arm arcs forward.

I grab Vander's torso.

The whip whistles, cutting through the air at blinding speed.

I twist until Vander is beneath me and gather the magic of the realm around us. Sharp pain ignites between my shoulders, running from arm to arm, and tears a scream from my throat as I step through the void.

The moment we're on Dusk land, I fall to my knees with a piercing cry. Pure agony flares along my shoulders, pulsing and stabbing with licks of fire. Black encroaches on the sides of my vision. Red spots flash in the darkness. My head swims or rocks or shakes. I'm not sure. The world turns blurry. In the back of my mind, a spot of warmth tells me Vander is right beside me.

Oblivion claims me.

Chapter 16

I WAKE TO A fire scorching my back and my front pushed into something firm yet soft. The scream that pulls at my throat is guttural and agonising. I try twisting away from the pain, but something pins me down. My arms flail as I thrash wildly against whoever is holding me. I will not be trapped again. I won't.

"Calm down." Vander's voice is strained, but the soft yet commanding tone I adore is still there. The deep and rough baritone calms me enough that I settle, and he purrs, "That's it. Let us heal you."

I twist my face to the side and peel my eyes open to squint at Penna, the healer from the Dawn Court. Her silver hair still has that tint of blue I found so strange the first time she mended me, and she still has the flair of rebellion I liked so much.

Her cobalt eyes flash. "Your wound is deep. Lie still and allow me to work."

"Perhaps it's better if she's unconscious," says Vander, his grip loosening.

"They say healing the gash from a bone whip is more painful than most other wounds," says Penna, turning to the bench behind her. She returns with a matte pink powder in her palm and blows it onto my face. "Sleep. When you wake, Vander will have collected the molten sand of Summer and your back will be healed."

❧ ❧

The next time I wake, I'm alone.

The infirmary is silent, peaceful. By the hue of the light shining through the windows to my left, I assume Penna is sleeping. The moon must be close to its zenith.

I roll on to my side and pull the blanket tighter. I'm asleep before I can marvel at the lack of pain in my back.

❧ ❧

I spend the entire next day doing nothing but twiddling my thumbs and lying in the most uncomfortable bed I have ever had the displeasure of sleeping in. The infirmary is most definitely not my favourite place at Dusk Manor, but at least Penna is good company.

She tells me of her youngling years, when she would sneak from her home in Dawn and meet with her lover by the lake. The two would spend hours together, hiding from both Penna's father and Sylvia's four brothers. I envy the freedom she found at such a young age, but enjoy her tales all the same.

Wyn visits at noontime, bringing a luncheon of pastries and fruit. She tells me of the mission to the Summer Court to collect molten sand and how they managed it without issue. No guards saw them, no creatures tried to attack, and Nyree was on her best behaviour. Concerning, though, is the silence from Rennyn.

He has not sent a messenger allowing us entry to the Autumn Court. It's a problem for tomorrow, when Penna releases me from her care at last. I will go to Autumn and face my brother. If he has pledged allegiance to Tohminic instead of us, he can damn well tell me to my face.

Chapter 17

"A RE YOU SURE ABOUT this?" Wyn asks for the seventh time, though it feels like at least two hundred with all the worried glances and face pulling she's been doing. "He could have you killed on sight just for entering his land."

"Rennyn may be a coward, but he's still my brother. Besides, I'm still an Autumn fae, even if I live in Dusk. He cannot forbid me from entering my own home." I twist my upper body around to test the strength in my back. The scar — a horrible shining thing that runs in a horizontal line between my shoulder blades — pulls a little, but the pain's manageable.

"Have you told Van where you're going?"

I pause mid-stretch to glance at her. "Why would I? I'm a free fae and can go wherever I choose."

"For three reasons. One, he's our High Lord and deserves to know when one of our denizens is walking into enemy territory. Two, he worries about you. And three..." She narrows her eyes as if daring me to challenge her next words. "Three, you love him. Don't you dare try to deny it."

"I share a soul bond with him. There's a difference."

She scoffs. "I'm not blind, Bria. Torin and I were both trying to get through to you in the Day forest, and you only heard

Vander's voice. You only responded to *him*. You allow him to fold you everywhere without question because you enjoy it. There's nothing wrong with loving him. Don't tarnish such a sacred emotion by refusing to acknowledge it. It's the only good thing to happen lately."

I snatch a dagger from the bench and slide it into the sheath at my thigh. "Fine. You're right." I grab a second blade, sheathing it on my other leg. "But it means nothing. He's not looking for love, remember?"

"How do you know he hasn't changed his mind? Have you told him about the twin soul bond?"

I place the last two daggers in their sheathes against my ribs as fast as I can and head for the door. I cannot look Wyn in the eye and admit I haven't told Vander about our bond. It's loathsome of me to keep it to myself, yet I cannot find it within me to tell him.

It is possible he knows there's *something* between us, though I'm sure he cannot determine the details. Until I saved him from the Dullahan's whip, all we had was a connection and a thread between our emotions. Now, the bond has strengthened.

I always know where he is.

He knows where I am.

"If you don't tell him, I will." Her voice is sterner than I have ever heard it. "This isn't something you should keep to yourself."

He will put the pieces together in time, and I cannot allow him to discover the bond on his own. Out loud, I say, "I know I have to tell him, but the timing has to be right. Give me more time, Wyn."

She says nothing more when I exit the infirmary, and surprises me by not following. Instead of trailing behind me as I take the winding stairs to the ground floor of Dusk Manor, she turns right and enters the training room, where I know Vander and Torin to be sparring.

I'm not bothered she's telling them where I'm going. Our bond will urge him to follow me, anyway.

Though I know my friends will come to Autumn with me, I'm surprised at how fast they catch up. The forest is only silent for a moment before their hurried footsteps sound from behind. I pause, watching over my shoulder as they race down the slope towards me.

My mouth runs dry.

Both males are without their shirts, the bundles of leather gripped in their fists.

Torin's lean but muscular frame is more tanned than I thought, and the golden hue to his skin shimmers in the late morning light. I can appreciate the brilliance of his body, but my eyes don't linger, not with Vander beside him.

His light brown skin is silky smooth and ripples over his defined abdominals with each step he takes closer. The dips and grooves of his chest beg me to trace my fingers through them. My gaze moves higher, trailing to the fury contorting the features of his face. Even with the look of absolute horror and rage, I'm forced to clench my thighs against the throb of desire that pulses in my core. Though he's the epitome of beauty, I think he could be an ogre and I would still want him.

He crawled for me, and that is but one reason I love him.

Mother Star, I admitted it.

"Where the fuck do you think you're going?" Vander growls.

I face him and shrug. "To the Autumn Court to smack some sense into my brother. We have to strengthen the wards to protect the humans. I'm not waiting any longer."

"You can't go alone," says Torin. "It's not safe."

"Don't tell me what to do."

Vander comes to a stop a little closer than is necessary. "We're not. All we're saying is we don't trust Autumn. We're coming with you." He pulls on his leather jacket, zipping it to his neck over his bare chest. "I don't trust Rennyn."

"And you're looking for a reason to give him matching black eyes." Torin smirks at the idea.

Wyn laughs. "I'm sure the first one has faded by now."

"If you're so intent on witnessing a family squabble, be my guest." I spin and march towards the beach. "I'll be seeing my father, too. If Spring won't ally with us from the good of their hearts, they'll do it for a member of their court. I'm going to find out who my mother is."

"Are you... ready for that?" asks Wyn, jogging to catch up to me.

"Probably not, but we need all the help we can get if Tohminic attacks, and Spring's psychic power will be an asset in the war."

Vander grabs me by the shoulder and spins me around. He takes in every line of my face before asking, "That's not a reason to do something you've avoided for years. Are you certain?"

"Yes." I push my emotions towards him, letting him feel the calmness, the certainty, and the hint of frustration at the delay.

He doesn't argue after that, but dips his chin in acknowledgement and waves me forward. Though he's allowing me to take the lead, he remains close behind and reaches for my hand the moment we step through the wards. He says nothing as we both use our magic in sync to fold from Dusk to the castle of Autumn.

I do not stop as we pass under the outpost, do not so much as acknowledge to sentries when they call out from the gatehouse, and I don't glance at any of the fatigued guards within either bailey. I am determined, and nothing will prevent me from facing Rennyn. At least, that's what I believe until I step into the grand foyer and almost collide with Father.

Dressed in nothing but his sleep clothes, Father's usually neat silver hair is in disarray. His arms are slimmer than I remember, and there are more lines carved into the pale skin of his face. His green eyes, identical to mine, are duller than a cloudy day.

"Father, why are you down here?" Rennyn enters from the dining hall and pauses. "Sister."

I ignore him and take Father's hands. I distantly register my friends from Dusk gather around me in an arc of support, but I don't acknowledge them, either. Kerym Sutherland is all I can think of; my father's state claims every thought.

"Father? It's me, Bria." I keep my tone soft. There's a glint in his eyes that reminds me of all those times he would stagger from his study, drunk on plum wine.

Slowly, so slowly, he lifts his eyes to mine. "So much like your mother. Not my darling Fayeth. No." He slurs his words, as if he has indeed enjoyed several chalices of wine. He curls his fists into his sleep shirt. "No. You are just like the Winter female I bedded to drown my sorrows when Zentha mated. Oh, I loved Zentha so very much. Except your eyes, of course. Your eyes are mine. It is no wonder my mate never did like you."

"That's enough, Father." Rennyn grips Father's upper arm and shoves him towards a guard.

I cannot focus on how the guards treat their former High Lord. I cannot even *breathe*. Winter? Not Spring, like I have always believed.

And the copper hair... I sink to the ground and cover my face with my hands. Father has always said red hair is a mark of the Spring Court, but apparently there is another. There is only one female in Radelea with red hair who does not belong to Spring. I have never thought her to be my mother because if she is — a shudder runs through me — Winter and Autumn will be at war.

"Bria?" Wyn kneels beside me. "I know it's hard to discover you're not who you always thought, but belonging to Winter isn't such a terrible thing."

I lift my tear-filled eyes to her strong silvers. "Oh, how wrong you are, Wyn."

A thud behind me causes me to twist, and a gasp escapes.

Vander has Rennyn pinned against the wall, his fist pressing against my brother's throat. "Why is she so upset? Tell me. Now!"

Rennyn's golden-brown eyes narrow to slits. "She has never known her mother's identity. She just uncovered a well-kept secret. This is not my doing, Dusk scum. Release me at once."

"Van," Torin warns. Gone is the ever-present smirk, replaced by tight lips and assessing eyes.

Wind billows around them, churning faster and faster with every harsh pant from Vander's mouth. "Tell me!" he shouts.

"Her mother is not just a Winter fae." Vander lowers him to the floor and Rennyn meets my eye. "Bria is the illegitimate daughter of High Lady Uma of Winter. As far as we are aware, the High Lord does not know."

My nostrils flare as hot rage blazes through me. I leap up, ignoring Wyn's plea to leave. "You have known all this time, and you didn't tell me. Does Tohminic know? Was my identity the secret your bitch of a mother told him?"

He spits at my feet. His soft features contort into fury, those sharp angles becoming prominent. "You are the reason she is dead. If you did not exist, she would not have abandoned Father and left him to this fate. She would not have gone to Summer thinking *that* information was important to Tohminic. You are a *disgrace* to the Sutherland name."

A current of adrenaline courses through me, making me feel more alive than I have in moons. I flip a dagger from my thigh and charge for Rennyn with a raging war cry. The consequences of attacking Autumn's High Lord mean nothing to me as I lunge for his chest with the blade. All I see is red. Not the crimson staining my hands and soul, but the deep, visceral red of anger and betrayal.

A hard body slams into me from the side and pins me against the wall. Sharp bones dig into my hips, tight fists clench around my wrists, and a heaving chest bumps against my own. "As much as I'd love to see you get your revenge, I think you'll regret it."

I gather my magic in my palms, feeling every blade in the castle. The guards by the door startle when their long swords slide from their holsters.

"Bria!" Wyn shouts.

Rennyn's eyes are wide as he backs away with his hands raised. Wide and filled with fear. Fear of *me*.

The realisation crashes into me with more force than Vander's tackle. He's scared of me. Me. The fight seeps from my pores in an instant.

"We'll spend the next several hours in the southern forest. You will not hinder our search. Do you understand, *brother*?" I spit the last word like it's poison. I face Vander, our noses brushing. "Get me out of here before I do something we all regret."

"With pleasure."

Before we exit the Autumn castle, I turn back to Rennyn. "We may be blood, Rennyn, but you are not my family."

Chapter 18

THE AUTUMN FOREST IS just as I remember it. Pine is all I can smell as we weave between the twisting trees. Time has woven the branches overhead together to form a canopy of green, and the branches curl around one another like snakes fighting for survival. Meagre rays of light filter through the leaves and throw misshapen spots of amber on the leaf-strewn ground.

I keep my eyes trained low, searching for signs of the ogres in the moss and mud. The deformed breed of fae live within this forest and have warded their territory with a curious magic that alerts them to trespassers. Warding is the only gift the creatures kept after being created from the souls of a power-hungry High Lady, and their skill is exceptional.

We have long since crossed the line of their wards, and we should soon stumble upon the fabled hut of Baba Yaga. They say she built it from the bones of the younglings she feasts on, and it emanates magic in sickly waves. A shiver runs down my spine at the thought.

The forest grows quiet. The birds cease their melodies, the leaves no longer rustle, and the scattering of insects fades.

"We're close," I whisper to Vander.

He steps closer to my side and signals to Torin and Wyn, who move closer to better hear his whisper of, "Stay on alert. We'll be at the hut soon."

My skin prickles as magic washes over me, Vander's illusion of an ogre settling over me like a cloak. Behind, I know Wyn is doing the same to herself and Torin. I cannot help but feel exposed as I twist around a low-hanging pine branch. The ogres, with their grey-green skin and beady eyes, blend with the trees well. We need to be careful.

I bring my animalistic power to the forefront of my mind and send pulses through the forest. The birds are hiding among the branches overhead, rodents are panting beneath arching roots and in the deep grooves of the tree trunks, and something larger and much more sinister slumbers nearby. Beyond that, nothing.

Vander stills when I jab him with my elbow and point ahead, his eyes narrowing at the large pine tree and what looks to be a broken branch jutting out from behind it. Though it looks like a branch, I know it to be one of the makeshift clubs the ogres carry.

Our feet are silent as we move left, away from the sleeping creature, and deeper into the forest. Vander and Wyn cannot keep illusions over themselves and one other for extended lengths of time; we need to find Baba Yaga's hut, and soon.

The trees are so close together here, we're forced to walk in a line rather than side-by-side. And through the browning pines and thinning moss, is a small clearing. At the far end of the open space is a bone-white hut that uses the dead trunks of four pines as the corners.

We stop in our tracks, each of us eyeing the dozen ogres in the cramped area. Many of them are male, with only three females among them — none of them are Baba Yaga, who must be inside her hut — grunting unintelligible words to one another.

Memories of that day flash through my mind, sending a cold sweat trickling down my nape. The ogres tower over me, and I know their hands fit perfectly around my waist. A flash of silver hurtles through the memory, and Vander's axe imbeds in the skull of the ogre holding me.

I shake the memory away, though my hand gropes at my throat. I was only in the forest that day because Tohminic had threatened me in the Autumn gardens, choking me before throwing me to the ground as if I weighed nothing more than a quill.

Movement within the bone hut draws my eye, and I squint at the shadow in the small house. Small for an ogre, but the hut could fit a family of five fae with ease.

My pulse races and my eyes bulge as Baba Yaga steps before the cracked and yellowed window. Her bulbous nose curves down, hiding most of her thin lips. Her brow dips after the nose, and her face resembles that of a lizard, all deep wrinkles and flaking skin. She's an ogre, that much is certain. Even with the pointed ears and the pale skin revealing her fae origin.

She flexes a gnarled hand around a long staff, the tendons clear even from here. She slams the rod of timber against the floor of her hut and spins to look straight at me. "We have imposters among us," she grunts, the words clearer than that of her offspring.

"Fuck." Torin whips into action, drawing both short swords and darting for the hut.

Vander races after him, wisps of wind licking out from his palms like tongues. He doesn't run in a direct path for the bones, but leaps to the side every so often to avoid the groping hands of the roaring ogres.

Wyn jerks me back and shoves me behind a tree. "Remember your part."

I nod and take a deep breath. If I'm to fold Vander from harm's way, I must be ready, and I cannot be calm if I watch the mayhem unfold. They will be okay. They have more experience in combat and evasive techniques than I do.

Wyn turns to face the fray of stumbling ogres — the thuds of their frantic feet shake the ground we stand on — sending blasts of air towards whichever ogre she decides is dangerous. The sound of the creatures stumbling back and colliding with the trees is deafening.

Branches crack like exploding stone, roars pierce the forest, and a gleeful cackle sounds from within the hut. But I do not dare turn and look. I focus on the realm's power, concentrate on drawing it around me so I'm ready to fold.

With Vander keeping the ogre illusion over me, even while using his air magic to aid Torin in collecting a finger bone from the hut's exterior wall, he will not have the energy to fold himself. He's relying on me.

We just have to make it through the wards first.

So, even when I hear his cry of pain, even when I feel the agony of a leg wound through our bond, I do not look. I remind myself he needs me, not now, but once he has the last piece of the relic for our wards. The realm's magic courses through me, ready and waiting for my command. All I need is to take a single step, and we're free.

"Five heartbeats, Bria," says Wyn, her voice strained. She's struggling to remain by my side, as Vander ordered. "Four."

Shouts of victory from the males.

Sweat dots my forehead.

"Three."

Whistling gusts of wind. Thudding footsteps. A scream of rage.

"Two."

A grunted warning from Vander, the name he chose for me slipping from his lips like a caress. *Princess.*

My heart flutters, even through the fear and adrenaline.

"One."

I stretch my hand out, waiting for Vander's warmth to encase me. The moment his fingers graze against my palm, I pull on the threads of magic surrounding me and dart forwards. I keep putting one foot in front of the other, keep running as hard as I can until I feel the ripple of the ogres' wards wash over me.

Then I fold.

I don't make sure Wyn and Torin are following, don't make sure the ogres aren't chasing us, and I don't give a damn about anything other than getting Vander to safety. I leap into the void and concentrate on the morning glow of the Dawn Court.

Within moments, the dark forest disappears, replaced by a shining lake filled with merfolk and an azure building to the east. The golden balconies jutting from every side mark the five levels of Jonik's palace.

"We made it," I say, turning to Vander. The moment my eyes land on him, the fleeting happiness morphs into dread.

He sags to the ground with a groan, the pool of blood at his feet too large for the mere heartbeat we have been standing on Dawn soil.

"We expected you hours ago." Ulakas races ahead of his brothers, his black hair bouncing against his shoulders. His dark eyes widen as he skids around the lake. "Mother Star, what happened?"

He and Larrad kneel beside Vander, showing no hesitation in calling upon their healing powers, while Tasar folds back to their father's palace.

The slither of Van that lives in my soul goes quiet before his presence disappears altogether. His mind slips away as he loses consciousness, but I'm not worried. Not with both Larrad and Ulakas healing him.

"What the fuck?" Torin's exclamation is a mere whisper. "What happened?"

I spin to face him and jab a finger into his chest. "You tell me. This was supposed to be a simple retrieval." I haven't made myself look at the wound yet, though I should if I'm going to throw accusations around.

Torin throws his hands in the air and backs up a pace, almost stepping on Wyn's toes. "Everything went to plan... until it didn't. The ogress wielded that damn staff like a sword."

I make myself look at the wound. Nausea clenches my stomach, and I throw a hand to my mouth to keep the bile from surging forth. There is a clear hole through Vander's thigh. Blood trickles in a steady flow from the gaping wound, the torn muscle is pale, and I can see straight through his leg to the blood-soaked grass below.

Wyn makes a choking sound in the back of her throat.

"I need better access," says Larrad. His voice is terse, strained from concentrating as a smoky white light emanates from his fingers and seeps into Vander's leg, probing and searching for the best way to heal.

I throw myself at the ground beside Van, snatching a dagger from my thigh as I fall. Taking deep breaths through my nose, and taking as much care as I can, I peel his leathers away from the open wound and cut down the length of his leg. His tawny skin is already beginning to pale, and the dark hairs of his thigh are sticking to the sweat beading on his skin.

"Thank you," says Ulakas, his voice just as strained as his brother's.

The moment Tasar and Jonik arrive, my heart ceases its rapid beating. The High Lord of Dawn can heal any wound or ailment entirely, as long as the fae isn't too far gone by the time he reaches them.

Knowing Vander will be okay with the High Lord here, I sit back on my heels and close my eyes. I let the tears fall free at last. They're not only from the fear of such a gruesome wound or the paralysing terror from the ogres. They're tears for a life I will never have. I'm not a Spring fae, though I have spent five and seventy years imagining my life in their court. I'm a Winter fae, a female of shadow and ice, metal and animal.

Bria Sutherland, of two warring courts.

Not an hour later, the males declare Vander fit enough to travel via wagon to the palace, and our anxious group retreats to Jonik's home. Wyn disappears down one of the long, golden hallways while Torin heads off in search of a female to bed in order to take his mind off everything.

I don't leave Vander's side for the rest of the day. I sit with him while Jonik finishes healing his leg, sending prayer after prayer to the Mother Star. When the thoughts no longer feel like they're enough, I speak my prayers out loud.

She has not listened to my pleas for many a moon, but I am determined she guides Vander through this. My mind is so full of begging the sun to heal him, I do not so much as acknowledge the colour of the walls or layout of the room. As far as I'm concerned, there is me, Vander, the wooden seat I sit in, and the Mother Star. Nothing else.

He remains unconscious all day and all night. When I demand to know why he will not wake, Jonik says it's normal, that his body needs time to recover. Still, I worry. I worry while Wyn and Torin stop in to ask if I want to help create the ward relic at dawn, when I tell them no and wish them luck, and as I fall into a fitful sleep and dream of horrible wounds and raging ogres. The worry follows me through my slumber until a cool hand brushes against mine and jerks me awake.

"You didn't have to stay," Vander croaks. He pushes himself up and throws his legs over the side of the bed. His knees graze mine, sending pulses of reassurance through my veins. He's alive. He's awake and moving and alive.

"I thought you were going to die. Of course I stayed." My hand shakes from lack of sleep as I rub my eyes, but shakes harder when I grab hold of his hand for dear life. "You should rest, Van. Lie back down."

He runs his free hand down his face. "I could feel it, you know. Your worry. Even while unconscious, I can feel you. Why?"

At first, I'm afraid of where this question leads. The potential for rejection makes my mouth run dry. Then I remember how I felt when I realised just how bad his injury was, how my heart fractured a little at the thought of him dying. I remember I love him and he deserves to know about our twin souls. So I explain it all.

"I knew something was different about the Dusk Court the moment I laid eyes on it. There was something that drew me to it, as if my very bones yearned to step foot on the land and relish in its scent and feel. I couldn't think past the island that night on Zentha's ship. I fell overboard because I couldn't control myself and stepped towards you. *You* Vander, not the land. Though I didn't realise at the time why I was so drawn to Dusk, there's no question."

"I still don't understand. Something draws you to me, but that doesn't explain why I can feel you in here." He points to his temple and a groove forms between his brows.

"Since we first met, we have both felt a burning desire to see the other succeed. You fought for me during my father's ridiculous tournament, and I chose you in return. Did you ever wonder why? Did you ever consider your thoughts were being guided by something more, something greater than you and me?"

He shakes his head. "I have never understood my need to protect you. It ruled my actions when you almost drowned. It rules me still. If you have the answers I seek, tell me. I'm tired of being commanded by something I don't understand."

"I didn't understand it myself. At least, not until our trip to the Day Court, when Zentha allowed me access to her archives and I found a text on twin souls." His eyes dart to mine, a spark of curiosity shining within the silver. I sigh. "We're bonded. Our souls complete one another. You may know the bond as true mates. The title is a misconception. We're not mates in a romantic sense, but a necessity of life."

He blinks. Once, twice, then a third time. "Twin souls." He says the words as if testing how they feel.

I figure we might as well put everything on the table. Wyn's right. I can't go on ignoring my feelings for him. If he chooses to respect the bond between us, he deserves to know just how deep those feelings run.

"There's something else." I can't keep the nerves from my voice.

"What is it?"

I stand and cup his face. "My entire body burns when I think of how you crawled for me, of how you fight for me without question. I'm a raging fire and you are the air that feeds me. I love you, Vander, and I think you love me, too." My lips part and I lean down to press them gently against his. Only for a moment, before I pull away.

He says nothing. He doesn't appear to breathe.

I have laid my whole heart out for him, and I cannot stand the silence, so I turn and flee the infirmary. I flee the rejection forming in his mind, flee the heartache and pain, leaving them for me to deal with another day.

Chapter 19

THREE MOONS PASS BEFORE Jonik tells us Vander is well enough to fold home. The triplets offer to come with us and use their combined magic to fold us safely, but Van refuses.

He tells them he's fine, but I think he wants less fae knowing about where we place the ward relic as possible. If we can keep that information between the four of us — I'm hoping no one tells Nyree or the other Ill-fated — we might just have a chance at keeping the humans safe.

Vander doesn't take my hand to fold to Dusk like he has in the past, and I'm left to step through the void on my own, my thoughts spinning and confused. His emotions have been conflicted since I revealed our bond to him. Sometimes, I think he is almost eager, and others, there's a simmering rage. I can understand both. I should have told him the moment I knew, instead of leaving him to wonder about the presence in the back of his mind.

Wyn was mistaken. I should never have told him how I feel.

He deserved to know about the twin souls, but my love for him? My heart clenches. Perhaps I went too far with the whole fire and air thing. He told me he's not my knight in shining armour, that he was only vying for my hand in mateship because he detests how females are treated in Radelea. He told me, and I did not believe.

Since the very beginning, he has been honest. *Love isn't something I'm interested in. Any ideas you have of falling for me… you can forget them right now. With my father's death, my home under scrutiny, and the possibility of war on the horizon, I don't have time for anything other than protecting my court.* His words from the garden will haunt me forever.

I step onto Dusk soil with a heavy heart to find only Wyn waiting for my arrival. "We're going into the village to celebrate," she says. "Then, once the Mother Star has set, we'll place the relic."

She and Torin had no issues imbuing it with magic. From what they have told me, it was a sight to behold. The moment the Mother Star shone her first ray of light over the land, the items blazed with a light of their own and melded together to form a glowing stone.

"Perhaps I should retire to my room. I don't feel like socialising at the tavern," I say as we enter the forest. I graze my fingers along the needle-like leaves. It is a habit I won't suppress.

"You've been acting strange since we faced the ogres. Do you want to talk about it?"

I flick her a glance. "I told Vander about our twin souls. Then I did the most foolish thing I could have done. I told him I love him."

She sucks on her teeth. "What did he say?"

"Nothing. He just sat there looking at me."

"He had to have said *something*, Bria."

The look I give her conveys all she needs to know. We break through the forest, the manor stark against the pale sky, and fall into a comfortable silence. It is likely Wyn is trying to think up an excuse for her brother's lack of opinion on my feelings, or she's contemplating how to broach the subject with him without starting a war of words. Either way, I wish she wouldn't.

I tell her as much as we climb the hill.

She scoffs. "If you think I'm not going to defend my best friend, you're wrong. He shouldn't have treated you like that. He deserves to know he acted like a dick."

My groan is one of frustration and understanding, understanding I will not win this fight. "If he had any interest in pursuing a romantic relationship with me, he would not have remained silent."

"Who remained silent?" Torin asks as he slides down the hill towards us.

I shake my head. "Never you mind." Blessed Mother Star, if he ever finds out what I did, he will never let me live it down. I'm surprised he let the whole dating me thing go so easily.

"Come on," he says, begging me with his eyes. "I thought we were friends."

"We are friends. That doesn't mean I want to tell you all my secrets."

"What is it you want, Torin?" asks Wyn, saving me from further embarrassment. We both know he will not let the subject drop if he's determined.

He scowls between us for a moment before deciding he cannot win this round. "Van wants to head into the village now, rather than wait hours for the two of you to change and do your hair or whatever it is you females do. He's gone on ahead. I'm to escort you." The smugness in his tone brings a smile to my face.

"Then we thank you for your protection." I laugh at Wyn's deadpan tone.

"The ward stone is safe?" I ask as we turn west, away from Dusk Manor.

"Of course it is." He links his arm through mine, clamping his hand around my forearm. It's enough for me to know he did not, in fact, let the subject drop. "Now, what were you and Wyn talking about before I graced you with my presence?"

"Let it rest, Torin," says Wyn. There's a hint of resignation to her tone.

He glares at her. "I won't. Tell me, or I'll be forced to guess. Or, better yet, I'll read the memories of the grass you walk on."

"Guess away," I say. There's no way he's so observant he will guess correctly.

I am proven wrong with his first words. "You love Vander and you told him as much. Now you're avoiding one another because you're both stubborn and foolish. Tell me I'm mistaken." When we are both silent, he adds, "The wind whispers to me, remember?"

He does not let the subject drop until we're inside the village tavern, though Wyn and I both keep our lips sealed. He may have guessed correctly, but that does not mean we have to tell him he's right. The gloating would be unbearable.

From the outside, no one would guess the tavern to be so spacious. I'm pleasantly surprised by how open the vaulted ceiling makes the space feel. The dark timber arches are lower than normal and give vibes of archives and dungeons. Where the timber boards do not line the beige walls, paintings, plates, and the heads of too many animals draw the eye.

Against the far wall, a fae male with dull indigo skin and webbed fingers polishes a tankard, solely for something to do. There are only two other patrons: a hooded fae in the corner, and Alizeh, the wind wraith.

The table Vander has claimed is a small circle surrounded by wooden chairs, with four ales resting atop. He looks up as we sit. "I hope ale is okay?"

"Thanks, Van," says Torin. He doesn't sit before taking a long, exaggerated drink. When the mug is empty, he burps and wipes the back of his hand over his mouth. "That hit the spot. Another round?"

I shake my head then claim the seat across from Vander and take in the welcoming tavern while Wyn sits between us, leaving the last seat for Torin once he gets himself another ale. I'm just admiring the tracery of the reticulated windows when a shout sounds from the rear of the tavern.

"Fire! Fire!"

Torin and the indigo-skinned male are the closest. They both dart behind the bar and into the kitchens beyond. Alizeh and the other patron — the hooded fae in the corner, though I swear I see a flash of pearlescent hair beneath the dark grey cloak — race for the door, leaving Wyn, Vander, and me the only fae left.

"There's something blocking the back door." Torin's voice comes on a whisper of wind.

"Make sure that front door stays open!" Vander shouts over the crackling of fire, which is growing louder with every rapid beat of my heart. His chair skitters back as he launches to his feet and disappears behind the bar with the other males.

"I'll head outside and see if I can get the kitchen door open," I say, knocking a mug of ale to the ground in my haste.

I pause outside and check both directions. The buildings along this street are all joined, which worries me a great deal. If the fire spreads... I dare not think about it.

Some parts of the western village are still foreign to me, and I am not sure how to get to the back of the tavern. There's no sign of an alley or road, so I make an in-the-moment decision and race for the left. When I realise the street turns away from village square, I double back.

Smoke is billowing from the open tavern door by the time I race past once more, though I do not stop to help. I keep running. If Vander, Torin, and the staff are stuck in those kitchens, they will need a fast escape.

It takes too long for me to reach the end and find the narrow alley that snakes behind the irregularly shaped buildings. The dirt path is tight, not large enough for a wagon with the crates and barrels lining the sides. As I race down, it becomes harder to breathe through the clouds of smoke that are seeping through a window above the tavern's rear door. The hand covering my mouth and nose does little to block the acrid odour, and I have no hope of covering my face with my leathers.

I almost crash into the wooden door when I make it to the tavern at last, but save myself from injury by colliding with a wooden barrel instead. The pain from my ribs smashing against the rim only lasts two heartbeats.

The door is a simple one, though the brass handle is red hot. I coax my metal bending magic to my palms before making a claw with my hands and twisting. My magic curls around the glowing door handle, invisible to anyone but me as it contorts the rounded knob and aids the flames from within in melting the weak metal.

Once the brass drips from the now smoking door — plumes of black seep through the joins in the wood — and the telltale click of the lock doesn't ring through the roar of flames, I send the threads of my power into the lock and force it open.

The moment the door swings inward, I'm engulfed in an enormous cloud of black. I cough and fan it away from my face while jumping out of the way of a scampering rat. The frightened rodent gives me an idea, and I swap my metal bending power for my animalistic magic.

One heartbeat later, I'm smaller than my fae foot and darting into the kitchens. It is difficult to tell where to run in such a small body; everything is distorted, flickering in amber and red, and hazy from the smoke. I scurry along the side of a wall and over a rounded bump in the floor. My tiny paws dig into the floorboards when I skid to a stop. That is not a bump, but a leg.

"I can't see anything." Torin's voice is distant, drowned out by the roaring fire. "Blow the smoke away, Van. She's in here somewhere!"

The shadow of a male crosses the kitchen, moving closer at rapid speed, and I freeze in a crouch. The instincts of the rat are strong, and I cannot fight the urge to remain immobile, even with a heavy boot mere heartbeats from stepping on me.

With no other option, I snatch my soul back into my fae body. Stupid rodents and their foolish instincts. I rouse with a gasp and leap to my feet. Racing into the kitchen, I dive to my knees and crawl along the floor, groping around with my hands. With my eyes squinted against the sting of smoke, the already arduous task becomes more dangerous.

The cook's boot is the first thing I find. I wrap a hand around the toe and drag her towards me through the curtain of smoke. To my left, the fire moves closer, catching on a rack of dried spices. Ahead, two shadows move on the other side of the flames, frantically searching for a way through. A gust of wind parts the amber and red with ease, and Vander's face swims through the waves of heat.

He jabs Torin with an elbow and nods in my direction. They both watch me for a moment as I drag the cook to safety, then they turn and run.

Tongues of flame lick at my leathers, but never catch on the black fabric, though I swat at my hair when a tendril catches on the copper strands. My knees throb with the effort of pulling the cook from the kitchen. My lungs ache, and every draw of tainted air burns as hot as the fire surrounding me. As much as I wish to close my watering eyes to the heat and smoke, I keep them open enough to see.

Hands grab at my ankles and take hold, pulling me faster. I tighten my grip on the cook as Vander and Torin work to free us from the fire. The flames on my left are close now, too close, their intense heat trying to burn me from the inside out.

"You foolish female. What were you thinking?" Vander shouts the very heartbeat he pulls me through the doorway. "You could have died!"

"You didn't know where she was. I did."

He growls and lunges forward to help pull the cook from the alley, all the while muttering about females who take stupid risks.

I crawl out of the way and use a barrel to hoist myself upright. My arms and legs shake with the effort, and another cough tears at my raw throat. My mouth tastes of ash and rust and my lungs *burn*. It does not stop me from running after Vander and Torin as they carry the cook into the village square, where fae pass buckets of blissfully cool water along a line to the tavern's front.

"Bria!" Wyn hurries over from where she's helping an elderly fae fill buckets at the well. "Blessed Mother Star, did you go in?"

"Yes," I croak.

"Vander? Torin?" she asks, angling my face to check for burns.

I nod in their direction. "Made it out. Van gave me a scalding hotter than the flames, too."

"Because he cares. As much as he likes to deny it, he worries about you."

When I catch sight of Vander frowning at me with much intensity, I doubt Wyn's words. I doubt them very much.

Chapter 20

"TILT YOUR FACE TO the side," says Penna. She tuts as she assesses the left side of my face for injury — she has already healed my throat, lungs, and a minor burn on my right hand after Vander called her down from the manor. "Another small one. Hold still."

I almost laugh at her command. Sitting still is all I have been doing since I helped free the cook from the fire. Wyn is beside me, her sharp silver eyes watching Vander, Torin, and a handful of village fae clean the ebony smoke scars within the tavern. We are blessed with the view through a shattered window.

Vander has not spoken to me since he whipped those angry words my way in the alley. Though I know he's busy, it stings. The cook would be dead if it were not for my quick thinking. I do not wish for the praise or acknowledgement, but I would appreciate a damn smile.

Penna's warm magic seeps into my jaw. The wound itches. I refrain from rubbing my fingers over it, knowing she will only smack my hand away if I try. The sensation only lasts a moment, then she's asking me if I am injured anywhere else.

"I don't believe so," I say, peeling my eyes away from the tavern. "The flames got close to my left, but they didn't burn through the leathers."

She moves to my side, hovering her palms over my legs, my ribs, then my arm. "All seems in order. Though I cannot say the same about your hair."

"My hair?" My hand shoots to my copper locks.

"Yes, dear. You will need to cut the burned parts." She looks to Wyn, who is still focused on Torin and her brother. "Wyn can help you if you cannot find the strength to do it yourself. I have healed you as much as I can. I should get to the infirmary. Will you be okay?"

"I'll be fine. Thank you, Penna."

She offers me a tight smile before joining the group of four who are carrying the cook on a kind of bed made of canvas and timber. For such a rebellious soul, she does not handle the horrors of war all that well. I suppose no one can. War is not something you can ever get used to. It is not something a fae would wish for or condone. If there were a way to bring peace to Radelea without fighting, even if it required my soul as a sacrifice, I would do it.

Now we are alone, I turn to Wyn. "What's wrong? You have been unusually quiet."

"I'm just thinking... It's as if whoever's attacking us knew we were about to place the relic. Uncanny timing, don't you think?"

"Let's be real for a moment, Wyn." She looks at me with a raised brow. I arch mine back. "It's quite clear who's behind the attacks. Tohminic. And I know who is helping him."

She groans as she stands. "If you say Nyree, I swear to the Mother Star I'll scream. Get over your dislike of her. It isn't healthy." She walks away before I can say anything more.

I'm surprised the sting of tears does not assault my eyes like it often would in a situation like this. My best friend, because that is what Wyn is to me, refuses to listen to my concerns. Bria of Autumn would have thought Wyn's actions a betrayal, but I now see them for what they are.

Denial. Fear. Hurt. No one wants to believe a fae they have known their entire lives, let alone one they have granted freedoms to and worked closely with for years, is a betraying them.

But I know what I saw. That flash of pearlescent hair beneath the traveller's cloak could belong to no one else. I am sure of my assumption the Ill-fated are behind the attacks. Worse, is each attack appears to be caused by the Summer Court. Fire and undead, their magic branches, belong to none other. Tohminic and Nyree are working together.

I'm determined. The others will see the truth, even if forcing them to see it causes me to lose those close friendships.

I stand and wander closer to the tavern to help, deciding I will tell them when we place the relic. No one stops me when I enter, or when I move through the bar to the rear and into the kitchens.

Vander and Torin are still here, moving damaged timber with their air magic and clearing a space for the villagers to assess the structure.

"Is there much damage?" I ask. My words startle them both.

Vander's eyes dart straight to the frayed ends of my hair, then meet mine, and he seems to struggle with himself for a moment before he shakes his head and turns away to continue removing mounds of ash.

"Look for yourself," says Torin. "This whole side will need to be rebuilt."

I would rather not witness the scars left behind by an unnecessary attack, but I force myself to take in the blackened walls, the smouldering remains of the stone that separates the kitchen from the main part of the tavern, and the puddles of onyx-coloured water on the floor.

"It will take time," I say.

He grunts and heaves a wide beam of timber onto his shoulder. "It will. The villagers will have to drink their ale elsewhere for the time being."

"The tavern will close?"

"There's no choice," he says as Vander takes the other end. They carry it to the rear door and throw it into the alley.

I graze my teeth along my bottom lip before asking, "Have you viewed the memories of the timber, Torin?" His unique magic allows him to access the magic of any object and sort through the recent memories stored within. If the walls saw whoever did this...

"They were wearing a hooded cloak." His voice is tense, as if he remembers the fae sitting in the tavern's corner. "I couldn't see past it."

"Can I help at all?" I ask, gesturing to a pile of much smaller beams and hoping to steer the conversation away from the tension brewing in Vander. Both males shake their heads, so I add, "Then I'll return to the manor and prepare dinner before we head out to place the relic. The moon's rise is not far away."

They're too busy sorting through the debris to acknowledge my words, and I leave without saying goodbye. Just like when I entered the tavern, not a single fae stops me on my exit. I have never felt more like an outsider than I do at this moment.

It's calmer outside now, with less fae dashing from store to store to discuss the fire, and more denizens working to clear the rubble instead of gaping at the ruins. I do not see Wyn anywhere, but Alizeh is flitting from fae to fae with chalices of brandy. I decline when she offers me one.

My walk to the manor is slow. I take the extra time to bask in the glory of the she-oaks, running my hands through the branches and letting the feel of nature centre me. I always thought my love of nature stemmed from my Spring Court heritage. Now, I'm realising it is just who I am. Slowly, as if piecing a puzzle together, I am discovering who I am beyond the tiaras, balls, and gowns. Just as Vander said I would.

Although I'm aware knowing where you come from is important to discovering who you are, I'm finding that knowing where I *don't* come from is shining a light on the aspects of me I always thought were from my birth mother.

I am still pondering the marvel when I enter the manor and head straight for the bathing chamber. First, I scrub all evidence of the fire from my skin, then stand before the distorted mirror with my dagger. The singed hair on my left is browned and curls in on itself. I use slow strokes to shave the damaged strands away, but no matter how I cut the fine hair, I cannot make it look even halfway decent.

So I shave it off.

I angle the blade against my scalp and drag it over the hairs, and in doing so, I feel as if I am cutting away a part of my old life. Every copper strand means something. Father and his strict rules, Fayeth and her cruel words, Rennyn and his omission. The Autumn fae and their scowls, having no friends, losing the younglings I was teaching... I cut away every hurt and every part of the life I once lived. I disown my family and my home court.

By the end, I decide I look kind of rebellious. It's an ironic thought, given Father would always refer to me as such and I would argue I was merely jaded. I have cut away my old life, and now I appear just as my father thought of me.

The left of my hair is nothing more than a shadow of copper against pale skin from the tip of my pointed ear to halfway up the side of my head. I braid the long strands on the right and drape it over my shoulder. I will wear the new style with pride, thinking of it as yet another scar to match the flames and crosses of Summer. The scar from an attack on my new home, and a scar from cutting away who I once was.

When I am happy with the neat job — and impressed I did not cut my scalp — I dress in the second set of leathers Wyn had made for me, and join the others in the dining room.

"What the fuck have you done?" Torin exclaims as he accepts an empty plate from Vander.

Wyn chokes on her wine. "Damn, Bria. When Penna told you to cut away the burned bits, I doubt that's what she meant."

"I couldn't make it look right, so I just got rid of it all. Do you not like it?" I avoid looking at Vander to gauge his reaction.

Wyn chuckles. "Like it? No. I *love* it. It's badarse."

A smile pulls at my lips as I take my seat and help myself to boiled potatoes and sliced ham. Guilt tightens my stomach as I load my plate. I allowed myself to get so distracted with my hair, I forgot to prepare dinner.

Wyn doesn't stop there. She makes Torin agree my hair is 'gnarly', whatever that means. I figure it's a saying from the human realm and shrug it off. Then she leans across to Vander and smacks him up the side of the head. "It looks good. Right, Van?"

He does not take his eyes off his food when he reluctantly he agrees.

The rest of our meal passes in tense silence. We are all concerned for our court, worried about the attacks and who is behind them, and thinking of the tavern rebuild. Though for me, I am also eager to broach the subject of Nyree and Tohminic working together.

I think on the matter so much, I lose my appetite halfway through the meal. I'm more than thankful when Vander declares it time to place the relic.

A little east of the manor, a towering mountain ash tree sits atop a small hill, marking the island's centre. It's a eucalyptus, and for some reason, it stands alone in a field of long grass. Soft moss grows on the exposed roots that stretch for the ground in straight lines, and the undulating trunk is wider than the four of us standing side-by-side. Strings of bark fold downwards from above, but I cannot see higher. The tree is black against the oranges and pinks of the setting sun, clawing for the sky and imposing in its height.

"We set the relic inside the trunk," says Vander, turning to me. "Right?"

I shrug. "The details on placement were vague. I think we just need to place it and hit it with a blast of magic to activate its power. As long as this is the centre of all other ward stones, it should work."

I pull my fur-lined cloak tighter around me — it's not cold this evening, but I will need the warmth later — as we follow Vander around the tree and come to a stop in front of a narrow opening in the trunk. It is as if the tree knew we would need this location and created a hollow while it grew.

Van slips his hand inside, drops the relic, then draws back. "Wyn, you have the honours."

She rubs her palms together, then splays her fingers, sending a gust of cool air into the hollow. She holds her magic for several heartbeats before the wind simmers down.

We wait in silence, but only for a moment.

A gentle hum pierces the quiet, followed by streams of golden magic racing along the trunk like pulsing veins. They climb higher and higher, illuminating the entire mountain ash and spreading through the branches before shooting from the leaves in glittering arcs.

Eight arcs, all racing in different directions. To each of the already placed ward stones, I realise when the first arc lands beyond the she-oak forest. Once the golden arc has linked the relic with the ward stone, the shimmering fades, leaving nothing but the hum of magic behind.

Eight arcs come and go, all within heartbeats. With each disappearing link, the magic at the tree's base grows stronger. It grows so strong it forces us to stumble away. Currents of power trickle over my skin, bringing gooseflesh to my arms and making the hairs on my nape stand on end.

I can only imagine the damage this relic could do if imbued with the wrong magic. For there is a warning that comes with creating this relic, one I have told no one. If a fae is to feed their magic into this tree, the ward will change. It will turn hostile and torture any within the Dusk Court it deems an enemy.

A shiver runs down my spine at the thought.

Once the magic of the wards has settled, and we're on our return to the manor, I walk beside Torin and ask, "When you saw the memory of the hooded fae in the kitchens, did you catch any details about them? Eye colour, build... hair?"

"No. Why?"

"Are you sure? Because when we were in the tavern, I saw a hooded fae in the corner. They ran when the cook shouted her warning, and I saw a flash of pearlescent hair beneath the hood."

"Bria," Wyn sighs. "We've been through this."

This is just how everyone in Autumn would act around me. "I'm tired of no one listening to me. The Ill-fated lit that fire."

Wyn comes to a stop. "You don't know her like we do. Enough of this. I won't hear more on the matter." She turns towards the manor and storms up the hill.

Vander follows, glancing over his shoulder with a frown.

Torin places his hand on my shoulder. "Best drop the subject, love. You won't win this fight." He gives me a light squeeze before following the Theron siblings.

And I'm alone. Just as I thought I would be.

I spin on my heel, break through the she-oaks, then step onto the beach. The magic of the realm wraps around me in a heartbeat, and I fold away from the Dusk Court.

Chapter 21

T HE BRISK AIR OF Winter stings the tip of my nose and flecks of snow cling to my eyelashes. Although I wish for nothing more than a hot bath beside a roaring fire, I do not dare fold to Dusk. Not until I have found Uma and begged for Winter's allegiance.

The mountain range I walk on is precarious. Steep slopes threaten to give way beneath my careful feet, slick patches of ice on the rare flat parts crack under my weight, and the bitter cold could bring me to my knees if I let it. But I persevere.

I have visited the Winter Court only once in my life, with Father, Fayeth, and Rennyn. I wonder now if Fayeth knew my birth mother lived in the mountain castle in which Ruith and his wife live. Thinking back to when I was two and twenty, a mere babe on the verge of becoming a youngling, she was especially vicious during that trip. It was the first time she told me I am worthless.

Having come here only once, I am struggling to remember where the entrance to the castle is. Every peak, every flat, they all look the same: grey rock covered in blinding snow. I recall a valley lined with obsidian statues and a twisted peak at the end of the Path of Shadows. Though where that path and peak are... I do not know.

I draw my hood over my head, the fur lining offering a layer of warmth that does little against the cold, and collect the large branch I found upon arriving to use as a crutch to hike these precarious mountains. My eyes track over the slope I am about to climb, and my heart sinks.

The stars are a beautiful backdrop. There's not a cloud in sight to hide their magnificence. Only the gigantic mountain before me cuts through the night sky. I hoped to conserve my magic, but I think... just this once. I pull on the threads of the realm's power and fold to the peak of the mountain.

The wind whips at my travelling cloak, trying to tear it from my body. I grip it harder and push away the pang of regret. Perhaps I should have told someone I intended to come here. Perhaps I should have brought someone with me.

There's no time for indecision. For the first time in my life, I am doing something selfless. I do not wish to meet the female who handed me over without a thought, but I will do it if it means Winter severs their alliance with Summer, gaining us another ally.

I spin in a slow circle, taking in the mountainous landscape. It is difficult in the dark of night, but something within me calls to the south. The peak I am looking for bisects the sky far in the distance. Twisted and capped with snow, the apex of the largest mountain in the Bolbala Ranges is my destination. Kol, Ruith's castle.

My mother's home.

I gather my magic and surround myself with it, then fold to the very peak of Kol. Below me, at the midpoint of this mountain, the line of statues. A sense of satisfaction fills me. I have found the castle of the Winter Court. I did it alone, without aid from a male or servant.

Bria Sutherland, independent female.

The happiness is fleeting.

"Halt." A guard appears from nowhere, his translucent skin both familiar and unnerving. "State your business or relinquish your claim to life."

"It's me, Tarathiel. Bria of Dusk. I'm here to speak with Lady Uma."

"Bria? Why are you arriving in the dead of night?"

I scoff. "It's hardly the dead of night. The Mother Star has not long disappeared beyond the mountains."

"The High Lady does not take visitors. Has not for five and seventy years."

"Then take me to your High Lord."

"Very well."

Tarathiel leads me to a hidden cave entrance, one I would not have found on my own, and throws an orb of fae light into the air once inside. "May I ask the reasons for your unannounced visit?"

"It's private." My tone is terse. I'm glad to make small talk, but this has nothing to do with Tarathiel.

We take a sharp left from the antechamber and enter a grand foyer made of polished rock. Magnificent pillars of obsidian line either side, six in total, with intricate carvings depicting scenes from Winter's history. I remember the pillars from my only visit to the court, and remember the stories of horrific wars with Night, who believed the power to wield shadows should belong to them, and Winter fae being forced into hiding within the mountain.

The last pillar, my favourite, shows the love story of the High Lord and his mate. I suppose the images are a lie, though, given Uma betrayed Ruith and bedded another male.

Tarathiel asks nothing more as he leads me through the castle. We descend a grand staircase of onyx, turn down a wide corridor of black marble, and pause beside a heavy-set door painted black. I think the Winter fae take their love of shadows and darkness too far, though the effect is mesmerising.

Tarathiel knocks before letting himself into a large dining hall. The cluster of tables baffled me upon my first visit, and they confuse me still. Every other court dines at one large table. Every fae shares food. Not Winter. In Winter, each denizen has their own meal, with no shared carafes or platters.

Fortunately for me, Ruith and his guards are the only fae in the dining hall tonight.

"Princess Bria Sutherland of Autumn, My Lord. She has —"

"Actually," I say, cutting Tarathiel's words short, "I'm Bria of Dusk. I do not belong to the Autumn Court." I look to the far end of the hall, meet Ruith's dark brown eyes, and curtsey as well as I can in leathers and a cloak. "Well met."

"Well met," he says. He gestures to a seat at his table. "Sit. I will have someone fetch the wine."

Tarathiel exits on silent feet, leaving me alone with the High Lord and four guards.

"What brings you to my court?" Ruith asks. His skin seems a darker brown than it was when I last saw him at Rennyn's born day celebrations, as if he has spent time in the sun. If he is so close to Tohminic that he has been to the Summer Court recently... Have I just walked right into enemy territory?

Ruith's young for a High Lord. His skin still holds the shine of youth, and his muscular yet lean build is visible beneath his tight-fitting tunic. I think if the white fabric were to get wet, I would see every dip and groove of his chest.

"I had hoped to speak with Lady Uma."

He freezes and orders the guards to leave. It is sign enough he knows. "She has been waiting for this day," is all he says once we're alone. He runs a hand over his short hair, which is a black so deep it seems to absorb the light.

"May I see her?"

He beckons a servant over, who fills two chalices with a deep red wine before scurrying away.

"First, allow me to explain." He waits until I give him permission before saying something I never thought I would hear, "Uma's betrayal almost cost me everything. When I discovered she was to birth a babe of Autumn, I was..." He sighs. "I very much regret my actions."

"The strongest of fae would have felt such heartache. I'm sure you did no wrong."

"I thank you for your words. Still, I spend every day working to atone for my sins. Uma has not yet forgiven me for my behaviour all those years ago, but I have forgiven her. I love your mother with my entire heart. That is why I had to send you away."

I blink back tears. "It was you?"

He dips his chin. "The members of my court do not know of her night of lust, mere moons before our mating ceremony. If they were to discover what she did, they would force her to walk the path of shame."

My eyes flutter closed. Every fae in Radelea knows of Winter's path of shame, where fae who have done wrong walk before their court and have stones and food thrown at them.

"The denizens would have made her carry you along the path. I did not care for your life then, but I cared for Uma's. I hid her in the castle until she gave birth, then sent you to your father. No one has ever uncovered her betrayal or my deception. Until now, it seems."

"What a disgusting way to do things."

"It is our way," he says, simply.

Guilt burns through me. "Tarathiel said she hasn't taken visitors since I was born."

"She refuses to meet with another fae until the day you walk through her door." His dark eyes grow darker, and shadows curl from his palms. "I do not know why you have come, Bria, and I will not prevent you from meeting my chosen mate, but if your reasons put her in danger, I will retaliate."

"I expect nothing less." A tangy burst of fruit fills my mouth as I sip my wine and contemplate my choices. Meeting Uma would be uncomfortable, but knowing she did not *choose* to hand me over to Father makes me think of her differently. On the other hand, I believe Ruith will throw me in his dungeons if I so much as mention the war efforts to my mother.

"You should know I came here with less than honourable intentions," I say. "I wished to use my status as Uma's daughter to gain allies in the war. I will not meet with her if you do not wish for me to, but please know I no longer wish to see her conflicted. Especially if telling every fae in Radelea I'm her daughter puts her in danger."

"Your honesty surprises me. We have seldom spoken, but I am pleasantly surprised to find you are most unlike your father."

I dip my head in thanks. "It is the highest praise you could offer."

He snorts. The High Lord of Winter actually snorts. It is so... normal, and I believe I can trust him.

"My life has not been easy," I say. "While I would have faced the stones of shame in Winter, even as a babe, I have endured ridicule at the hands of my father's court. None shunned me more than Fayeth. Unwanted in my own home... It was difficult growing up in Autumn."

"I heard of your time in Ad'Starrag." His words shock me into stillness. "I was horrified on your behalf. Uma does not know of what happened to you. You may see her if you vow to keep all mentions of war to yourself. Do this, and I will consider severing my alliance with Tohminic."

"Just like that?"

"My mate means more to me than an allegiance to the Summer Court, Bria. Many think me to be harsh, but my only goal in this life is to see my denizens happy and my mate free of anguish." His shadows slither back into his palms. "Do we have an understanding?"

It is the best outcome I could hope for. For a High Lord to even *consider* turning his back on their allies after millennia is a huge chance I cannot refuse.

"Deal."

We finish our wines while talking about the war. Ruith shares information I cannot wait to hand over to Torin and Vander. I believe it is a sign of trust, a test of sorts.

Soon after, I am standing beside a set of ornate double doors waiting for Ruith to return. He claims my arrival will be a shock to Uma, and it is best she's prepared for such an event.

He pokes his head through a small gap in the doors, looking every bit the uncomfortable mate and nothing like the fearsome High Lord he is. "She is ready for you."

I smooth my leathers, though they are little more than a second skin and have no creases to speak of, then flatten the wispy strands that have blown free of the braid on my right.

Walking into another High Lord's bedchamber is strange, to say the least. But I feel welcome the moment I step foot inside. It could be the light walls and furniture that does it, or the warm smile on Ruith's face, or more likely, it's the warmth of Uma as she wraps her arms around my shoulders and pulls me in for a tight embrace.

"Oh, my darling daughter, I thought this day would never come." Her words are choked and filled with more emotion than one fae should ever carry.

I catch a glimpse of her features before her wild copper curls block out the world. It's clear she has spent the past five and seventy years hidden in these chambers. Her skin is pale, almost translucent like Tarathiel's, and her ice-blue eyes are dull.

"I never knew," I say, struggling to free my arms enough to hold her in return. "I'm so sorry I never knew."

The longer I hold her, the more something within me fractures, as if piece by piece, the ice encasing my heart and soul is thawing. All my life, I have imagined this moment. I have tried to think of what I would say and how I would feel and act, yet none of that compares to this moment. The female holding me has always wanted me. I have not spent my entire life unwanted by all. There's always been Uma, waiting in Winter for me to realise who I am.

Something cool rushes through me, cool and foreign yet so very wholesome. I feel... almost complete, like my mind has waited for this moment to heal.

"Easy there, Bria."

I pull away from my mother and frown at Ruith. "Excuse me?"

He jerks his chin towards my hands.

I look down, and shock rushes through my veins. Shadows. Black, impenetrable shadows curl from my hands. I lift my palms higher and inspect the wispy darkness, greeting them like an old friend after eons of being apart.

When I think I would like them to take the shape of a galloping horse, they bend to that command with ease. A simple thought, and the shadows retract. They disappear into my palms, where I can feel them just below the surface, waiting for another order.

My eyes lift and clash with Uma's. "I have your magic," I whisper. "The darkness I have always thought clouded my mind... It was shadows all along. I truly am your daughter. I did not dare believe it until now."

She cups my face. "You have always been my daughter, regardless of you not knowing who you are. I would very much like to get to know you. Stay tonight, and we can have breakfast together once the Mother Star shines?"

A small smile plays on my lips, and though I know I should return to Dusk, where Vander and Wyn are likely beside themselves with worry, I cannot stop myself from agreeing to Uma's request.

A morning with my mother is just what I need.

Chapter 22

T HE FOLLOWING MORNING PASSES in a blur of information. I learn everything there is to know about my mother, from growing up at the base of the Bolbala Ranges with her two brothers to meeting Ruith by chance in a tavern in the cliff city to the south.

I share Uma's love of reading history and we both prefer to travel by horse rather than folding; I invite her to the Dusk Court so she may meet my mare, Solana.

We're both grinning by the end of breakfast.

It's as if a weight has lifted from my shoulders. Throughout my time in Winter, I have not thought of all the red coating my hands or the fate of the realm. War does not exist in the bubble of happiness I share with my birth mother, and I wish I had fought harder to find her, and sooner. If I had, perhaps I would not have felt so alone all my life.

But I have met her now, and I'm certain we will be in each other's lives until the Mother Star deems us ready to move to the next.

I learn of Uma's snow and ice power and how she has never grasped it well enough to wield. She can bring bitter cold to her palms, and that is the extent of it. We assume I will be the same, or have less control of the Winter element than she does.

Ruith joins us for a walk through the cliff-side village of Apricity, where we meet traders of every description — my favourite are those who deal with stories woven into tapestries — and stop at the tavern where Ruith and Uma met to enjoy a brandy. Four guards trail behind us the entire time, their ever-watchful eyes startling in their brightness.

When it's time for me to return home, I bid a teary farewell to my mother before the guards escort her back to Kol, then turn to Ruith. "I have one last request, if you would be so kind to grant it."

"Please," he says, watching the guards and his chosen mate disappear, "ask away. You have given Uma a rare happiness that I could never dream of gifting her. I am forever in your debt."

"In fact, it's two things now. First, how do you feel about me calling you Stepfather? Second, would you be so kind as to escort me home? Only, I didn't tell anyone I was coming here. Vander will be in a right state upon my return."

His dark eyes brighten. "You may call me whatever you please, daughter. And I would be delighted to escort you. In fact, I believe your Lord and I have many things to discuss."

Daughter. Not Stepdaughter. Not Bria.

Daughter.

I do not think my father ever referred to me as such without grimacing.

My fingers tremble as I take his hand. Together, as father and daughter, we fold to Dusk... only to almost collide with Wyn,

Vander, and Torin as they prepare to fold away from the island court.

"Bria!" shouts Wyn. "Where the fuck have you been?"

I take in their panicked faces, and a niggle of pain ignites in the back of my throat, followed by a heavy burn in my stomach. Each of them wears leathers with uncountable daggers and blades strapped to their bodies. They are ready to fight for me, and I could not give them the respect they deserve by telling them where I was going.

Ruith releases my hand and steps forward. "Well met, Lord Vander." He dips his chin to the others. "Wyn. Torin."

"Well met," they echo.

It's Vander who steps forward. "She's been with you? Safe?" His hand rests on his battle axe.

"She has. She will always be safe in my court. We have brokered a deal. Do you have a place where we may talk?" Ruith's tone is calm but carries a hint of authority he has not used with me since I arrived in Winter.

Wyn and Torin look at me with raised eyebrows, but Vander keeps his silver eyes pinned on Winter's High Lord. I don't blame him for not trusting Ruith, especially because Winter is supposed to be loyal to Summer, our enemy.

"We can talk here," says Vander. Unlike Ruith, there is no hint of kindness to Van's tone, only distrust and unease.

I realised this morning that I have to protect Ruith in order to protect my mother. Even without that understanding, though, he's my stepfather. I may love Vander, but he does not choose me as I choose him. Ruith and Uma will always be there. Vander will not.

"I would rather find somewhere private. It is a sensitive matter I wish to discuss," says Ruith.

Vander steps forward, flicking open the clip on his axe.

Shadows lick across my palms as I step in front of Ruith. "Harming him harms me. Back off."

Vander's eyes flick to my shadowed palms and widen. "One night in Winter and they've turned you against us. You move fast, Princess." Is that hurt lacing his tone?

I withdraw the shadows and shove against his chest. "Stop being a jerk and listen. He isn't here to harm any of us, but wishes to speak to you *in private* about a sensitive matter. Think, Van. Why would the High Lord of Winter wish for no fae to overhear this discussion?"

Wyn grips Vander's arm and drags him back. "Listen to her, brother. The panic of waking to find her gone is ruling your actions. Let's see what the Winter Lord has to say."

Vander shrugs Wyn off and jabs a finger at Ruith. "If this is a trick, you will not leave this court unharmed."

"He will," I say, my shadows returning and whipping out in dark curls.

"I think we better head inside before Bria sends a blanket of shadow over the court," says Torin. He winks at me before adding, "It's kind of sexy how you reacted like that."

"That's enough," Vander snaps.

Torin only chuckles and leads the way to the manor. He walks beside me, and Wyn walks on my other side. There is still tension weighing down their shoulders as we enter, and I know they must be wondering what's happening and why I am so calm around someone we thought to be an enemy just yesterday.

"I take it you met your mother?" asks Wyn as we turn towards the war room. "How did it go?"

"She's everything I could have asked for in a mother. And Ruith is a bonus I didn't expect. I'm happy, Wyn."

"Then I'm happy."

Torin, not one to be excluded, says, "I'm happy, too. But this tension between you and Vander needs to stop, or I won't be happy, and there's not a single fae in Radelea who deserves to endure me when I'm mad."

We pass through the illusioned statue — Ruith cringes — and enter the room as a group to find Nyree pouring over the map yet again.

I turn to Ruith and shake my head. We had discussed my suspicions of Nyree over wine last night. He knows I am not comfortable with her here.

"I do not wish the Ill-fated to be here." His words are for everyone, though he looks only at Nyree.

"This is my home," she says, turning to face us. "I have every right to be here."

Wyn opens her mouth to argue in Nyree's favour, but I interrupt her before she can begin. "Ruith and I refuse to have this conversation with her here. If you wish to hear what we have to say, then you will make her leave. I won't hear any more on the matter." I meet Vander's gaze, so he knows I will not budge on this.

He sighs. "Fine. Nyree, get out."

She obeys, but not before offering me the deadliest look she can muster.

Once the door is closed, and we're sure Nyree is not lurking beyond the wooden planks, we all take our seats at the table.

Ruith clears his throat. "I am informed of your hardships, and you should know I am sympathetic. My pity was not enough to turn on my allies."

"Then why are you here?" asks Vander. He is the only one who has refused to sit.

"Although my sympathy was not cause enough for me to shun Tohminic and his court, my daughter *is*. Bria is not my blood, but she is my mate's blood. It is one and the same. I have agreed to ally with Dusk on one condition: my mate must never know of the war."

Wyn scoffs. "That'll be hard, given battles and death will fall upon your court should Summer choose to attack."

"Allow me to finish," says Ruith, his tone still calm. "My mate shall never know of the war, at least not until I believe she is ready. It will take time for her to adjust to her new life as a mother and a member of society. She will learn of the conflict once life has settled for her."

Wyn's brows raise, and I mouth, "I'll explain later."

"You'll sever your allegiance to Summer?" asks Torin, leaning his elbows on the table. "Just because your wife bedded another male and ended up pregnant?"

I close my eyes against his words. "Torin, you're out of line. He's agreeing because it's the right thing to do, and he won't make enemies out of two females who have spent enough time away from one another."

"I could not have said it better," says Ruith.

"What do you offer?" Vander asks, sitting at last.

Ruith leans back in his chair and crosses an ankle over his knee. "You will have my infantry at your disposal, as well as an offer of sanctuary, should you need it. If I had an armada, you would be welcome to that, too."

"And in return?" asks Wyn.

"In return, you allow Bria to come and go between our courts as she pleases, and you keep the knowledge of who her mother is to yourselves. Winter customs leave no room for debate and I will not see my mate harmed."

"You've agreed to this?" Wyn asks me. I nod — I wish only for Uma's safety — and she turns back to Ruith. "You have my word that I won't reveal the knowledge to anyone."

Ruith tells them what we discussed last night, that Tohminic has not left his keep since my escape. He claims the High Lord is frightened of retaliation should he show himself, but he's certain the Summer fae are plotting something big. He overheard them speaking of undead armies and selkie attacks, due to move out any day now.

Once he has given us any information on Summer he has, he explains he needs time to put things in order within his court before declaring Winter their enemy. He will return in a few days to sign a treaty between Winter and Dusk, then the entire realm will know he sides with us.

He ends his claims with a question. One I'm not sure will be well received. "Bria has alluded to another reason behind the war, one that is much more reasonable than the claim of land this all began with. May I hear your reasons?"

Before anyone can answer, I say, "I trust him, Van. With my life."

Vander pushes away from the table and paces the length of the room. He passes the stand of weapons and runs a hand over his long stubble, then turns at the tapestries, a crease forming between his brows.

Eventually, he stops beside us. "I cannot tell you yet. Once you have signed the treaty, I will explain everything. It's the best I can offer."

Ruith stands and extends a hand. "Then we agree? Our courts are allies?"

Vander takes the proffered hand. "Allies."

It's so simple, a handshake between males. Yet I cannot help but wonder if this is the start of something big. A handshake. A beginning. It is a new era.

Chapter 23

I SPEND THE REST of the day training with Torin and Wyn. We work on my combat skills, which I'm pleased to notice have improved a lot since my first lesson some forty moons ago, then move to developing my metal bending magic.

Throughout the entire afternoon, Nyree sits on the edge of the training field and offers cruel words of advice to Torin and Wyn on how to bring me down. Her suggestions begin with simple acts, like feigning to the left, but soon evolve to more drastic measures like tripping me or not pulling punches. She even suggests shaving the other side of my hair to make it match, claiming I look ridiculous and lop-sided with only one side shaved.

Vander does not show. Before we moved from the war room to the training field, he claimed he needed to check on the relic ward, but that should only have taken him an hour. He has not returned since.

There is a point where I show off my new shadow magic. Torin and Wyn are both in awe of how I can wield the darkness so well with no training. I think there's just a part of me that relishes in the knowledge the shadows don't come from my father. It is the first thing I have had in life that was not of him. It's... freeing.

When we retire for the evening, we find Vander already eating dinner in the manor.

He says nothing to me for the rest of the night.

Vander does not train me again today. This time, it's the tavern's progress he needs to check on.

Another day, and more excuses from Vander. There's nothing but frustration thrumming from his end of our bond. Again, he ignores me at dinner and retires early. It's becoming routine.

It has been three days since Ruith agreed to be our ally. Torin and Vander venture to Spring and Autumn to demand answers for their silence. Even with Winter as our ally, our numbers are smaller than we had hoped.

The males reappear during the night, and Vander takes his dinner in his room. I am certain he's avoiding me; angry that I left without a word, and conflicted over my claim of love. Perhaps one and not the other, or both. If he will not talk to me, I will never know why he's giving me the cold shoulder.

Wyn tells me not to worry about it, that Van just has a lot on his mind.

I can't help but wonder... Does he regret saving me from Ad'Starrag?

On the fourth day after my return from Winter, I struggle to read in the archives. There is something that has been bothering me for days now, and I haven't been able to put my finger on what's worrying me.

I skim over the same line of cursive letters for the seventh time, and shove the tome away with a sigh. I cannot concentrate, not with my mind trying to remember something else and the incessant worry about Vander avoiding me.

The others have gone with Torin to the tavern, so he can rewatch the memories held within the walls. He's not confident he will find anything new, but after I begged him to assess it again, he agreed.

My eyes travel to the windows, where the full moon waits for the Mother Star to disappear. It's one of those days where we can see the moon throughout the day, one of those days we must be weary of, for the moon's presence during the Mother Star's reign is a warning. An omen of things to come.

It could mean anything. Autumn could choose to side with Summer and Night — who have declared themselves allies of Summer — the new alliance with Winter could fall through, or Nyree could finally...

The niggling in the back of my mind pushes to the front of my thoughts, and I gasp as the question that has been bothering me makes itself known: why is Nyree always looking at the map in the war room?

The book lover within me does not allow me to just get up and leave the small table in the archives. I place the two tomes and a single scroll back on their shelves before slipping through the statue of the wind wielder and into the antechamber before the war room.

A sudden desire to flee in the other direction thrums through my veins, and my muscles twitch in response as if to obey that command. I rebel against the feeling and shake out my hands before pressing both palms against the wooden wall.

Wyn had shown me only yesterday how to trigger the door by pushing my intention into the timber and activating the magic, and if it deems me trustworthy, it will swing open.

I wish to look at the map and will touch nothing else, I think with as much strength of inner voice as I can, then wrap a slither of my shadow magic around the thought before sending it into the fibres of wood. A click, then the door swings open. And I face an empty room.

The nerves clenching my stomach retreat, replaced by the face-reddening feeling of acting a fool. I must admit, if some part of me is afraid of being alone with Nyree, I should very well acknowledge it and obey. The subconscious is a marvellous thing.

I don't bother to close the door behind me before stepping onto the platform and leaning on the table to view the map.

The wooden pieces that depict each court remain on the parchment. Summer's red flames remain at their keep, Winter's white icicles are at the north-western mountain ranges, the green leaves of Spring are in the northern lands, and Night's black bones are on each of the four western Islands. Dusk's pieces, silver spirals of wind, are scattered in every court, though most of them remain within our land.

Day and Dawn, the cresting wave and golden sun, are mostly within the north-eastern courts, but some of them are standing in the seas, where their armadas are still watching our enemies. And Autumn's brown paw remains in our south-east.

Assuming my home court is among them, our enemies curl around our southern border and most of the east and west. Our allies in Day and Dawn are the farthest from us, and our new allies in Winter provide an escape route in the north-west should we need it.

The closest land to us is Autumn, with their western village reaching for us like an old friend. And from that little dock-side village, there's a smear in the dust that trails across the sea to the she-oak forest in Dusk.

Autumn is aiding Summer. Whether Rennyn knows of this is irrelevant. We now know how the undead were breaching our borders and can keep a closer watch on our eastern shore.

But who made the smear in the dust collecting atop this map? It could have been anyone, but I have a sneaking suspicion Vander and the others do not know. Other than coming here to meet with Ruith, we have not met in the war room for many moons. If anyone were to see Zentha and Jonik coming and going, the entire realm would know we're allies.

Keeping our alliance a secret has kept their courts safe for now, though I'm not sure we can keep the information hidden for much longer. Most fae within Radelea will know already.

Another smear in the dust catches my eye, and I trace my eyes over the line that moves from the Night Islands to the western shore of Dusk. It matches a line that travels through Summer from Ad'Starrag and meets our eastern shore. "He was right. Summer is going to attack."

"I can't allow you to tell anyone," says a voice from behind, a voice that sends an icy shiver down my spine.

I jerk upright and spin to face Nyree. "You're working for Tohminic, aren't you?"

"That fool? No." She prowls closer, her hands never leaving the pockets sewn into her travelling cloak. "It was too easy, how the others believed he was behind every attack. They didn't once consider them a ruse."

The blood drains from my face. If what she says is true, then the Summer Court has nothing to do with the fire and the undead attacks. But that doesn't make sense. "If he's not responsible, then how were you controlling the undead?"

Her smirk is as cruel as the glint in her eyes. "Oh, those fae were not dead, Bria. At least, they weren't until you lot killed them. I merely had one of my Ill-fated control their minds. They were *acting* like the undead, but were very much alive."

I recoil from her words. If what she says is true, Rennyn burned his mother alive. He killed her. The five souls we offered to Blodwen, tortured.

The urge to scrub myself clean threatens to bring me to my knees, and my hand moves to my mouth to hold in the excess saliva, as I recall every time we have fought the undead. The two fights I can recall, I cannot remember seeing rotted flesh or sagging skin or anything that proves those fae had already passed from this world. Only... Only Nik.

"But Nikolai..." I cannot make sense of her words.

"A gesture of good faith from the High Lord you hate so much. You don't think I would imitate an entire court without permission, do you?" She steps forward again, then again, until she is within reach.

I'm not wearing my daggers today, instead relishing in the freedom of a flowing gown, but the rack of weapons is in the corner should I need it. Although, I do not think I can make it in time. My metal bending power thrashes inside, and I free several threads of magic and wrap them around a sword in preparation. Then I split my concentration and look over my shoulder for the rock I know to be holding the corner of the map down.

My divided attention works to Nyree's advantage. The moment I turn to grab the rock — while simultaneously yanking the sword free with my magic — something hard smacks against the side of my head.

Stars blaze across my vision and pain flares. I wobble and slam into the large table, then sink to my knees. I press a gentle hand against the throbbing wound. It comes away slick with blood.

"You... jerk —" My words are sluggish.

"I can't let you tell anyone," Nyree repeats. Her face is blurry as she kneels in front of me, and I cannot tell if the face on the left is real or the face on the right. "I can't let you ruin our plans. You might as well know how badly you messed up by not closing that door. You won't be conscious to do anything about it, anyway. I'm going to remove the relic, Bria. And when I do, the Dusk Court will fall."

"You can't." I sag to the side, my shoulder pressing into the wooden chair.

Both of her faces smirk. "Oh, I can. I have proven myself. The Ill-fated will have this place for themselves. You're lucky we still need you. If we didn't, well, you'd be dead by now. Instead..." She raises her fist, and I catch sight of a bloodied rock in her hand. I do not have time to react before she slams the stone against the side of my head once more.

I'm unconscious before I hit the floor.

Chapter
24

I GROAN AND ROLL to the side, my hand shooting to my aching head. I squint my eyes open but see only darkness. There's a hint of mildew in the air mixed with the tang of blood. The fae light I throw up is a dull, flickering amber, but it's strong enough to cast a glow over hewn rock walls and dribbles of water tracking to the ground.

I recognise it as the tunnel below the war room, the one that leads to the portal to the human realm.

Vander has spent the past four moons ignoring me. Wyn is furious that I keep trying to frame the Ill-fated. Torin doesn't want to cause tension between everyone. Even with all that playing on my mind, I know I have no choice.

Even if I had the strength to climb the ladder, the hatch is heavy, and I cannot open it on my own. Besides, Nyree has likely placed something over it to prevent my escape.

I pull on the thread that connects my soul to Vander's and send every throb of pain, every slither of fear, and a pulsing beat of my location straight to him.

Surprise and anger thrum back at me, followed by a blanket of calm. I don't know how I know it, but Vander is coming for me. At least he still cares for my wellbeing, even through his anger and reluctance to acknowledge our bond.

I pull away from our connection and focus on staggering to my feet. My vision is still a little blurred, and there's a strange weakness in my limbs, but I manage to use my hands to claw my way up the rock until I'm standing. My breaths turn ragged as I lean against the wall and rest my head against the cool stone. Drips of water collect in my tangled hair, but the drops are a welcome reprieve to the throbbing headache.

How could I let this happen? Nyree was acting stranger than normal; knowing that, I tried to attack first, but failed. I can only put it down to a moment of foolishness. Turning away from someone I knew to be working against me is a mistake I will never make again. Yes, I was searching for a second weapon. Still, it is inexcusable. I turned away from an attacker.

It's the first rule Vander ever taught me in combat. *Always keep your eye on your enemy.* He will be so disappointed.

I distract myself from the pain by counting my heartbeats. After almost fifteen hundred beats of my calming heart, the hatch above my head groans open, and light filters into the tunnel. From the weakness of it, I guess the full moon is ruling the sky.

I was unconscious for hours.

"Bria?" Wyn calls down. "Are you okay?"

"A little sore, but I'll live." I cannot say the same for the fae we killed without thought or mercy. "Get me out of here, please."

A black blur flashes in front of me. Vander lands in a crouch. "What happened?"

My emerald eyes clash with his, and I cannot pull my gaze away. "Nyree. I was wondering why she's always looking at the map in the war room, and went to see it for myself. I left the door open, and she let herself in. We spoke for a moment, then she hit me over the head with a rock. Ironic, given I come from the court of earth."

He crooks a finger beneath my chin and turns my head to the side to inspect the wound. "It has stopped bleeding, but we'll get Penna to have a look." His face twists as he whispers, "I didn't feel it."

"You were ignoring both me and our bond, Van. And I understand why. I... I'm sorry I said all those things. I should have kept it to myself."

"Let's not talk about it right now. You need to heal."

"No," I say. I shake my head, but stop when the throbbing gets worse. "We don't have time."

Torin and Wyn drop beside me, both of them looking over me with concern.

"I'm sorry." My voice is a mere whisper. "I didn't want to be right."

"Right about what?" asks Vander.

Wyn's face falls, and she places a hand on my arm. "I'm sorry I didn't believe you. I should have listened."

"Listened to what?" Vander growls.

Rage twists Torin's face. The war room's memories would have showed him everything. He loses control and punches the rock wall. The crack that booms through the tunnel is sickening. "That fucking bitch Nyree attacked Bria. She's going for the relic."

"Calm down. We'll add extra protections," says Vander. "She won't get within a sword's length of the mountain ash tree."

"You're not understanding, brother. She's already gone. Nyree attacked after gloating about her deception, threw Bria into this tunnel, then left to retrieve the relic," says Wyn. "Bria was right all along."

Though it warms me to know everyone sees the truth after all this time, repeating it does not help anyone. "We don't need to keep acknowledging I was right. We need to go. Now. If she gets her hands on that relic, we're vulnerable once more." I look to my right and squint into the darkness ahead, where I know the portal to Earth to be. "The humans will be at risk. This would all have been for nothing."

"She's right," says Vander. "There's no point praising her good instincts or apologising for our lack of trust in her. If we don't stop Nyree from taking the relic, we'll have enemies on all sides."

"What do you mean?" I ask.

It's Wyn who answers. "Did you ever wonder why we glamour our ears when we're in the human realm?" She doesn't wait for my response. "The supernaturals there don't trust us. In fact, their leader said in no uncertain terms the supernatural beings would band together and wage war on our kind should we continue to pry into their business."

All this time, I have been thinking of the humans on Earth and have given no thought to the other creatures who roam the land. Vampires, shifters of every description… they would attack us. Without knowing what kind of power they hold, we would be walking into a war blind.

Ascending the ladder is a struggle I'm not prepared for. My arms shake with the effort, and my feet slip on the wooden rungs, but I continue climbing while ignoring the throbs of pain in my skull. Humans may have the protection of their supernatural government on Earth, but no one in their realm knows of the war in Radelea. They're vulnerable.

"Tell me about this government on Earth," I say through my ragged breaths to Wyn. I need a distraction from the weakness in my limbs and the pain in my head.

"There are two. A human government and the supernatural one."

"Why?"

Torin says, "The humans don't know supernaturals exist. The two species live together on Earth, but as far as humans are concerned, they're the only beings in existence."

"The human government knows about us, and they're happy for us to come and go as we please as long as we don't show our true selves," says Wyn. "The supernaturals, though, see us as a threat. They mostly deal with rogue supes, keep order between wolf packs or vampire nests, or hand down punishments to wrongdoers."

"Punishment?" I pant.

"If anyone threatens the existence of supernaturals," says Torin, "they deal with them. Swiftly. Say a bear shifter turns from man to bear in front of a human. The government will step in by altering the memory of the human and killing the shifter."

I pull myself into the war room and remain on all fours while I catch my breath. "That's horrible."

"It's their way and we have no right to judge," says Vander. He squats in front of me. "Are you okay?" His hand twitches, as if he means to help me to my feet.

"Just weak."

His eyes narrow and he grazes a thumb across my upper lip. The simple move sends a ripple of sensation from my mouth, through my entire body, and all the way to my toes. I close my eyes and drag in a harsh breath. When he pulls his thumb away, a warmth remains. Like an echo of pressure, the feel of him touching me with such gentleness lingers on my lips, and I fight the urge to run my tongue across them.

When I open my eyes, Vander is raising his hand to his own mouth. His tongue darts out and grazes over the pad of his thumb, and a delicious throb ignites between my legs until I almost combust on the spot.

His eyes jerk to mine, widening slightly. He clears his throat and looks away, his face twisting with an emotion I cannot place. "Powder of the blue mock lotus. She drugged you."

"We need Penna to give her the antidote. She'll only get worse if she's not healed," says Wyn.

"Take her to Penna while Vander and I get weapons. Meet us in the armoury if you're finished before we collect you," says Torin.

Vander offers me one last look before following his second from the war room. Guilt crashes through me. I cannot control my body, but it is clear he doesn't want to feel what I'm feeling. I make a mental note to research how to suppress a twin soul bond. It will mean a trip to Day, but I think Vander will allow me to leave if it means he is free of my emotions.

Wyn helps me to my feet. "You okay? You're looking a little flushed."

"I'm fine. Let's just find Penna so we can help Van and Torin. The sooner I'm healed, the sooner we can confront Nyree."

We walk through the silent manor, flashes of moonlight illuminating the path from the many windows. It's bright tonight with the full moon, which is both good and bad. Good, we will find the Ill-fated if they're out in the open. Bad, we won't be able to hide if we need to.

Descending the stairs drains what little remains of my energy. By the time we reach the infirmary, Wyn is all but carrying me.

Penna sighs when we enter. "What has she done now?"

"I didn't do anything," I slur. Even my thoughts are sluggish.

"Nyree dosed her with blue mock," says Wyn. "Can you heal her and give her an energy boost? It's important Bria has strength enough to leave within the hour."

"I was about to retire for the night. You are lucky to have caught me." Penna gestures to my least favourite bed. "Sit her down, then." She rummages in one of the glass cabinets before returning with a small vial of pink liquid. She hands it to me and orders me to drink.

I try. I really do. But my hand shakes so much I risk losing half of the antidote to the floor, so Wyn takes the vial, which is smaller than her palm, and presses it against my lips. The liquid tastes of sweet musk, and I have a moment where I think the flavour should be used to make some kind of confectionary.

My arms stop shaking straight away. I'm able to straighten, rather than lean to the side against the head of the bed, and my thoughts clear.

"And this," says Penna, handing me a second vial, this one filled with a shimmering blue liquid. She heals the wound on my head while saying, "It will boost your energy, but you will crash hard after three or four hours."

The pink liquid fooled me. When I drink the blue potion in one gulp, I choke on the bitterness.

"Did you expect honeyed mead?" Penna laughs. "This one will work in a moment. You are free to leave once you feel the effects." She turns to Wyn. "Can I help with anything else?"

Wyn shakes her head. "We're okay. Thank you for this. Go enjoy what remains of your night." She hesitates before adding, "But be on alert. We may need you at some point."

"It is clear you lot are up to something. I will remain here tonight."

A rush of energy crashes through me in a wave. It fills me with a tingling, cool sensation that begs me to move. I leap from the bed and jump from foot to foot. "We should get going, Wyn. Time is of the essence."

We bid goodnight to Penna after thanking her again, then walk the short distance from the infirmary to the weapons room, where the males are just finishing loading their leathers with daggers, swords, and axes.

"We're really doing this, then?" Wyn asks. "We're going to fight Nyree and the other Ill-fated?"

"We can't let her take the relic, Wyn," says Torin.

Wyn doesn't say anything more and slides daggers into the inbuilt sheathes of her leather pants. Though she will fight with us, there's a small frown playing on her full lips. It cannot be easy to realise someone you have always thought to be a friend is, in fact, your enemy.

I move to the far wall, the one that gleams with every type of dagger imaginable, and start plucking blades from their hooks and sliding them into my leathers. I try not to think of what we're doing tonight. Even so, the thoughts invade my mind.

Fighting is not something I wish to partake in, but to save Dusk and the humans, I will do it. My hands will be heavy with red, but the safety of this court is more important than the sanctuary of my mind. Preventing the Ill-fated from taking that relic saves more lives than we will take in defending our court. I just have to remember that once the night is through.

Images of the Summer fae in the rotunda flash across my mind's eye, reminders of what I did to ensure my safety. If I can live through the nightmares that haunt me after that... Perhaps I cannot move past it this time. The horrors that will haunt me after tonight will be worse. Of that, I am certain.

I think of Nyree, and how her pearlescent hair will shine with red if she so much as touches the relic. Vander will not let her betrayal go unpunished, even after centuries of knowing her.

Red, red, red.

Dusk will be bathed in it.

Vander's face looms before me. "Breathe."

I had not realised I had frozen while collecting another dagger from the wall. My eyes drift to my pale fingers wrapped around the black hilt, and all I can see is red. It's funny how my thoughts can overcome me at random moments, funny how I can be fine, then change in a heartbeat.

"Can we do this without violence?" I whisper. My tear-filled eyes find Vander's face.

Understanding crosses his features. "They won't give up without a fight. If you wish to sit this out, we'll understand."

"And wait in my room wondering what has happened, wondering if I could have helped?" I shake my head. "I want to be there, I just... Everything is red again. It's all I can see."

"Breathe," he repeats. He tucks a strand of copper behind my right ear. "You're strong enough for this. Just remember what you're fighting for."

I nod along with his words. "For Dusk and the humans. For Wyn and Torin and you. I'm fighting for my family."

"That's right. And tonight, your family needs you to be strong. If you need to break down, I will stand with you and hold you while you cry. *After* we secure the relic. I will stand with you, Princess."

Chapter 25

WE MOVE TOGETHER THROUGH the terrace floor, all of us tense. We are four fae dressed in leathers, each of us with too many blades strapped to our bodies. Though the manor is silent in the heart of the night, I know the rooms on either side of the hallway to host sleeping fae. We do not wake them, and we do not call for the Dusk army to gather.

If we can secure the relic and banish the Ill-fated without word spreading... It is the best outcome. If the denizens hear of this betrayal, a wave of panic will pass over the island.

The ground level is much the same: silent. It's eerie to wander through the dark and quiet hallways, and my magic thrums in response.

"How many Ill-fated live here?" I ask as we approach the exit.

"Eleven," says Torin. "Five of them female."

"You should know," says Wyn. She jabs her elbow into his ribs. "You've taken them all to bed at least once."

Torin grins. "Was worth the effort, too."

I cannot help but smile, even with anxiety thrumming through me. If Torin can still joke during such a time, I believe all will be well. He trusts in his magic, his skill, and his friends, and I should, too.

When we step into the night air, a cool breeze wraps around us. The middle of the year is creeping up on us, and winter will be here in a matter of months. It will work to our advantage if deadly battles fall upon the land now that the season's namesake is our ally.

True to my word, I do not think of crimson as we descend the manor's sloping hill. I push every negative thought and emotion to the far reaches of my mind, ready to overwhelm me at a later time.

"Bria." Torin's single word is a command.

I pull on the threads of my animalistic powers and search for a bird sleeping in the she-oak forest to our south. It does not take long for me to find a small blackbird; I don't hesitate to send my soul across the land until I am looking through its beady, sleepy eyes.

I stretch my wings out wide and launch into the sky from the highest branch of a pine. The crisp air is delightful against my sleek feathers as I rise higher, my body blending with the night. Dense clouds hide the stars, and there's a kind of pressure in the air I could not feel in my fae body. A storm is on the way.

Banking east, my sharp eyesight finds the lone mountain ash tree with ease. The centre of the island is empty of anything but the tree. None of the Ill-fated are running for the relic or sprinting home after retrieving it. I twist to the west, searching along the dirt path I know leads to a row of houses on the northern shore, homes that are owned by Nyree's fae.

That's when I spot them. Eleven fae dressed in leathers and black cloaks with their hoods drawn. Gleaming blades shine from their bodies, revealed with every swish of a cloak, and there's one male among them with a longbow.

I guide the blackbird's body to the wide branch of a pine, encourage it to return to slumber, and send my soul back to its rightful body.

I come to with a gasp. "They're on the way. Halfway between the Ill-fated village and the tree."

Vander, who has his arm wrapped around my waist to hold me upright, says, "The timing will be close. They may make it there before us."

"Are they armed?" asks Torin.

I nod. "Mainly swords. Some daggers. One archer."

"Then we run," says Vander. He turns towards me. "Are you ready?"

I search his eyes, finding nothing but trust and determination. I dip my chin. "Let's save our court."

Something akin to pride flashes across his face before he releases me and turns to the east. It stuns me for a moment, that look. And I have to force my legs to move and follow him. I remind myself he has been ignoring me for the past four days and make myself believe the look was one of relief that I'm fighting for the safety of his court.

"Remember," says Vander, "only use illusions as a last defence. The energy needed isn't worth it if we can win with weapons and wind."

Vander takes the lead. I'm the slowest and take the rear. While we run, I replay his words from the armoury. I'm strong enough for this. What we're fighting for is worth it.

Breathe.

Breathe through the red and the anguish.

The mountain ash looms ahead just as my thighs begin to ache, and I welcome the sight of the lone tree. No one knows why it grows alone. Perhaps, long ago, this tree served as a kind of meeting place or the site of a different strengthening relic. Perhaps we may never know why this tree is here.

To our left, the group of eleven Ill-fated close in, the fae in the lead already at the long, exposed roots that stretch towards the ground. We're not going to make it in time.

I grope for my metal bending power and tease four ribbons of silver free. The magic thrashes with glee as I send it to my palms. I skid to a stop and focus on the power, allowing the others to race ahead without me. My skill with daggers and swords is nowhere near ready to test in a real world fight, and my help is best given from afar.

Before I can close my eyes and focus on the specks of light that are the swords and daggers, Vander, Torin, and Wyn meet the Ill-fated.

Nyree shouts in rage and draws a sword of her own while commanding her followers to attack. Her short blade won't do much against Torin's dual long swords or Vander's axe. The thought should make me glad, but all I feel is remorse. Remorse that I could not prevent this. Guilt that I didn't try harder to make the others see Nyree's true colours. For if I gave her a colour, it would be crimson.

Wyn screams, her body contorting though there's no one near her.

Torin twirls both swords and arcs them through the air, one of them slicing along the thigh of an Ill-fated male.

Wyn stops screaming.

I remember the Ill-fated are Night fae with power over blood and bone, and suddenly I wish for nothing more than to run. I could make it to the edge of the wards before anyone caught me.

Before I can so much as turn and set a foot down, I remind myself that I always run. I ran to Nikolai when Father declared me ready for mating, and Nikolai refused to flee with me. It broke my heart. I ran to the forest after Tohminic attacked me in the gardens, only to have an ogre almost squeeze me to death. I have spent my life running, and it has never proved to benefit me or anyone else.

No longer. I will not run from my problems any longer. Vander's right. I *am* strong, and I *can* do this.

Wyn sends powerful gusts of air in every direction, and I watch in horrified awe as a female tumbles backwards and rolls down the hill. Her head slams against a protruding rock halfway down. She does not move once she reaches the bottom.

An arrow whizzes through the air, grazing against Vander's cheek but not causing major damage. Even from here, I can see the dribble of red that trickles to his jaw and disappears in the scruff lining his chin.

Torin is locked in a duel with two males, somehow meeting each of their attacks with a clang of metal.

I force my eyes closed at the sight of Vander slamming his axe into the forehead of a male — though blocking the image does little to deaden the sound of the male's cries — and focus on the power within me.

Dozens of lights ignite in my mind, each of them a sword, dagger, axe, or arrowhead. Once I have a grip on where the weapons are, I open my eyes. The flashes of light remain. I pull on every dagger the Ill-fated wear and pull them from their sheaths. They hurtle through the air towards me, but I bring them to a stop when they are halfway across the small clearing atop the hill.

I turn them. All of them. Towards a retreating female.

Ten daggers race for her and imbed in her legs before she even knows what's happening. I do not waste time by waiting to see how injured she is. I can determine such a thing later, when my friends aren't in danger.

Our enemies realise what I have done within a heartbeat, and Nyree calls for them to retreat. Her scream rings out through the night as if no other sound exists.

Four of her followers are writhing on the ground in pain, but the remaining six turn and run.

I watch as if in slow motion as Wyn, with her face screwed in anger, throws two daggers at Nyree's back. Her throw is hard, and her aim is true. Both blades sink into Nyree's flesh with dull thuds.

Nyree's keening cry will forever be etched into my memories. Although her injury is severe, the leader of the Ill-fated does not stop running.

Not when Torin's sword pierces the heart of another female. Not when he pulls his sword free and spins, the bloodied blade severing the arm of a male who Vander has just struck in the neck with his axe. She does not stop for the cries of her fae, but runs for her life like the coward she is.

I'm about to pull my wide eyes from Vander's axe when I see a female creep up behind him with her sword raised.

"Not on my watch, bitch." My words are a venomous mutter as I yank on my power and steal the sword right from her hands.

Her eyes widen and jerk in my direction. She spins as if she can outrun two Dusk fae, a hybrid Night and Dusk, and me. She is the only Ill-fated who remains on this hill of blood and gore and power.

How dare she approach Vander from behind. My twin soul, the male I love with all my heart, will not fall victim to a sneak attack tonight. Blinding rage obscures my every sense, and something within me snaps.

I wrap my magic tighter around the sword I still have in my grip. The blade turns mid-air before sinking into the female's stomach with a squelch. The wound will not kill her, not if she finds a healer before the Mother Star appears on the eastern horizon.

This is how I fight. I cannot stand to end the life of another, but I can injure our enemies to the point they cannot fight back. I can help to turn the tides of this war without sacrificing a moral of my own, a belief that all life is equal and murder is wrong.

When the female I impaled turns and runs, still with the sword jutting from the side of her stomach, I race for the hill.

"I know you said to stay by your side," I rush to say before Vander can scold me, "but I thought my skills lie elsewhere. If I were here fighting sword with sword, I would only have been a hinderance."

He brushes a thumb across my cheek. "You did well, Princess. So well."

I cup his face, but instead of the gentle caress I wish to give, I grip harder and force his head to turn to the side so I can see the wound on his cheek.

"It's just a graze." His voice is strained.

"I'll be the judge of that."

I don't release him until I'm certain he's right. It is just a graze. His fae body will heal it before the Mother Star is at her highest and brightest. Still, I had to be sure.

"What now?" Wyn asks as she collects fallen weapons from the grass.

Torin pulls an arrow free from his arm and tosses it aside. "Now we retaliate. At least five got away with minor injuries. Two with severe wounds."

"And the other four?" I dare to ask.

"Dead."

I'm not brave enough to ask about the injuries that caused the deaths. I'm more comfortable believing the wounds I inflicted were not so terrible they cannot be healed. Instead I ask, "And the relic?"

Vander pulls away from my tight grip and moves to inspect the tree, but my metal bending magic is still coursing into my palms, so I search the surrounding area for any hint of atryxium. It flashes in bursts of blue-grey from within the hollow of the mountain ash. It's duller than it would normally be, given the atryxium is now a part of the relic.

"No need to check. I can feel it in there. It's safe," I say.

He turns to me with his brow raised. "You can feel the metal, even though it has been absorbed into everything else?"

I shrug. "Atryxium is the strongest, rarest metal in Radelea. It's essence is just as strong."

"What do we do now?" Wyn repeats.

"Now, we take me to that lovely female in our infirmary," groans Torin. He has a hand pressed against his upper arm where he pulled the arrow free. "It's been too long since I graced Penna with my presence."

I arch a brow at him. "Are you sure that's the only reason you need to see her?" I make a pointed look at the blood seeping between his fingers.

"Of course." He gives me one of his signature smirks, then a wink. A dreamy look crosses his face. "I'll have to take my leathers off."

The laugh that bursts from my mouth is loud. "How do you not know she prefers females?"

His face falls, and I laugh harder. "Are you serious?" he asks as we head back to the manor. "You mean if she sets those brilliant blue eyes on all this" — he waves his free hand over his lean muscles — "she'll *pass it up*?"

"She has her preferences, just as you have yours," says Wyn. "Maybe Alizeh is free tonight?"

Torin's eyes brighten.

Wyn goes on ahead to rouse several guards to keep watch over the mountain ash, leaving me to deal with a heartbroken and injured Torin, and a contemplative Vander. He keeps shooting strange glances my way, but whenever I assess our bond to determine what he's feeling, it's a jumble of confused thoughts and conflicting emotions, so I leave it be.

Chapter 26

V ANDER AND I WALK through the manor together after leaving Torin in the infirmary, and it's clear something is bothering him.

The horizon is just beginning to lighten, but I will not make it through the hour, even to eat. The energy booster Penna gave me is wearing off, and I wish for nothing more than a soft bed, warm blankets, and hours of sleep.

"What's wrong?" I ask Vander, gripping his arm once we're off the stairs and entering the hallway to his bedchambers.

He pauses and looks at my hand. A shudder runs through him. It's clear from his expression he is warring within himself, and I give him the time to consider what he wants to say. Waiting isn't my strong suit, but I give him that because I can feel that he needs it. He needs the moment to collect himself. To breathe, as he so often tells me to.

Prying into his emotions feels like overstepping a boundary, but the uncertainty and frustration pulsing along our bond is too strong to ignore. There's something else entwined with the two feelings, something I cannot put my finger on.

I try to be patient. Although when several moments pass and he has not said a word — or even dragged his eyes from where my hand still rests on his arm — I have to try again.

"Vander?" I slide my hand down his arm and grip his hand with every intention of turning him until he's facing me. "This is obviously difficult for you. I... I request permission to travel to the Day Court, where I might uncover a way to sever our bond."

In a move too fast to track, he twists and pins me against the wall. One hand braces above my head, and the other grips my hip in a tight hold. His fingers press into my skin as if he can't control them.

"I told you I wasn't interested in love. You know my reasons, yet you let your emotions run rampant."

"What are you talking about?"

"When I discovered she had drugged you with blue mock."

The memory crashes into my mind. I was... influenced by his touch. Just the memory of him running his thumb over my upper lip sends a pulse of bliss through me. "I can't help what I feel. And I do try. I know you don't want anything from me, and that's okay, but you can't honestly expect me to have that much control over my body?"

"It's not that I don't want you. The Mother Star knows I do."

My heart races at his admission. I have always believed he doesn't want me. His reasons for ignoring me are something else altogether, and if I can just discover what they are... "Then what is it? Why do you ignore what you're feeling?"

His glorious silver eyes flare. "Because I'm frightened. I have lost enough in this life to last several more. Why do you think

I'm fighting so hard for my court? I can't stand to lose anything, or anyone, else."

He leans closer, so close I could reach up and brush my lips over his if I wished. But this needs to be his decision. I can't force it on him, and I cannot influence his emotions. So I push all my thoughts away so they won't filter into Vander's.

"We're at war, Van." I keep my tone calm. "Death is inevitable. Do you want to spend the rest of your days fearing loss, or do you want to *live*? I know I'd rather enjoy what time I have left. I'd rather show those I love just how much I need them."

The indecision is clear in his eyes. "And if we're not right for each other? If we do this and fail?"

I meet his gaze. "Fear does more damage than failure ever will."

I feel like I'm fighting to convince him, and that's not what I want. I can't coerce him into giving in to his feelings, and I cannot use sweet words to encourage him to make a move.

Vander fears loss. He has every right to that fear.

I move to twist from his hold, but the hand holding my hip tightens, and he pulls me against him. Our eyes lock, silver and green, and his breaths turn harsh. The hairs on my arms prickle and rise, and the scent of home swells as his magic thrashes around us. Pine, cedar, the ocean's salt, and a sweet musk. I love everything about his scent.

My fingers ache with the need to touch him, but I keep my hands loose at my sides and fight the urge. "Vander." His name is but a whisper on my lips.

"I can feel your desire to leave," he says, his tongue darting out to wet his lips. "You don't want to influence me with your words and emotions. It's a little late for that." He keeps eye contact and lowers his face slowly.

Remaining still is the most difficult thing I have done, yet I manage it.

He brushes his nose against my throat and inhales. His masculine groan sends a shiver dancing down my spine. His eyes meet mine once more. "I have thought of you every night since I first realised we had a mental connection." He drags me with him while he walks backwards, but I don't dare take my eyes off his to see where he's leading me. "I lie awake wondering if you're brave enough to pleasure yourself like that again, and whether you thought of me when you touched yourself."

All my inhibitions disappear the moment we enter his bedchamber. Our bodies are so close together, not a breath of Vander's wind could flutter between us.

"I was thinking of you," I say, my voice husky. "Yes, I touched myself to the image of you pinned beneath me. Yes, I enjoyed it. But my touch was nothing, *nothing*, compared to what I felt from your end. Even then, you desired me."

"Maybe the bond we share is ruling my actions, or maybe you're just too alluring to resist," he says as he slams the door behind us. "I don't give a damn if this ruins me. I'm all in, Princess."

My shadows whip out from my palms and swirl around us. They flutter on Vander's breeze and tangle with his wind, entwining and caressing in tongues of darkness.

It's becoming more and more difficult to hold myself back. Every fibre of my being yearns to touch him. I need to feel his soft brown skin beneath my fingertips, to relish in the stubble on his chin and the curve of his muscular arms.

My lips part. I clench my thighs.

"Don't say it unless you're sure. I'm not a female who lets go of things easily. If you tell me you're all in, you must mean it. Because if you mean it..." I lose the fight with my hands and drag them up his chest until I'm cupping his face. "You're mine, Vander Theron, and I won't ever let you go."

His wind blows harder; the drapes framing the window ripple. With my hands still gripping his face, he leans down and grazes his teeth over my earlobe and whispers, "Fuck fearing loss. Fuck being ruined. I'm all in, Bria."

I pull back and search his blazing eyes for any sign of hesitation. Using my name for the first time since we met should be sign enough, but I don't believe his words until I see the sincerity and burning desire swirling within the silver. A whimper tears from my throat.

Our mouths crash together.

His lips are soft against mine as he coaxes my mouth open. Our shared breath heats the miniscule space between us, and our hearts pound together as our hands grope for buckles and clasps.

I flick my tongue along the curve of his bottom lip, tasting the remnants of his evening brandy, but only for a mere moment before he slants his mouth over mine and captures my every breath.

All I know is Vander.

Our magic roils and crashes through the room, weaving threads of destruction and chaos I pay no mind to. I snag a ribbon of metal bending power and wrap it around every weapon on our bodies, then discard the blades on the wooden dresser in the corner.

He pushes me back, and I bump into the exposed brick wall. He lifts a lazy hand, and a patch of dense air caresses the tender flesh of my throat before pinching my leathers and dragging them down my body.

Though he is only touching me with his magic, I have never been more aroused. I'm panting, my eyes never leaving his and his never leaving mine as he undresses me with his power. The dampness between my legs only increases when a whisper of wind grazes across my bare legs and blows against my throbbing clitoris.

He guides the air to my swollen nipples, where it flicks against the sensitive buds until I'm moaning with desire. "So beautiful," he says, his voice rough and seductive. His eyes greedily drink in every part of my naked body, from my parted lips to my full breasts, from the gooseflesh covering my arms to the glistening moisture between my legs.

I can take it no longer. I grope at his leather jacket and drag the zipper down in one rough pull, revealing the smooth skin of his chest. His arms are not even free before I run my palms over the dips and grooves of his defined abdominal muscles. I can only liken the softness of his skin to the finest of silks, and I yearn to trail kisses from neck to hip. My fingers slip beneath the leather of his pants and yank them down. His erection springs free, delicious in size and throbbing for me. I follow the path of my hands with soft kisses and flicks of my tongue until I'm kneeling before him and looking up at him through hooded eyes.

"Bria," he warns, though he fists a hand in my hair. "I want to take my time with you. If you continue to —"

I draw him into my mouth with a deep groan, taking him deeper and deeper until I feel him at the back of my throat.

"Fuck," he hisses, sliding his other hand into my hair to join the first. The strands pull a little, but the pressure is both welcome and delightful. Air, in the shape of a hand, trails down my stomach, leaving a scorching fire in its wake. My eyes roll back, and I moan around his cock when his magic strokes my clitoris.

I wrap my hand around his hard length as I drag my mouth back to the tip, flicking my tongue over the bead of salty liquid gathered there. "I have waited so long for this, Van. We have all the time in the world to savour one another, but right now... Right now I need you."

"As you command." He roughly pulls me to my feet and throws me onto the bed. He's on top of me in one heartbeat, and driving into me in the next. One powerful thrust is all it takes to have me quivering beneath him. Our roiling magic tears at the walls, the drapes, the ceiling, and we both ignore the destruction of the room.

He fills me with such perfection, I feel every throbbing vein. It's a fullness I will never tire of, even once I have passed from this life. To feel his bare chest against mine, to have my legs pressed against his silken skin... It's desire and pleasure, and it completes me.

Vander wraps a hand around my thigh and lifts my leg until it rests on his shoulder, and just the sight of my pale skin against his golden glow and the bulging muscles of his arms is enough to send a fierce pulse of ecstasy tearing through me.

I press a hand to the nape of his neck and drag his head down until I can reach his mouth. My other hand has a vice grip on his waist, pulling and pushing with him while he thrusts. I slip my tongue between his lips and open myself up to him.

Adoration and fierce protectiveness surge through our bond from his end, almost shattering me here and now. I send pulses of respect and love back to him, struggling to think clearly through the throbbing bliss building in my core.

I already love this male. Every time our bodies collide, and every glide of skin against skin fills my heart with joy. There's a sadness there, too, though. A pang of regret that we do not have the chance to worship one another, as we both deserve. If I could devote all the time in the world to pleasuring Vander, I think I would.

He pulls back, those silver eyes intent on my face. "I want to look at you while you scream my name." Vander's strained voice mingles with our ragged pants.

My mouth pops open when he angles his hips and takes me deeper. The swollen head of his cock hits that sweet spot inside, and my limbs shake from both exertion and ecstasy. The sound I make is unlike anything I have heard. It's primal, animalistic. It is pure.

His pace increases, his thrusts becoming wonderfully rougher. Beads of sweat form on his forehead. It's the sexiest sight known to fae kind. His wind and my shadows thrash through the room, whistling and humming in sync.

A blazing fire swells inside me as I rock against his rhythm, building and building until my core tightens to the point of agony. I never thought I would experience an orgasm so overwhelming I would scream a male's name, but scream I do.

"Vander!"

I clench hard around him as my orgasm rips through my body, and cling to his shoulders for dear life. Wave upon wave of bliss curls my toes. I throw my head into the pillow but keep my eyes on my High Lord.

Even through the aftershocks, I make myself watch him come undone. He jerks his hips with no obvious rhythm and groans as he loses himself in me. As the Mother Star rises and shines her light upon a new day, Vander and I cement our bond for all eternity.

We both feel the moment our souls collide. It's a deep knowing, a prickle of pain, a blanket of ice, and a raging fire all at once. He's there. He is in my mind and soul. His thoughts, his emotions, his words... I am Vander, and Vander is me.

Chapter
27

M Y ENTIRE BODY ACHES when I wake. My arms are heavy, my legs are numb, my thoughts are sluggish, and there's a smile curving my lips. Memories of giving myself to Vander flood in, creating a very welcome waking dream.

"You're awake." He speaks straight into my mind, though he is not beside me in the enormous bed.

I know the mind link is a part of the twin soul bond we share, but even that knowledge could not prepare me for the absurdity of it. I can hear him as if he is right next to me, and I am sure it will be difficult to tell if he's truly speaking or whispering into my thoughts when we are together.

Replying is easy. I only have to grasp the golden thread of our bond and send a thought towards him. *"Yes. Where are you?"*

"On my way."

The way he says it... My smile grows wider. Waking up to those memories, then spending hours tangled in bed with him is a kind of happiness I never thought I would have. With anyone.

I climb out of bed, pull a woollen blanket free, and wrap it around me as I stand at the window and look out over the eastern shore of Dusk. The view from Vander's bedchamber is breathtaking. Four guards patrol the lone mountain ash. The sea where I fell overboard on Zentha's ship is calm. The distant land mass that I know to be the border of Autumn and Summer is bright in the mid-morning light.

Either I have not slept for long, and Penna will scold me, or I have slept for more than a day. The latter is more likely, given the stiffness of my limbs.

"It's about time you got out of bed," says Vander from the door.

I turn and smile. "How long was I asleep?"

"A day and a half." He saunters over and tucks me into the curve of his shoulder, both of us looking out over our home court. "How are you feeling?"

"Well rested. Is there news of Nyree and the other Ill-fated who got away?"

"No. We assume they've fled to another court. Night or Summer, we're not sure. We have scouts looking for them, and Torin's listening for whispers." He hesitates for a moment, and I urge him to continue. His next words make every thought of losing myself in Vander disappear faster than they came. "Torin and Wyn know we have been intimate."

All the blood drains from my face. Torin will be unbearable. "You told them?"

"I had no choice. Wyn went to check on you in your room. When you weren't there, she was ready to storm the entire court to find you. She was rather smug when I told her where you were. Expect questions. Not to mention, we were not exactly quiet."

I tilt my face to see him and fight the urge to kiss the length of his jaw. "You don't mind if I answer Wyn's questions?"

He cringes, but says, "You have to talk to someone. I have long since learned females have an ingrained need to gossip. Without it, they may just explode." He smirks.

I nudge him with my shoulder. "I don't have to tell her anything if it makes you uncomfortable. But Van? What are we?"

"There's no word for it," he says, dragging his gaze back to the landscape. "I suppose you could call it a mate bond, to save tedious explanations?"

I follow his line of sight and watch as the guards at the mountain ash are replaced by four others. "Mates." I test the word. "You don't regret it?"

"I spent months ignoring what I felt, determined to believe the emotions were either yours or a product of our twin souls. I realised I was mistaken when you attacked that female who was sneaking up behind me. Because you were feeling relief, and all I could feel was a burning need to pleasure you as thanks."

"There's time," I say with a smirk.

Torin disagrees. He bangs his fist on the door before letting himself in. "You'll have time to get better acquainted with Van's spitting lizard later, Bria." He waggles his eyebrows before turning to Vander. "We should get going."

I groan. "Please don't refer to it as that."

His eyes flash with mirth. "As what, a spitting lizard?"

"Go get dressed. I'll deal with this fool before we head to the human realm." Upon seeing the question in my eyes, he adds, "We decided it's time to alert them to what's happening in Radelea. If Nyree and whoever she's working for are attempting to infiltrate Earth like we believe, the humans need to prepare themselves. You can stay here, if you wish."

I shake my head. "No. I want to come. Seeing what we're fighting for will help me move past things."

Torin calls after me when I slip past him, still wearing the blanket from Vander's bed. "Why not stay? I'm only just getting started."

I think every fae inside the manor hears me groan, perhaps even those in the stables outside. They also hear the thud of Vander's first against Torin's ribs. I walk away smiling wider than I have in moons.

❦ ❦

Entering the tunnel below the war room makes my chest constrict with pain. There's something about the confined space and darkness that makes my skin crawl after waking up down here on my own.

I remind myself to breathe. Vander came for me without question. The walls are not closing in as I fear they are. If I can overcome a moment of panic about drowning, then I can overcome this.

Vander is at my back, and from his insistence he walks behind me rather than beside me, I fear his actions are being ruled by the bond. It's well known that mates are protective of one another, but what of twin souls who fall in love? It is something to keep in mind if I ever fall victim to the bond's demands.

Approaching the shimmering curtain of water that is the portal takes less time than I remember, but once again, I marvel at the sight. The gleaming waterfall — still with no sound, no beginning, and no end — is a rainbow of colours that begs me to step closer.

Wyn and Torin disappear beyond the veil without slowing their pace, leaving Vander and me alone.

"How do I do it?" I ask. "You guided me through last time."

"I can guide you again."

Linking my fingers through his feels as natural as breathing. "I'd still like to know how to step through on my own, just in case."

"Think of the alleyway in which we enter, and only that alleyway. It's just like folding."

Green, blue, red, purple, the mirage of colours is forever changing. We step through the veil together; the void pulling at me like I'm folding. My skin is too tight and too loose, my limbs lock in place, and my chest tightens. All I know is darkness and the feel of my hand joined with Vander's. It's over before the panic sets in, and we are soon standing in an alleyway beside a tall brick building and placing glamours over our pointed ears.

We're moving onto the street within heartbeats. Having only stepped foot outside the alley once, I don't know where to look first. The humans are extraordinary with their advancements.

The towering buildings are just as intimidating a second time, and my metal bending power thrums with all the steel. "How marvellous," I say when we pass a low but wide building of seven floors. "Their dwellings are all made of metal. And a lot of humans have metal *in* their bodies."

"They call them piercings. Some have them in their eyebrows, belly buttons, even their tongues," says Wyn. "We explained this last time."

"I once met a female who had both nipples pierced," says Torin.

Of course he did.

"I remember from last time," I tell Wyn, ignoring Torin's remark, "but I didn't think so many of them would enjoy it."

"Wait until you hear about tattoos," says Torin with a wink. "They draw on their skin with ink. It's *permanent*."

I don't have time to question him further.

"We're here," says Vander, waving to an ivory building across the street.

I cannot tell if it's two storeys or three, though both ends of the house are taller than the middle. The large pillars that mark the front are beautiful, and I wonder if we can construct a similar building in Dusk.

I'm about to voice my question when a harried-looking guard rushes towards us. "Sorry, folks, Parliament House is closed today for a private meeting. Move along."

A subtle breeze rushes past and into the gigantic building, and we all turn to Torin, who has his head cocked to the side. He's quiet for a moment while he listens to the whispers coming from within Parliament House, returning to him on a gust of air.

"It's a supernatural meeting," he says at last. "They're discussing us."

"Then we have a right to be there, *officer*," says Vander, turning back to the guard.

Looking closer, his pale blue shirt and dark pants differ from a typical guard uniform. He has weapons I have never seen, and there's a strange device with a curled cord attached to his shoulder. The emblem on his sleeve says he is a member of Victoria Police.

The officer rests his hand on a black device on his hip. It's clear he knows we're not of this world. "No can do, pal. Go back to where you came from."

Vander rolls his eyes. "I'm High Lord Vander Theron of the Dusk Court. Move aside of your own accord, or I'll move you myself."

The officer steps aside while using the corded device on his shoulder. He speaks into it, telling whoever is listening that we're forcing entry.

"How does that work?" I wonder out loud as we ascend the steps and enter Parliament House.

"Don't try to understand the technology here. It'll give you a headache," says Torin. "Through the vestibule and right at the main hall into the council chambers."

We follow his directions, with Vander in the lead. Two guards, this time dressed in smart black jackets and white shirts, attempt to restrain him, but he sends a gust of wind at each of them and they tumble through the hall. Pride and lust course through me as he slams a hand against each of the double doors and bursts into the room.

Gasps of surprise and outrage filter through the open doors.

"High Lord Vander of Dusk," he says, pausing on the threshold, "here to offer you warning of a war among the fae."

I step beside him. I'm immediately horrified.

Everything is red. Crimson.

The carpet, the cushioned bench seats, and the swivelling chairs in the middle of the room. Even the timber seems to be painted with a kind of reddish varnish.

Breathe.

In through my nose, out through my mouth. Again and again, until I can focus on the smaller details. Like the clear divide.

On the right, pale beings with pointed teeth, or with fur prickling along their forearms, and a handful of normal-looking humans with vials strapped to their chests. On the left, humans dressed in business attire.

There are two humans standing at the head of the room, one a male with a kind but lined face, the other a severe female with bulging muscles. The head of the humans and leader of the supernaturals.

"Explain," says the female. She does not offer her name.

Vander takes three steps into the room, flanked by Wyn and Torin, though I remain slightly behind them. I can stand to be here, but I cannot force myself to enter the red room.

"We are at war," he says. "It all began with the reveal of my court, a land of air and illusion wielders. Several of the other high fae thought to claim my land for themselves, which resulted in my mate's capture by the High Lord of Summer."

"What does it have to do with us?" she asks, flexing her biceps. A flash of ebony fur runs along her arms and disappears beneath the tight shirt she wears.

"The Dusk fae have spent millennia protecting the portal to the human realm," says Wyn. "A portal that our enemies have uncovered. We don't know what they want with you, but assume their reasons are nefarious. This is a warning we're happy to give, so you may prepare."

"We have fought on your behalf, protecting you with great risk to ourselves. But we're not sure we can continue to do so," says Torin.

The human leader leans forward. "How do we know you're telling the truth?"

"Fae cannot lie," says Vander.

I whisper along our bond, *"But that is a lie."*

"A necessity. Protecting ourselves is more important than protecting the humans. If they trust our word, things will be easier."

"Why not just hand over the woman?" asks a male with pointed teeth.

Vander pins him with a glare, but it is the male with fur on his arms beside his toothy companion who says, "You vampires are disgusting. No wonder the moon didn't grant you mate bonds. Mates are sacred, bloodsucker."

The vampire hisses. "And where is yours, wolf?"

The wolf snarls.

"Settle," says the female at the head of the room. I figure she's a wolf, too, or some other type of shifter. Her eyes glow a bright amber. "Premier, what are your thoughts?"

The male beside her straightens his open jacket. "Close the portal. We want nothing to do with a war in Faerie."

"Faerie?" I ask Vander.

"What the humans call Radelea." Out loud, he says, "Will you not consider allowing our species to mingle?"

"Not this again," says the shifter female. "We've already told you we're not interested in letting fae on Earth. We have enough tension with the vampires and wolves at war." She pins the two males from earlier with a glare.

The premier says, "Your lot has caused enough damage, breaking into our police headquarters and trying to steal weapons. We don't make deals with thieves."

So Nyree did not wish to invade the human realm. She merely wanted their weapons.

"This is news to me," says Vander.

The premier waves a hand. "A woman with glowing white hair led a group of ten. It was as if they could read our thoughts, and they got away through sheer luck. It's why we're meeting today."

"Sounds like the Ill-fated," whispers Wyn. "I think we've made our point. If Nyree's stealing from the humans, they won't want anything to do with us. Besides, we have other things to worry about back home. Maude is moving, Van. We're wasting time here."

My mind spins with the revelation. Night is moving? To where? As much as I wish to contemplate the answers, I cannot focus on those thoughts while the shifter and premier are whispering to one another. From their scowls, whatever they're saying can't be good.

Torin nudges Vander with his elbow.

"You have been warned," says Vander.

He turns to exit, but the shifter female says, "If you or any creature like you enter Earth again, fae lord, we will consider it an act of war. Leave in peace today. But consider this *our* warning."

Chapter 28

"Tell me about the Night Court," I say, side-stepping a human female with black strings coming out of her ears.

"Torin has been keeping an ear open to their movements," says Wyn. "They've been more active since the Ill-fated showed their true colours."

Torin's greedy eyes follow the human female as he says, "They're gathering weapons and rousing their army. We don't know why."

"It's a little coincidental, don't you think?" I enter the alley behind Wyn. "Nyree tried to take the relic, then Night is on the move. Are you so certain they *chose* to remain in Dusk when High Lady Maude offered the Ill-fated a chance to return to their homes? Perhaps they have been working together all this time."

Vander growls from behind me. "It's a possibility." One that angers him. Rage flashes along our bond, burning hot and ice cold.

Torin enters the veil — it is a mere shimmer among the bricks — first. Once we're all in the tunnel beneath Dusk Manor, he says, "What other observations have you made that we've been too blind to see, Bria?"

"You've let her be a part of meetings in the war room. She knows every plan, every counter attack… She knows everything and she would have given that information to Maude if they're working together. Tohminic, too."

"So, we need to come up with a plan of attack she doesn't know about," says Wyn as she leads us down the tunnel. "We're back to square one."

"Fuck." Torin's expletive mirrors all our thoughts.

We're quiet while we make our way through the tunnel, up the ladder, and into the war room. If the Night fae are preparing for war, and the Ill-fated, who are Summer's allies, intend to fight with them, our chances of defending the human realm are slim. Though from the reactions of the supernaturals and humans, perhaps we should leave them to their fate.

The Summer fae can cause irreparable destruction, and with their undead and selkie armies, they're the largest force in Radelea. They will come from our east while Night and the Ill-fated come from our west, trapping us on an island.

"We need an escape route, should it come to that." I look at Vander, who is leaning over the map of Radelea. "Spring is yet to choose a side, but if Nyana joins forces with Tohminic and Maude, we'll have enemies on every side."

"Ruith has offered us sanctuary in Winter, but I don't think we should take the war there. The Winter fae would have the upper hand, but the terrain is treacherous. It's likely Night and Summer intend to surround us on this island, but if we move here," says Wyn, dragging a finger from the Bolbala Ranges to the dry mountains of Dawn, "it both buys us time and gives our healers a safe space to use their magic."

Torin leans on the table beside her. "We can't risk Dawn. If our enemies infiltrate their infirmary…"

"Jonik's armada needs to move. It's no use to us on the eastern shore. If they can sail to the south of us and hide among the cliffs and bays of Autumn, we can trap Summer," says Vander. He turns to me and asks, "Where does your brother stand?"

"Honestly? I'm not sure. He could go either way at this point. Do you want me to talk to him? I can go right now." I take a step towards the door.

He shakes his head and looks back at the map. "I don't think talking to him will help. If he hasn't already decided, he will soon. Spring, too. Everyone will be forced to show their hands by the next full moon."

"How many fae in the Night Court?" asks Wyn.

"Two hundred thousand," says Torin. "More than half of them ready and able to fight."

"Twice that for Summer. Then some, if you include the selkies," says Vander.

"Don't forget Tohminic's undead army. We would be fools to think he won't use them on the front line." My arm brushes against Vander's as I point to the western shore of Summer. "Getting them across the water will be his biggest obstacle. Can we have Jonik's armada watch these seas?"

"I'll send word right away," says Torin.

"I'll go," says Wyn. "You need to give Bria a lesson in Night fae. If they are planning to attack, she needs to be as prepared as possible."

Relief filters along the bond from Vander's end. Out loud, he says, "If you can teach her anything, teach her how to shield her mind."

Soon after, Torin and I are in the ground floor training room sitting opposite one another on the padded floor. The room is simple, with some kind of black foam covering the floorboards and walls, no windows, and only one door. There are no distractions, other than Vander checking in now and then to ensure I'm making progress.

Which I'm not.

"Imagine locking the hatch to your magic room, then cover that with a wall of atryxium. All imaginary, of course, but it's the best way I can describe how to block a mind reader," says Torin.

It is not the first time he's explained how to shield my thoughts from the Night fae, but no matter how many times I try, my metal bending power won't let me place the wall. It bursts out and crackles in my palms — we removed all our blades after one instance of my magic almost cutting through Torin's long hair — before slashing across the room like whip trying to find something to grasp.

"I must be doing something wrong. My shadows and animalistic magic don't mind the wall, but the metal bending power hates it," I say. "There's no way I can block the hatch."

He ties his hair back with a length of dark leather. "It has to be the atryxium. Try a weaker metal, though make sure it's still strong enough to shield your mind. Maybe —" He pauses and tilts his head to the side, then frowns. His frown grows deeper, more pronounced until anger contorts his soft features.

I wet my dry lips to ease the discomfort. My gaze flicks to the closed door as if it holds all the answers. The longer he's quiet, the more my heart races. "What is it? What does the wind say?"

He straightens; his face drains of colour, and his voice is a grating whisper when he says, "They're coming." He leaps to his feet and races for the door. "Night and the Ill-fated, they're coming."

"What does it mean, Torin?" I need him to say it. I won't believe it until he utters the words.

He looks back at me, the tension in his shoulders building. "We're at war."

"Fuck." It's the first time I've used the vulgar human word. I believe it's called for.

We sprint through the manor, then tear into the war room where Vander, Wyn, and the Dawn triplets are gathered.

Tasar, Ulakas, and Larrad arrived mere moments ago, it seems — they're still wearing their travelling cloaks, though the leathers and armour beneath say the trio are ready for battle. They must have folded here after Wyn sent word to move their armada.

"Zentha will be here any moment," says Wyn. She looks over her shoulder to face us, and freezes. "What's wrong?"

Everyone stills.

"They're coming." Torin's two words send a lick of fear through the room that leaves no one untouched. "We have hours."

"Wyn, call the army to the training grounds," says Vander. "If any do not wish to join us in defending our court, do not force them. Torin, as commander of my army, I expect you to keep them all calm until I arrive. I'm counting on you to have a plan."

Wyn rushes out the door without a word.

Torin follows behind, and the severity of the situation hits me when he doesn't make a smart remark.

"What can we do to help?" Tasar and Ulakas ask at once.

Larrad says, "I never trusted that Ill-fated bitch."

"Your father is commandeering the armada?" Vander asks.

Larrad nods, his silky black hair rippling with the movement. "He is, though it will be many moons before the ships can join the battle. Is there a way to delay the Night Court?"

"Nyree would have told them where to fold onto the island," says Vander. He runs a hand over his short hair. "Trusting her was a mistake we may never recover from."

"You can't change the past, Van. We just have to deal with the hand the Mother Star dealt us," I say.

He turns to the triplets. "Can you have as many fae as you can fold into Dusk? Our numbers are too small, especially if Summer and Autumn join Night and the Ill-fated. One of you fold to Winter and warn Ruith we'll be sending the vulnerable to Kol."

"We will do whatever we can," says Larrad.

Vander looks back to me, and we stare at one another for a long moment, ignoring the Dawn triplets as they leave. In that look is everything we don't have time to say. It's a look that conveys a fear of the future, regret we didn't find each other sooner, and a bittersweet goodbye.

"Run," he says. *"Run, Princess, and never look back."*

I cup his face and press my forehead against his. *"I'm not leaving you. We do this together. Fight or run, it's your choice, but we stay together. Swear it to me."*

His eyes flick between mine, and his emotions war within him. I see the moment he decides. *"We fight."*

"We fight, and we win."

⁂

The training field is full of fae. Dusk is a court of fifty thousand, with forty of those air and illusion wielders able to fight. The remaining ten thousand, those too young or frail to wield a sword, are here to farewell their friends and family. It's heartbreaking to see so many younglings with tears staining their cheeks as they farewell their mother or father, grandparent, or whoever else they love who is preparing for battle.

Mates stand with their heads bent together, and I hold Vander's hand a little tighter, the same fear coursing through me that courses through the veins of every fae here. Fear. It's a horrible feeling, but a necessary one.

Without fear, we are without care. We fear this war because we have so much to lose; we have so much we cherish that losing those treasured connections will cause more damage than the wounds of combat ever could. No, it is not our enemies we fear. It's loss. It's destruction. We fear life after the war, because we do not know how many of our loved ones will be here, we don't know if we'll have homes to come back to, and we don't know if the Dusk Court will still stand when the day is through.

The unknown is a fear every fae shares.

I cannot help but marvel at our denizens. As I stand here clasping Vander's hand, I am in awe of the love here. When this same army surrounded Ad'Starrag and the Summer fae realised we were about to fight, there were no teary farewells among the fire wielders, no heartfelt pleas to be safe, and no children begging their parents to go with them to safety. Our two courts couldn't be more different, and I couldn't be prouder to belong to Dusk.

"It's time." Vander's voice is soft, but a whisper of wind carries the two words over the training field, where it reaches every pointed ear.

The fae offer a last goodbye to their loved ones, and those too young or weak or vulnerable to fight gather to the left of the field.

Van continues. "High Lord Ruith will protect our loved ones. You have my word. May the Mother Star bless your journey and watch over you."

One by one, the fae travelling to Winter fold. Vander has lifted the wards around the training field for this moment, and will replace them after the war. It's a risk, but a necessary one. A ripple of magic travels across the field, sending dust curling into the sky, and fizzles out on the grassy plain beyond. The choked sobs that fill the otherwise quiet space make my heart clench.

"Was it like this when you came to Summer for me?" I ask Vander.

"No. We took only half of our army then. This time it feels more... final. Like we could lose everything if we don't fight hard enough."

I squeeze his hand. *"We won't lose anything. I have a plan."* A plan I cannot think of, unless I wish for the Night fae to read my thoughts and discover what I intend to do.

"Care to share?"

"Not just yet. Right now, our court needs us."

I turn my attention back to the army, watching as weapons exchange hands and the fae strap shields to one another. They're a team. A unit.

But if the Dusk army is this good, how well do the Night fae work together when they have mind magic to use to their advantage? I push the thought away. Dwelling on the negatives won't save our court.

Torin moves between groups as they form to delegate tasks or places to defend. He's as serious as I have ever seen him as he adjusts the grip a young male has on his sword, then moves to a female to order her to tie her hair back in a tight braid. His words come back to us on the slight breeze that has been circling the field.

Wyn stands beside me and watches the army prepare. There are too many daggers to count sheathed on her body, and she keeps twisting the snake bangle on her wrist. I've long since learned it's the last item she has that belonged to her mother; it brings her solace in times of stress and fear.

"Any words for the fighters, Van?" Torin asks, his voice and the wind that carries it caressing our ears.

"They don't need words of courage or false assurance. I trust every fae in this field to do what they need to protect our court. We are strong, we are united, and we have more to fight for than the rest of Radelea." Vander drags his silver eyes over every fae. "I will fight alongside you until the end."

I clear my throat and add, "May the Mother Star bless every one of you."

A murmur of blessings rushes over the army like a wave. Whispers of gratitude for what we have, shouts of grace, and cries of mercy fill the field. The determination brings a tear to my eye.

That tear falls free as groups disappear. Torin has ordered some to the she-oak forest — I grip the branch in my hand tighter — some to the mountain ash tree, the manor, the villages, the academy... The list is endless of the locations we need to protect. Spreading our army so thin is a disadvantage we have to endure until we know where the Night fae will target first. Then, once the battle begins, we will call all to wherever they're needed.

The field slowly clears, leaving only Penna and three other Dawn Court healers. They dip their chins before folding to prepare the infirmary for the wounded. I believe the Dawn triplets have sent word ahead, begging High Lord Jonik for extra healers, though I am not certain he will receive the message in time.

Wyn pulls me in for a tight embrace. "Don't you dare die on me today. You're the closest thing to a sister I have. You're my best friend, Bria."

I hold her for as long as I can. "I'd be dead without you. There are not enough words in any world to describe just how much you mean to me. Be safe."

She moves to Vander and places a hand on his heart. "No matter what, little brother, I will always be in here. If anything should happen to me, take solace in Bria. You two are perfect for one another."

"I won't listen to your goodbye," he says. "You can apologise for it later."

Wyn scoffs before stepping through the void without another word. She's all Vander has in terms of blood relations. I send a desperate prayer to the Mother Star to look out for Wyn and Torin, if not for my peace of mind, then for Vander's.

Torin's face is a mask of calm when he approaches. "Don't die, Van."

"No goodbyes," Vander repeats.

I have no such qualms. I pull him in for a hug, whispering, "Be safe, Torin. Dusk wouldn't be the same without your inappropriate jokes and cunning smile."

"I'm not going to let some Night fae get the better of me. The Mother Star isn't so cruel that she would force you to go through life without my beauty and humour to entertain you." He folds away before I can laugh.

The moment I turn to Vander, he says, "No goodbyes." The last word hasn't fully passed his lips when he folds us to the edge of the she-oak forest, when he folds us to the front lines.

Chapter
29

OUR FRONT LINES COMPRISE fifteen thousand fighters. There's a mixture of air wielders, illusion experts, and those skilled in weaponry. Though he is not here, the fae obey Torin's order to split into five groups of three thousand and spread along the island's coast.

This area, where we fold into Dusk, is the most likely place our enemies will arrive. The Night Court does not have ships to sail from their four islands. It's safe to assume they will fold to the edge of the she-oak forest.

The army is quiet, but the forest behind us is singing. Fierce wisps of air rustle the leaves of the pines and she-oaks, creating a cacophony, only joined by the occasional whinny of a horse. I have always disagreed with using animals for war, so I do not look at the steel-clad stallions.

I think of Wyn, who is leading an infantry of five thousand in the northern village, and of Torin, who is at the manor with ten thousand, many of them crammed into the building itself to protect the human realm. And I think of the five thousand at both the academy grounds and the western village. The horses we are to sacrifice, the fae and families. I think of it all as I walk the length of the coast with Vander.

Every fae here wears leathers and armour. It's a sea of black and silver against the greens and browns of the forest at our backs. The rear of our infantry thins among the trees, the strongest of us acting as a last defence before the Night fae break through and move to the manor, where Torin and his soldiers will take over.

I don't like to dwell on how things will play out, but knowing where everyone is and knowing their roles helps to keep that one word at bay.

Because red will run through the streets of this island by the time the Mother Star sinks beyond the horizon. I look at her now and admire the brilliant glow of her noonday light, wondering what she makes of this. Does she reject the notion of war like I do, or does she relish in the fight for her approval?

Vander clenches his hand tighter. "Are you okay?"

"I'm fine. Just trying not to imagine the aftermath."

"We'll deal with it when it comes. Remember to breathe, Princess. Breathe, and clear your mind of anything but the present moment." We turn at the edge of the beach, where a rushing river cuts through the land and spears towards the centre of the island. "They will be here soon."

We have selected the eastern-most edge of the army as our fighting space for two reasons. I want to monitor the sea that separates us from Autumn and Summer, and the river offers a way for our enemies to sneak to the mountain ash that rests atop a hill at the river's end. We have to protect the humans and supernaturals of Earth, even if they don't wish for our aid. Protecting them feels right, as if the Mother Star yearns for their safety.

Vander offers me one last squeeze of the hand before unclasping the leather straps that secure his axes and gripping them tight in his palms. "If anything happens to me, I want you to fold to Winter. Your mother and Ruith will take care of you."

"No goodbyes, remember?" I take the two short swords from their holsters on my back. They're heavy compared to the many daggers strapped to my body, but they are my best defence when the battle is thin, which we're hoping for when it begins.

"They're here!" a voice shouts from the middle of the cavalry, the centre group of three thousand.

The clash of swords rings across the beach, louder than the whispering leaves and crashing waves. Screams, shouts, and the screech of horses fill what remains of the silence, causing my ears to buzz with the sound. A burning need to rush to their defence stings my eyes, and I force myself to remain here. If I race to help, I leave this section of beach open.

One moment the centre group is the only one fighting, and the next... The next, the beach is swarming with members of the Night Court, interspersed with undead. Their army is four times the size of ours. Dressed in nothing but black — even their armour is a flat onyx — with swords of a gleaming obsidian, they fold in on the run with their blades held high. Their shout of warning comes at the same moment the first sword clashes against a male beside me.

I stagger back as a wave of pale-skinned fae charge at us, intent on defeating the edge of the infantry before the battle can begin. The sword in my hand feels foreign and unwelcome as I raise my right arm and angle the blade across my body in defence. My legs threaten to crumble as I alter my stance. My breaths become ragged as I imagine blood dripping from the sword's tip.

"Breathe." Vander's word comes just as a female lunges for me.

There's no time for fear. No time for reassurance or second-guessing. I have less than a heartbeat to slam a weak sheet of metal over the hatch to protect my thoughts, but it's enough, and my metal bending power allows the intrusion.

The female comes at me with two wicked daggers. The curved blades are already slick with blood. She slides at the last moment, twisting her body until both daggers are coming straight for my ankles.

Instinct and muscle memory guide me and I pivot to the left while swinging my right arm down, my sword cutting through the air with ease until it slices clean through her wrist.

Her scream joins the others that haunt my mind.

There's no time to make sure she's down for good. I twist the other way and meet the sword of a male with a smear of food across his bottom lip.

"Bim?" The word comes out in a breath of disbelief.

His long sword will be no match for my two short swords, but I will need to be careful with my movements to avoid the black blade. The chest armour protecting his heart gleams like there are a thousand stars imbedded in the metal. It's distracting to look at, so I keep my eyes on his face, using my peripheral to watch his arms.

"Bria. How lovely to see you again." He steps to the right, and I move left. "Such a shame it is under such horrible circumstances."

I block out the fighting. The two fae coming to blows in the river, Vander and his two opponents, even the screams of the horses as they charge through the mayhem. It all fades away. There's only Bim and me on this blood-stained beach. His armour, which does not fit him as well as his fellow Night fae, is made to distract me from the weak points, but if I can just find one...

There. The way the metal curves around his armpit, where the leather ties are strained. I don't have much confidence in my combat abilities, but now isn't the time for self-doubt.

The moment Bim lunges, I drop my sword and slide a dagger from my thigh. I duck lower, and his blade skims my shoulder and cuts through the leather, only grazing my skin a little. To my advantage, he almost loses his balance. It's the perfect opening.

I stab the dagger into his armpit and yank it free. Springing back as his shout fills my ears, I slam my booted foot into his chest and send him crashing into the ocean, where he flails and gasps.

There are too many enemies for me to wonder about Bim's fate. I collect my short sword before spinning to help Vander with his two opponents, to see a female creeping up behind him while he's distracted with the two males.

Why do they always go for the sneak attack?

"Behind you!" I shout into Van's mind.

The Night fae's eyes dart to me, and a cunning smile curls her thin lips. In warning Vander — he blasts a gust of wind behind him that sends the female hurtling through the air — I have revealed our bond. It's a connection our enemies will fight hard to use against us.

A male Vander is fighting drops his weapons and claws at his throat. His dark eyes grow wide with fear and knowing as he sinks to his knees in the damp sand, the air from his lungs stolen by my mate's magic.

I turn away, unwilling to watch the life drain from his eyes, even if he is my enemy.

Things are worse than I thought if Vander's using his air magic. We determined swords were the best defence when we discussed battle plans, and if he's ignoring those plans...

I free the silver ribbons of my metal bending magic and find every speck of bright black around us. My magic strains against the sheer amount of obsidian blades on the beach. "More. I need more."

After teasing four more ribbons free, I ensure the hatch is firmly closed, then add those threads of magic to the others crackling in my palms. Instead of urging the blades to fly towards me, I entwine my thoughts with the magic like I would my animalistic powers and *command* the blades to bend to my will.

I am the true master of metal. Every speck of black light, of which there are at least two thousand, pulses within my mind. They're all under my control. With a single thought, the daggers, swords, arrows, and everything in between shoot from their holsters and into the raging ocean.

Before any of our enemies can take advantage of my exposed mind, I shove the metal plate back into place, protecting myself from the thought-stealing magic of the Night fae. It wouldn't do to have them figure out just how much Vander means to me.

There's a drain on my energy now, and I don't dare access my metal bending power again. I cannot move my soul into the body of an animal without putting my fae body at risk. That leaves my shadows and weapons unless I want to chance a full magical burnout.

"Good!" shouts Vander. "More when you're ready."

"I don't think I can." I slash my sword at the nearest fae, cutting through the leather covering his thigh. "It's too draining with so many blades."

A whisper of air caresses my ears, Torin's terse tone replacing the clash of the battle. "I've sent the Dawn triplets over to you and most of my fighters to Wyn. We have a small infantry of Night here, but I believe it's a distraction. We'll join you once we clear the manor."

The triplets arrive before he finishes speaking. "Tell us where to fight," they order as one.

"The west," Vander growls as he uses his left axe to cut through a female and his right hand to steal the breath from another's lungs. "One of you stay here."

I spin away from a flying dagger and throw one of my own. For a fleeting moment, relief fills me when the dagger finds a home in the chest of a Night fae. Before the glee can set in, pure agony engulfs me.

A scream rips from my throat. I swear my entire body is on fire, though when my frantic eyes and hands rove over my leathers, there is nothing out of the ordinary. I fall to my knees — the sting of rocks digging into my flesh is nothing compared to the fire scorching my veins — groping at my face and chest as if I can grab hold of the pain and rip it away.

"Bria!" Vander's shout is a distant cry, quiet compared to my screams.

"Hold on, Bria!" shouts Ulakas.

Tears blur my eyes as I fall backwards. The cool sand does little to ease the fire in my veins, and I can do nothing but scream through the pain and stare at the Mother Star's blinding wrath. Her glare is vicious and bright, and her heat beats down on the court as if to warn us against this chaos.

A hard body slams against me, followed by Ulakas rushing to say, "They cannot use their blood magic on you if they cannot see you. Do not move. I —" His words cut off with a gurgle.

As quick as it came, the fire retreats from my veins. I blink the tears away as my vision clears enough to see the crimson bubbling from his mouth. "Ulakas!"

My arms shake as I shove him off me. I roll him onto his side and yank the short sword free from between his shoulders. I whip my head in every direction, searching for Vander. In the distance, a fleet of ships bearing the Autumn emblem fights for my attention. I don't have time to ponder if Rennyn has come to aid us or fight against us. If I do not get Ulakas to the infirmary...

"Vander! I'm folding!"

I flip Ulakas onto his back and press both hands to the wound. Blood flows freely between my fingers and coats my hands like the sick glove that haunts my soul. "It's okay. I'm taking you to Penna. She'll heal you. It's okay. You're going to be okay."

A hand clamps around my upper arm. A heartbeat later, I'm kneeling on the hard floor of the infirmary.

"Bria?" Penna rushes over from where she's healing a gruesome leg wound. "What happened?"

I release a ragged breath. "He saved me. He saved me, and now he's dying. Help him. Please help him."

"We have to go back. He's in good hands." Vander's hand tightens around my arm and he folds us back to the beach. "Push it from your mind and breathe. Concentrate, or Ulakas will not be the only fae to fall."

"Autumn," I manage to say.

We both turn to face the ships that are moving fast on the churning ocean. The winds of Dusk are whipping at the waves and sending white spray into the air, where it crashes against the hulls. They're too far for me to determine if they're friend or foe.

I palm two daggers and race for the nearest Night fae. There's nothing I can do for Ulakas right now, but if I can thin our enemy's numbers by even one, and better our chances of survival, then I will put every effort into it.

Every spare moment — between dodging attacks and slashing with my blades — I flick glances at the Autumn fleet. Every time I spin away or duck or lunge, every movement to keep mobile and avoid the probing mind and body magic, I assess how near the ships are. They're coming hard and fast, the air magic churning the ocean and aiding the earth wielders.

I slash my blade across the chest of a male before spinning and stabbing it into the leg of another, and risk one more glance. I tell myself it will be the last time I allow myself to become distracted by the ships, though the thought is meaningless when I see the first fleet of arrows fly towards us.

Us.

Not Night; not our enemies.

Vander spins towards the whistling arrows and slams his palms towards the ocean. He pushes a raging wind at the iron-tipped weapons, sending them careening back to their wielders.

Another fleet bursts from the ships, thousands of arrows whistling towards us. The ground rumbles, the Autumn fae close enough to use their magic.

I roar at the ships as if the sound alone can send them back from where they came. The last of the cages in my mind fractures, and my hands turn to bitter ice. I clamp them over the face of the nearest Night fae, and I know... I know I will never forget this moment, the moment I lose control. I will never forget the look of pure terror on the male's face as frost creeps from beneath my palms and over his cheeks. There is not a world in which I will forget the way his eyes glaze over and his blood turns to ice.

I am Bria Sutherland, and I'm a killer.

Chapter 30

"SELKIE ARMY APPROACHING FROM the north. Maude has joined the fray." Wyn's warning comes on a vicious breeze that tears at my hair. "We're losing ground."

My dagger clashes against the blade of an obsidian sword, my arm shaking from the force. Daggers aren't enough against the swords of the Night fae, and I'm struggling to hold my stance.

"If the selkies are coming," I grit out, then rush to duck an arrow as it whistles past, "we need to abandon the front lines."

"There are no front lines," says Torin the moment he folds in beside us.

Vander sends a powerful illusion at an approaching foe, sending the male cowering into the ocean. "We're losing. As soon as the Autumn fae join the fray, we're done. Especially if the northern village is falling."

"Over my dead body. Torin, stay here." I twist away from the arc of a long sword and grab Vander's hand, then wrap the void around us. The realm's magic pulls at my hair and skin, fighting to shove me in whichever direction it sees fit. There are too many fae folding, and forcing my way through the darkness is like walking through the quicksand pits of Summer.

We step from the darkness and into a shadowed alley in the northern village, where thousands of fae are swarming the dirt streets. I gather those shadows around us, shielding us from prying eyes.

There are more still bodies here than on the beach. Whether the Dusk fae have passed or are unconscious from their injuries, I do not know.

The ocean rages beyond the village. Great waves of menacing grey and blue reach for the sky before crashing against the rocky shore. And within that grey-blue... thousands of silhouettes. The selkies.

In my peripheral, Wyn is fighting beside the butcher shop, and looks to be struggling against three males. Beyond them, Maude watches the mayhem with a smirk. There's something in the bright blue of her eyes that makes me pause, but I don't have time to wonder about it.

"Vander, cover me."

He adjusts his grip on the twin axes and faces away from me. There's a tension in his shoulders, and a pulse of uncertainty that thrums along the bond I share with him, but respect and trust are there, too. He does not know what I'm about to do — I'm certain he would forbid me from it if he did — but even with the assurance this village will fall, he's allowing me to do what I think is right.

Fat drops of rain fall from the sky as I sheathe my daggers and sink to the ground beside a large barrel, then rip open the hatch that keeps my magic from exploding out of me. The amber ribbons seem to know I need them, and burst free without command. I wrap them around my soul and send the magic blazing into the world. We pass over the village, where no animals remain, past Wyn and her three opponents who no longer fight, and into the depths of the churning water.

I whiz past selkies of every size, weight, gender, searching for the one bright spark I recognise. Menacing and cruel, filled with excitement and anticipation, I find Xaler in the middle of the draft. He's protected by eight guards somehow carrying tridents in their seal forms.

His mind thrashes when I slam my soul into his, though there is little he can do against my magic in this form. Before he can shift into his fae body, I wrap my soul around every fibre of his being. I take control.

The seal's body, which is large for a selkie, is sleek and fast in the ocean. I'm graceful and strong in this form, and pure joy courses through me as the water rushes along my brindle fur.

Retreat. The war is over, retreat. We have defeated Dusk. Return to the Summer Court to celebrate. I repeat the command over and over until Xaler believes every word. Then, I access the mind link that connects every selkie in his draft, and order them home, too.

It will do little to turn the tide in this war. But it's all I can give.

I make sure Xaler and his army are determined to head home before dragging my soul back to my body. I jerk upright with a gasp, and leap to my feet. "The selkies are retreating. Order our denizens out of the village, Van. We have to retreat."

"We can't leave," he says, sparing me a glance over his shoulder before returning to guarding the alley's entrance. "The Night fae will destroy it."

"We're losing. Send Wyn and her infantry to the front lines to hold steady. I have a plan. Do you trust me?"

He faces me fully. "Of course."

I place my hand against the side of his face and run my thumb over his bottom lip. "We need to sacrifice this village to save our court. The selkies have gone, but the fae here will not back down."

"What good will it do?"

"If they defeat Wyn's infantry, they will continue south to the mountain ash, where I will be. We need to keep them as far from the relic as possible. If Wyn retreats, they'll remain here and celebrate her yield by destroying everything. It's lose this village or lose the relic, the manor, and the western village. War demands sacrifices. This is one of them."

The indecision pulls at his features for a moment before he sighs and sends word to Wyn. "Retreat. You're needed at the beach."

"Are you certain?" She sounds exhausted.

"I'm trusting Bria here," he sends back. "You should trust her, too."

He doesn't mention the years of history I know by heart from my time educating the younglings in Autumn, though that is what he's implying. I have read of wars and battles and everything they entail, and I'm trusting my instincts here. Thank the Mother Star Van trusts them, too.

Another whisper comes with the wind. Penna's voice is tight with panic. "Night fae at the manor. Infirmary breached. Requesting aid to flee with the injured."

Vander and I meet each other's gaze. I say, "They must have been waiting for Torin to retreat."

A heartbeat later, we're reaching for one another and folding straight into the infirmary. There's no question whether the healers and injured deserve to see tomorrow. No question of defending the beach or manor.

The moment we step into the once sterile room, Vander sends word to Torin to bring six others and help us. It's the last words he speaks before meeting the sword of a Night fae with both axes.

My body is frozen and my eyes glued to the still chest of a male I adore. Ulakas does not move, he does not breathe or twitch. And his unseeing eyes...

"I'm so sorry, the prince of Dawn did not make —" Penna begins.

"Get them out, Penna!" I don't even look at her before I jump into the fight with my daggers, sending waves of metal bending magic to contort blades whenever I can. Ulakas will not die in vain. I'll defend his memory and rid this court of every one of my enemies, or die trying.

Blades flash, shouts echo, and grunts fade, the deafening sounds growing louder with Torin's arrival. It doesn't take long to clear the room. Then we fighting our way through the hallway while Penna and her Dawn Court friends fold in and out, getting the injured to safety.

Between one glance into the infirmary and a look over my shoulder towards the stairs, I glimpse a flash of pearlescent hair. My already raging mind does not allow me to consider the consequences of arcing my blade towards Nyree as she races along the hallway.

She meets the thrust of my dagger with a laugh. "You forget I watched you train, Bria. I know how you fight." She feigns left before slicing at my right and laughing once more.

Her black leathers hug every curve, and in the heartbeat it takes for me to assess her stance and armour, I know there are no weak points I can take advantage of. I cannot win this fight, but I am determined to take Nyree with me if I'm to fall.

"Not today," Vander growls into my mind.

Nyree lunges for my throat with her sword. Mid-lunge, the weapon clatters to the floor and she gropes at her chest with both hands, a choked gasp ripping from her lips. Her rage-filled lavender eyes shoot to Vander across the hallway; her face reddens and her lips turn a gruesome blue, but the wrath remains.

"This is just the beginning," she gasps.

I make myself watch as the life drains from Nyree. I force myself to witness her fall, force myself to notice the way her arms sag to the side. Her blood is not on my hands, it never will be, and there is no guilt clenching my stomach.

Her death is as unexceptional as she deserves. She deserves her fate. She deserves to die here, in the home she pretended to love among the fae she betrayed.

Only once her eyes are dull do I turn away. With my back against Vander's, I shout, "We have to get to the mountain ash. Can Torin hold the manor on his own?"

"Yes." He defends himself against two short swords, then adds, "Fold or fight?"

"Might as well do what we can and fight our way free."

Torin goes on ahead to clear the main floor of the house, leaving us with the dozen fae outside the infirmary.

We chose to fight.

And fight we do.

We dip and weave, dash and swing, lunge and parry. We fight hard and fierce to save our home. By the time we clear the ground floor, we are both sweating and panting. Vander has several minor cuts along his arms and legs, and I have a gaping wound on my hip that needs tending to, but we do not stop fighting.

We battle our way up the stairs. I lose my footing several times — each time directly after using my metal bending magic — and have to steady myself against the wall.

Vander shouts orders over the clash of his axe against swords.

I follow his instructions without hesitation.

Our enemies never relent.

It's chaos.

Somewhere along the way, the ground shakes harder, and I know the Autumn fae have stepped foot on our land. It only encourages me.

The Night fae never use their blood and bone magic against us, and I wonder if High Lady Maude sent the weakest of her army here to test our resistance. It's what I would do if I had no clue how the enemy would react.

At one point, I try encouraging Vander to go on ahead and leave me with the last two fae on the main floor, but he refuses, claiming he's not leaving my side. So we continue to fight together, Van with his expert skill and me as a fumbling companion.

By the time we break free of the manor, the Mother Star has disappeared beyond the horizon. It's a worrying sight to see her fading glow, as if the darkness is a mirror of our lives, an echo of the darkness swirling within us. Darkness and crimson. It's all I can see.

But unlike in the Summer Court, I don't let my red gloves take over my mind. I don't fall victim to the demons haunting me, and I don't fall to my knees with grief and remorse. No, I fight harder.

We fight our way down the hill, leaving a trail of bodies in our wake. Those who meet the deadly blades of Vander's axes will not rise again, but those who suffer at my hands have wounds that will heal, given time. It takes more effort to inflict such wounds, but it's a sacrifice I'm forced to make to keep myself sane.

As soon as the last fae outside the manor falls, we fold to the mountain ash.

It's quiet here at the crest of the hill, with the tree's branches swaying in the multi-directional winds that are ravaging our court. They drip rain onto the sodden ground, each splash thunderous in the sudden quiet. The ward relic pulses with energy, shimmering orbs flashing along the eight arcs that connect the other ward stones with the tree. It's beautiful and frightening.

"I don't want to do this." I step closer to the tree and press my hands against the peeling bark. "But if we're to survive this night, this is a necessity."

"What are you going to do?"

"There's something I didn't tell you. Something I didn't tell anyone. If we feed our magic into the tree, the wards will change."

He steps closer, a crease forming between his dark brows. "Change how? What are you doing, Princess?"

"This ward... It's hostile if fed magic after activation. It will torture any it deems an enemy. It's a temporary fix, and the relic will revert to its original state once I stop pushing my magic into it. I don't know if our enemies will die or if they'll flee, and I can't promise I'll come out of this alive. There was no information on what happens to the feeder of magic."

"Then we do it together." He places his hands on either side of mine, and his chest presses against my aching back. "Together, or not at all."

"Push your magic into the mountain ash. I don't know what happens after, but I'm sure we'll know when it's time to stop." I free my magic before I have finished speaking.

The hatch bursts open and what remains of my metal bending power surges forth in a tidal wave of silver and bitter rust. The tree, which I'm sure has power of its own, pulls on my magic as if drinking from my very essence. There's a moment where I can see the eight arcs connecting each of Dusk's ward stones. It's only a glimpse before I slam my eyes closed against the agony of my power draining.

The tree's magic grows stronger, so strong the need to stagger back almost overwhelms me. The gooseflesh that covers my entire body prickles with the slightest of pain, and my legs and arms shake viciously as currents of power wash over my skin.

A dense fog blankets my mind as my animalistic magic, the new and fearsome ice power, and my mother's shadows join the writhing of my metal bending gift. Together, they meld with Vander's air and illusions and seep into the peeling bark and smooth trunk beneath.

Van's solid body holds me steady as the energy drains from every pore I have. Though his support is not enough.

The last thing I hear before darkness claims me is the screams of thousands of fae as the relic pulses with negative energy. The last thing I know is this was a mistake I will never make again. Horrendous is the only word I can think of to describe the sound of torture filling my island home.

Chapter 31

"**D**AMN IT, PRINCESS. YOUR magic was already drained, wasn't it." Vander's tone is tight as I come to. Tight and overflowing with concern.

"How long was I out?" I groan. I blink my eyes open to see it is still night. The stars are still shining down on the Dusk Court, and there are still screams racing across the island.

He helps me to my feet and keeps a steady arm on my elbow. "Only a moment. Come, we should help clear the place of our enemies."

There are a lot of them now. The Ill-fated, the Night Court, Tohminic and the Summer Court, and now the Autumn fae. Autumn's betrayal stings more than I would like to admit.

In almost three full moons, I have gone from believing Rennyn to be my ally — we haven't always got along, and his hatred of me is surprising — to understanding he's my enemy, and I can no longer call on him should I need it.

Since the unveiling of Dusk, I have gone from having a father, brother, and a bitter stepmother to having no association with Autumn. Yes, I gained a birth mother and stepfather in Winter, but losing those I grew up thinking of as family hurts more than the throbbing wound on my hip curtesy of a Night fae.

I blink the blurred vision away and turn to the mountain ash. It looks just as it did before Vander and I pushed our magic into it. "Did it work?" I don't dare to meet his eyes after what we did.

"Yes, but we best make sure. I can still hear them." He trails his hand from my elbow to my hand. "Look at me."

My eyes shutter closed, but I turn towards him. "There's nothing you can say that will make this okay. After everything I endured at Ad'Starrag, I was the one to inflict such pain on my enemies. There is no world in which I believe torture is excusable."

"Maybe not. But you may have saved this court. In sacrificing yourself, you have given the families who live here their lives back. You have given them hope. Remember that when your red gloves return. Remember the younglings, the elderly, and the vulnerable who can return home because of what *we* have done." He tilts my face up with a finger beneath my chin. "Together, remember? We did this *together*. You do not shoulder this alone."

I nod along with his words. Some of them pierce through the fog of despair, though the demons haunting me are quick to tear them apart. I have to learn to live with what I have done. It will not be tonight, and not tomorrow. But I will learn to shoulder the burden. I will survive this.

"We can talk more of it later," I say, twisting my lips into a weak smile. "For now, let us reclaim our court."

He folds us away from the mountain ash before I can either change my mind or succumb to the crimson fighting to rule my thoughts.

We step through the void and onto the sandy shore on the eastern side of the island, where we fought on the front lines. The scene is as confronting as a nightmare. There are injured fae wherever I look, discarded weapons stained with crimson, and thousands of our enemies with their hands clamped on either side of their heads.

Torin darts through the mass of fae riddled with pain, sheathing both swords. "I don't know what happened," he pants. "Our enemies abandoned the fight as if commanded by an unseen force. I think they're in pain. Some of them moaned about folding out, but they don't have the strength to make it through the weaker wards."

"We'll explain everything later," says Vander. "For now, I'll lift the wards so our enemies may leave, then illusion any who linger to believe the island is sinking."

Torin's dark eyes flick between us, the crease between his brows becoming more pronounced. He tucks a loose strand of long, blonde hair behind his ear. "What can I do?"

"Send whispers on the wind, encouraging them all to fold home." Vander takes in the chaos of the beach. "Ask Wyn to help you. Meet us at the manor when you're done, and we'll go to the northern village and assess the damage."

I look to the east. The stars are bright tonight, more so than they usually are. There is no hint of dawn on the horizon. We have hours until the Mother Star shines down on the land. Hours of mending, moving bodies and debris, healing, and rebuilding. Hours of seeing the utter destruction of our home and thinking about the pain *I* caused.

Breathe.

In. Out. The slow breaths help to push away those unwanted thoughts, those nagging words from my inner demons.

Vander's magic teases my every sense as he lifts the wards. Illusion and air and home caress my skin and tired muscles.

I close my eyes against the blood, gore, and broken bodies littering the sand, and when I open them again, our enemies have folded away and I'm looking at the scene under a new light. Gone is the mayhem, pain, and heartache. Replaced by the caring touch of one mate to another, and faces relaxing from fear to relief, then twisting into heartache.

My eyes open to the love here, and my heart opens to the knowledge I'm responsible for it. Vander, too. Both of us, together.

It's difficult to see the Autumn armada in the darkness. With the stars and waning gibbous as our only light, I cannot tell where the water ends and the ships begin. Though I cannot see him, I know Rennyn is on one of those ships. I desperately want to know why he turned on me, why he would risk everything for the likes of Nyree, Maude, and Tohminic.

If Torin's sources are correct, the Summer fae have not left their sandstone keep since I escaped. They sent their selkies to aid the Ill-fated and Night fae, but I did not see a single flame in battle.

I voice the thought out loud. "Did Summer fight tonight, or just the selkies?"

Van frowns. "I didn't see them. Why?"

"It's unusual, isn't it? That Tohminic would go to such lengths to capture and torture me, yet when presented with an opportunity to fight me once more, he doesn't show."

"Are you upset by that?"

I scoff. "No. I just worry that he's planning something."

"I'll have Torin listen for whispers of his movements." He takes my hand in his. "We have a lot of work to do to rebuild. First, I would like to sit with Ulakas until his brothers arrive."

"Jonik and his ships have not yet docked?"

He shakes his head. "They're hours away." He gathers his wind around him and whispers, "Meet us at the manor." The breeze rushes past as it searches for Tasar and Larrad.

We are both too drained to fold, even with the wards lifted, so we walk, my muscles aching with every step. Even my fingers tremble as they dance across the leaves of the she-oaks. I could sleep from full moon to full moon and still crave the rest my body needs. But as much as I yearn for a soft bed and warm blankets, there is much to do. Sleep can wait.

The moment we exit the forest, Larrad and Tasar are racing towards us. They are both riddled with cuts and bruises, and Larrad is limping. Though they are both injured, they seem in good spirits.

My heart clenches.

I tell Vander I should be the one to tell the Dawn princes of their brother's fate, then meet the two males at the base of the manor's hill. I take in the relief on their faces, the blood splattered on their shining armour, and their identical dark eyes. "Larrad, Tasar..."

Their faces fall.

Larrad steps forward. "What is it?" He looks over my shoulder at Vander, as if he will see his brother laughing beside the High Lord of Dusk. "Where is Ulakas?"

Tears well in my eyes as I watch their faces transform from kind and laughing to confusion and grief. "I'm so sorry, so very sorry. Ulakas, he... didn't make it."

Larrad grasps my shoulders in a firm hold, shaking me slightly. "Best hope you are lying, Bria."

Tasar steps up beside his brother. "How?"

"Get your hands off my mate," growls Vander, pulling me from Larrad's hold. "I understand you're confused and grieving, but nothing, *nothing*, gives you the right to touch her."

Through choked sobs and a stream of tears, I tell the Dawn princes how their brother fell. I take full responsibility for his death, telling them how sorry I am for being weak and vulnerable, how much regret and guilt burns through me when I remember how Ulakas died saving me.

By the end of my story, a small group has formed around us — Penna is here to update us on the injured, Zentha, Elmon, and Kyra have arrived with a team of spirit fae to help the deceased come to terms with their fate, while Wyn and Torin are waiting to speak with Vander about setting up a larger infirmary — and the Dawn brothers' cheeks are blotched with pink and tear tracks are cutting through the grime and blood on their faces.

Again, I say, "Words will do little for you right now, but please know how sorry I am. If I could go back and change it —"

"Stop," says Tasar. "Ulakas died a hero. Do not take that away from him by apologising for his death. We came into this knowing we might not all make it out alive. You are worth saving."

"While we wish he was still with us," says Larrad, "we understand. It is not your fault."

I can only nod, for I know if I open my mouth to speak, another apology will slip past my lips. My hands shake, but I avoid looking at them. They are stained with crimson, both from those I injured tonight and the red that will forever haunt my soul.

"Come, I will take you to him," says Penna. Her silver-blue hair is in disarray, and her often bright eyes are dull. There's a certain stiffness to the way she walks as she leads the Dawn brothers to the manor.

"She needs to rest," I tell Vander.

He turns to Torin, but doesn't let go of my hand. "Could you ask Jonik to send more healers? Then have him meet us in the infirmary. I'll restore the wards upon your return."

"What do I tell him?"

"If he insists, you may tell him the truth. Although, I would rather speak to him myself. Just..." Vander runs a hand over his stubble and sighs. "Just do what you can."

Zentha murmurs something to her son and his future mate, and they disappear in a blink. She turns to us and says, "Elmon will gather any Day fae willing to help and bring them to the northern village. I am sorry we could not make it here in time." Anger flashes in her eyes. "Someone tampered with our ships."

"Selkies?" asks Wyn. At the surface, she's unharmed, though her face is pale and her movements are slow.

Zentha's tight coils sway as she nods. "We assume so. Why Jonik's ships remain unharmed, I may never know."

I grip her hand. "Thank you for coming. It means everything to us."

Her ever-assessing eyes crinkle at the sides. "Anything for you, dear. I am pleased to see you have worked things out with Vander. Your spirit sings with glee."

A murmur ripples through those who remain, through the Dusk fae arriving to help where needed and the Day fae folding in beside us, their groups small. The murmur grows louder with every fae who joins us, and even the branches of the she-oaks and pines at our backs seem to be restless.

The rain eases to a light sprinkle as Vander tenses beside me, and I pull my attention from Zentha to focus on the chatter of the group.

"Surely it should be lighter by now?"

"The Mother Star, she has forsaken us."

Vander does not say a word before he tightens his grip on my hand and folds us to the northern village. At the highest point of the island, this village offers a clear view of the entire realm. Radelea's land masses surround our island, and during the daylight hours, we can see our northern neighbour, Spring. We can see the Night Islands and Winter Court to our west and north-west. And Summer, Autumn, Day, and Dawn to our east. This village was bustling with activity just yesterday.

Now, it's quiet.

Vander gives me two heartbeats to take in the destruction. In the first, I notice the smouldering remains of the buildings and the smoke curling into the dark sky. In the next, I realise not a single dwelling remains.

We turn east.

"She should be rising," says Vander. "The Mother Star's glow should pierce the horizon, bathing the land in gold and shadow."

"Perhaps you're mistaken, and she will rise soon. I'm sure she will. Just give her time."

And so we wait.

We wait for so long, my legs shake and my back aches from standing. My eyes feel as though they are frozen wide as I stare at the horizon and beg the Mother Star to appear.

Fae fold in behind us. Torin returns with Jonik, Jonik's mate, and dozens of healers, Wyn appears with Penna and the Dawn princes, Zentha and her Day fae, Elmon and Kyra. Dusk, Dawn, and Day. We all gather and pray for the sun to appear in silence.

After hours, the fae fold away one at a time. Some of them with tears streaming down their faces, others with hatred gleaming in their eyes. They return to their homes or to the village to rebuild.

Zentha, her son, and Kyra linger, as do Jonik and his remaining sons. Wyn, Torin, Vander, me... We all refuse to tear our gazes from the east, none of us ready to speak the truth out loud. Our legs give way, and we sit for hours longer. All of us are quiet. All of us are tense with fear. But there comes a time when we're forced to acknowledge the truth.

Like the beginning of Radelea's history, the Mother Star has abandoned us. She will not rise until we prove our worth. Until then, darkness is all we will know.

Until then, shadow rules the land.

About the
Author

Samara is a fantasy author from Melbourne, Australia, where she lives with her partner, three kids, and an English Staffy named Boots. Though she loves Melbourne, she grew up surrounded by a large family in north-west Tasmania and misses the quiet life.

Some of her hobbies include reading, a good ol' Netflix binge, camping, and playing Monopoly with her kids.

You can follow her on social media for sneak peaks into up and coming works under the handle @samarasaward.author

Also by
Samara Saward

The Opal Wolf

Helios Mage
Heir of the Solstice
Prince of Persuasion
King of Deception

Dragon's Oath
Legacy
Enigma
Anarchy

9 781763 729919